BLACK AS SHE'S PAINTED

WILLIAM SAVAGE

Ridge & Bourne

No part of this book may be reproduced in any form or by any electronic or mechanical means, including information storage and retrieval systems, without written permission from the author, except for the use of brief quotations in a book review.

This is a work of fiction. All characters and events, other than those clearly in the public domain, are products of the author's imagination. Any resemblance to actual persons, living or dead, is unintended and entirely co-incidental.

In memory of
my grandmother and her sister,
Dorothy and Beatrice,
who both served "in the munitions"
in the Great War of 1914–18.
The poisonous chemicals used there
cost Beatrice her life,
aged 24.

PROLOGUE

Maria Worden, personal maid to the wife of a rich goldsmith and banker, was far from happy in her work. Her mistress, she told herself again and again, was a spoilt bitch; the very worst sort too. The kind who puts on airs and graces to hide the fact that she came from nothing and no more deserves her elevated position than a rat who crawls to the top of a dunghill. What on earth had that fool of a goldsmith seen in her? Of course, men were notoriously stupid when confronted — that was the only suitable word — by a woman possessed of a far more than ample bosom. Especially one with the morals of a West End whore. Mrs Eleanor Melanus, as she was now, might be stupid, greedy and promiscuous, but you couldn't deny she had the most prominent breasts in Norwich. She was also more than happy to put them on display and knew how to sell herself to men to the best advantage.

Maria shifted in the bed, trying to avoid a nasty little draught that had found its way to her left ear. Her movement disturbed Bessie Joiner. The girl gave a whimper like a lost kitten and pulled herself even more tightly against Maria's side, her skinny arms tight across her bedfellow's chest. Poor Bessie! She couldn't have been more than sixteen or seventeen years old, though she looked younger. The kind of plain, stick-thin girl who had probably never been offered a decent meal — or many kind words — in the whole of her short life. She had her own bed, of course, in the small attic next door to Maria's room, but she preferred to share Maria's whenever she could — especially when the wind howled and rattled the skylights as it did tonight. God, it was cold! Only September and it felt more like January. Not that anyone cared about the lower servants being half-frozen in their beds. Maria knew there was plenty of wood and coal in the cellar, but that was for the master and mistress — all except the generous amounts she suspected the butler and his wife, the housekeeper, took for themselves. They'd be snug and cosy in their room on the ground floor, not like her tucked just under the roof three floors above and perished with cold.

She shifted again, trying to free her squashed breasts from the death-grip Bessie seemed to have on her chest. They weren't especially large, but she didn't want them made any smaller. She wouldn't mind Bessie clinging to her for warmth, if only she didn't hold her so tightly. The poor child had responded to Maria's simple act of kindness in inviting her to share her bed one cold night with overwhelming gratitude. After that, there was no way Bessie could be sent back to sleep on her own. Besides, Maria knew that cow Eleanor Melanus would put her out on the street in a moment if she found her personal maid in bed with a man. Returning Bessie's clumsy embraces was better than nothing. She could always imagine she was sharing her bed with some handsome, lusty young fellow, eager to prove his worth, before carrying her away to his fine house and making her his wife.

Maria realised she was far too cold now to go back to sleep. She moved again and this time managed to put her own arms around Bessie, although she knew she'd find little warmth or pleasure by doing it. Poor Bessie was nothing but skin and bones. Sometimes, Maria managed to steal one or two titbits from her mistress's table to give to the girl. They made little difference, save to provoke fresh outpourings of devotion. You couldn't help but love Bessie, in the same way you couldn't turn away from a lost kitten or a half-starved puppy. You cuddled her and comforted her and told her everything would be alright, even when you didn't believe it for a moment.

What was that? Not the wind this time. More like muffled laughter, followed by a sound half-way between a moan and a squeal. The mistress up to her tricks, most likely. The master had gone away that morning, as he often did, and wasn't back yet, so the coast would be clear for her to invite someone in to share her bed. The mistress's room was on the floor below them, almost underneath the attic where Maria and Bessie clung to each other under the thin blankets trying to keep out the cold. Most personal maids had a room close to their mistress's bedroom, but this was an old house. All four rooms on the floor below were properly furnished bedrooms for family or guests. The mistress didn't sleep with the master, of course. People of their class didn't share a bedroom, unlike ordinary folk. She had a large room and dressing room on the second floor at the front of the house. He had an equally large room, with a smaller dressing room, on the same floor at the back.

More noises from below, coupled with a muffled, but rhythmic, thumping. No prizes for guessing what that would be. Eleanor had been unfaithful to her husband almost from the moment they arrived in Norwich. Of course, he was a good deal older than her — perhaps almost sixty against her supposed twenty-nine. Maria smiled into the darkness. If you'd believe that, you'd believe anything. Thirty-five was more likely. Those much-vaunted breasts were already beginning to sag a good deal. Even the thick make-up her mistress wore couldn't hide the lines around her mouth or those on her neck. The maid, secure in the knowledge that she far surpassed her mistress in beauty, as well as being more than ten years younger, might have to dissemble in the mistress's presence. Alone, she enjoyed the feeling of well-deserved superiority.

Louder thumping now. Faster. In a moment there would be a crescendo of squeals and gasps. There was nothing discreet about the mistress's enjoyment of the act of love. Yes, there she went. It would soon be over and it would be quiet again, though not usually for long. Once was never enough for Eleanor Melanus. She'd give her partner a few minutes to recover then expect him to start again.

That night, the second round began more quickly than usual. Either the fellow possessed considerable resilience, or there was more than one of them. That wasn't unknown. Maria stroked Bessie's hair and tried to picture herself enjoying the attentions of two lusty young men. Carried away by her own imaginings, she squeezed Bessie hard and planted a long, passionate kiss on the girl's lips.

'What? What you doin', Maria?' Naturally, Bessie woke up, confused by this sudden show of affection. 'Did you just kiss me?'

The sound of a hard, masculine voice from below saved Maria from a reply. That voice seemed to be snapping orders, not exchanging sweet nothings.

Hell fire! Don't say the master had come home and caught his wife on the job with someone. This she had to see!

'Leave off, Bessie dear,' Maria said. 'Another time. Something's goin' on down below and I'm goin' to take me a look. Let go of me now, so's I can get up.'

'Don't leave me, Maria! You knows I be afraid o' the dark on me own.'

'Come with me then,' Maria snapped. 'Only quiet like a mouse. We don't want to get caught, do we?'

Whoever it had been who spoke so forcefully, he wasn't doing it now. There was talking going on, that was for certain. Male and female voices, one after another. Not very loud, but somehow suggesting the two were arguing, not exchanging endearments. That was odd in itself. Eleanor Melanus didn't invite men into her bedroom at night to talk to her.

Quiet as they could, the two maids tiptoed to the door of their room and tried to ease it open without producing the usual squeaking from the hinges. The way down from their attic was by means of a short, steep flight of rough wooden stairs, which led to another door at the bottom. That door opened onto the landing of the second floor. For the moment, they stood at the top of these stairs, Bessie clinging to Maria's hand, trying to make out what the confused noises from below might mean.

The talking had stopped almost at the moment they left their room. Now came more of the usual rhythmic thumping, only somehow louder and more violent than usual.

'Let's go back to bed,' Bessie whispered in Maria's ear. ''Tis only mistress up to 'er usual tricks. Gawd! Listen to 'em goin' at it! She'll be shiftin' an' wrigglin' on 'er chair all day tomorrer, like she often does after one of 'er men friends comes a-visitin'. 'Ave you ever 'ad anyone do that kind o' thing to you?'

'Me? Chance would be a fine thing!'

They had decided to go back to bed. It was much too cold to stay where they were, just to hear their mistress enjoying herself. Then the thumping stopped, not with the usual crescendo of squeals and moans, but with a sharp cry. After that followed a series of gurgles and rustles and, finally, silence.

'Let's go back to bed, Maria, please! I be awful frightened. Whatever it is, 'tis no concern of ours. What if the Devil 'as come an took the mistress off to 'ell for her sinful ways?'

'That weren't no devil,' Maria said. 'Hush! Someone's movin' about.' Bessie began to whimper and moan in fear, making Maria hold her close to try to keep her quiet. 'Hush! Hush! There's a sweet girl. Maria will look after you. Don't you be working' yourself into a state. Just stay here, nice an' safe, while I takes a look around.'

'Don't leave me, Maria! Promise you won't leave me for the Devil to find me out.'

'You an' your devils! There ain't no such thing, whatever that ole fool of a vicar says. Now, be a good girl and stay here. Soon as I gets back, we'll go back to bed an' I'll give you a nice cuddle to warm you up. 'Ow's that?'

'Will you kiss me too, like you were doin' when I woke up?' The girl had most likely never been kissed by anyone before, let alone with that kind of fervour. The master of the house, Mr Melanus, was old enough to be their grandfather. He had never displayed the slightest interest in either of them. Maria suspected he would find it difficult, if not impossible, to recall their names, should anyone ever ask him. Mr Simmonds, the butler, was dry and withered up like last years' reeds. He also went in mortal fear of his wife, the housekeeper. Maria couldn't imagine him taking a second look at poor, plain Bessie, let alone trying to take advantage of her. Her own striking looks had no effect on him, so Bessie's homely face and flat chest would certainly not.

She sighed. The world was such a complicated place. 'Yes, I'll kiss you as well. Twice, even,' she said. 'Now, nip back an' get a blanket off our bed then sit 'ere on this step. I won't be long, I promise.'

By the time Bessie was settled, all sounds from below had ceased. Maria moved as quietly as she could down the stairs, feeling her way in the darkness. At the bottom, she fumbled for the latch and opened the door to the landing by the merest crack. As she did so, from far below came the unmistakable sound of someone closing the front door behind them.

I

On the fateful morning, following Maria and Bessie's night-time excitements, Mr Ashmole Foxe could be found in his library, sitting in front of a blazing fire. The bitter gale outside, which had been rattling his windows all night, showed no sign of abating. The few people who had ventured out on that miserable Wednesday were wrapped in heavy winter coats and scarves. It was Foxe's usual habit, after breakfasting, to walk to a coffeehouse nearby, then take a turn around Norwich's vast marketplace for exercise, before attending to whatever business lay before him. That day, however, he had stood at his window, noted the reddened faces and pinched looks of people in the street outside, and decided to stay at home. Now, sitting listlessly before the fire, he was yet again wondering what to do with himself, until some new investigation arose to claim his attention.

Summer had declined into autumn, with an unseasonal run of strong easterly winds blowing across the German Ocean. Winters of late had been long and hard. This year, snow, hardened into ice by many nights of bitter frost, had lingered in hollows and under hedge-banks well into April. The summer, such as it was, had been marred by days and weeks of heavy cloud, dragging down the temperature and causing the farmers to

7

despair of getting even a moderate harvest. As a result, the price of wheat had soared and there were riots and attacks on millers all over the county. The rioters claimed the endless demand for flour in London, which meant too much of what there was went there instead of being used to feed the families of those who had brought in the harvest. Now the hoped-for golden autumn, rich with harvest, bright with tints of russet and copper in the trees, had proved to be simply a dream. Many of the trees were already bare of leaves, while the wheat and barley crop was even more wretched than that of the previous year. The hardships typical of the lives of the many landless labourers in the countryside would be intensified by constant hunger and bitter cold for months to come.

On the surface, Foxe was a bookseller by profession; a man of culture, with a taste for fashionable clothes and a decidedly unconventional style of life. In many people's eyes, his willingness to flout society's norms was the most notable thing about him. That and his unabashed delight in female company. Despite being unmarried, Foxe rarely lacked for bedtime companionship. His household servants, well used to finding a procession of different young ladies arrive at the breakfast table, referred to them as 'the master's pets' and took no notice. The censorious and puritanical wagged their heads and muttered words like 'dissolute' and 'libertine'. Most others smiled and professed tolerance, while secretly wishing they had the courage to act themselves as 'that naughty Mr Foxe' did.

Few of these people, envious or disapproving, knew that Foxe's dandyish style of dress and scandalous reputation concealed a more serious side to his character. On several occasions of late, he had acted as the mayor's unofficial agent in undertaking investigations into such crimes or mysteries as seemed too serious to ignore and too complex for the more usual methods, which involved relying on informers and 'thief-takers' seeking the reward money. He had proved discreet, inconspicuous, and, so far, successful.

He had also found in these activities exactly the kind of stimulus his mind craved. Foxe and boredom were poor bedfellows. Without something to occupy his mind, Foxe was a trial to himself and those about him. That was why he had first become involved in seeking out the answers to some of the more mysterious and important crimes which upset the smooth running of his native city. Simply to avoid boredom. Naturally, this was not how he characterised his actions to others if they asked. Then words like 'civic duty' and 'reluctant involvement' laced his explanations.

On a sudden whim — or was it a movement ordained by providence — Foxe decided to venture out after all. Not to the coffeehouse, but in search of a sympathetic ear into which to pour his various woes. He thrust himself into the wind which whirled around Norwich's vast marketplace, like the lion 'seeking whom he may devour' he knew from his bible, found temporary refuge in the narrow streets which led down to the river, and then crossed over into the northern quarter of the city known as 'Over the Water'. There he turned left and, with the bitter easterly wind now behind him, made his way along the river bank to where a mass of trees and shrubs nearly concealed the house he was heading for. Within moments, he was seated in Mistress Tabby's parlour, trying to bring some warmth back into his limbs and already complaining to her that solving mysteries kept distracting him from finding a proper and gentlemanly way to occupy his time to his advantage.

Her weary expression should have told him he would not find the sympathy he craved in her house. She had heard it all before, many times, and no longer took Foxe's regular bouts of depression and self-pity seriously. The moment a new mystery was on hand he would be up and away, all lethargy and melancholy forgotten.

'There's no reason you should involve yourself in the investigation of any crime,' the Cunning Woman said. 'Not unless it's directed against you personally. Why not admit the truth? You don't rush around seeking out murderers and criminals out of civic duty. You enjoy it. It stimulates your mind. You are a wealthy young man with nothing much to occupy your time, so you get bored. Others in your position turn to gambling for excitement, or build themselves ever grander houses, or get involved in politics. You investigate wrongdoing. All your talk of distraction from the proper business of life by feelings of civic duty is nothing. Look at you now! You've been what — two weeks? — without a mystery to get your teeth into and you're as bored as you always are when that happens.'

'It's not a proper activity for a gentleman though, is it? Investigating crimes, I mean, Tabby,' Foxe said. 'Crimes should be reported to the appropriate magistrate. In our fine city of Norwich in the reign of His Majesty, King George the Third, this means the mayor. After that, it's up to the person injured, or his friends, to bring a prosecution.'

'Or the magistrate himself. Why not see if the Lord Lieutenant of the county can be persuaded to appoint you to such a position?'

'Me? A justice?'

'Of course, most justices are sober, serious fellows with fat bellies and excellent wine-cellars. Not young men who chase women and snap their fingers at convention.'

'I do not chase women, Tabby.'

'I believe that to be true, odd as it appears. Most of them seem to sit still and hope for you to come upon them. You're like a fox who trots though the fields amongst a hoard of fat rabbits, all of them sitting there patiently, eager to be eaten.'

'I didn't ask to get involved in this business, Tabby. Sometimes it seems the mayor assumes I'll take on whatever task he cares to put my way.'

'Don't play hard to get, Ash,' Mistress Tabby said. 'If he didn't ask you, you'd be furious. If nothing turns up soon, simply go to the mayor, or your friend Alderman Halloran, and ask. You won't be happy until you're on the hunt again. You know that as well as I do. In the meantime, why not spend some time on your business of selling books? Talk with Mrs Crombie. She might be glad of your company. Seems to me you hardly go into your own shop anymore.'

'You know as well as I do, Tabby, how matters stand. Mrs Crombie has turned that shop into her kingdom. My presence is rarely, if ever, needed. When I do venture into the place, it's only to hear the latest gossip culled from customers. She needs neither advice nor assistance, since she runs that shop more successfully than I've ever done.'

'Maybe, but on an afternoon like this there'll be few, if any, customers, so she's almost certain to have time on her hands. She might be happy to spend it in conversation.'

'I can't go in there every day, can I?'

'Why not? It's your shop?'

'You know perfectly well why not.'

Mistress Tabby sighed and got up from her chair. In a mood like this, Foxe was perfectly capable of disagreeing with every suggestion she might make. She might as well save her breath.

'Do you enjoy being a Cunning Woman, Tabby?' Foxe said.

'Mostly, yes. Sometimes I do not. That's life, Ash. Your father was a bookseller and printer — a very good one too — and you followed him into the business. My grandmother was a Cunning Woman — and far more skilled than I shall ever be — and I followed her.'

'Not your mother?'

'My dear mother was kind and loving, yet somehow the gift passed her by. It sometimes does that. Now, stop bothering me, leave that chair and go and find something more useful to do. Why not sell Alderman Halloran some old books? He's always eager to add to your wealth in that way.'

'I have none to sell him.'

'Go and look for some then! Anything to save my ears from your outpourings of pointless melancholia.'

'Captain Brock is coming home. I had a letter from him today.'

'Good! You'll have someone else to plague with your complainings. Didn't I hear he's married Lady Julia at last? Now, there's an idea to keep you out of mischief. You could always find yourself a wife.'

'Another good man fallen into the bottomless pit of matrimony.'

'There speaks a fellow who has never tried it. Has it ever occurred to you, Ash, that marriage might be a pleasurable state?'

'I note you don't have a husband, Tabby.'

'I never had time for one, what with ministering to the *genuinely* ill and unhappy people of this city, while giving up the rest of my time to caring for a veritable nest of Foxes. Doesn't mean I might not have liked to find a husband. Now in your case, I can think of just the —'

'I'm leaving, Tabby,' Foxe said, laughing despite himself. 'You women are all the same. As soon as you see a fine young fellow like myself you start trying to fit him with the encumbrance of a wife. Can you imagine any woman would be willing to have me as a husband?'

'Sadly, I can. All too easily. We women are sometimes prone to undertake desperate tasks like that.'

'There! You've said it. If a woman was willing to wed with me how could I ever respect her, let alone love her, when she had just proved herself so desperate?'

'Enough, Ash! Don't you have things to do?'

'As it happens, I do. Three of those sober, serious fellows with fat bellies and excellent wine-cellars you mentioned earlier are coming to see me this afternoon. I do not know all are magistrates, but I wager at least one of them must be. All three are exceedingly wealthy merchants, influential in the politics of this city. That I know for certain.'

'Do you know what they want, Ash?'

'No, but I can guess.'

☙❧

FOXE'S SKILLS AS AN INVESTIGATOR HAD BEEN DULY NOTED AND considered by those who mattered in the city. The mercantile elite who governed the city of Norwich rarely made decisions without what they called 'taking soundings' — and others characterised as making sure they always protected their backsides. Now, having reached a conclusion they judged safe enough they acted swiftly and in concert. They had decided Foxe's services were too important to be given up. They had also delegated the means of making the current loose arrangement with him more definite to a small group of the most influential amongst them. The outcome still had to be unofficial, of course. There was no provision in either the law or the charters of the city for an investigative office of the kind now being established by the magistracy of London's Bow Street court. During their discussions, due note had, however, been taken of the success of that operation. It had come to include its own constables, generally referred to as the "Bow Street Runners", but it must be made clear to Foxe he could expect nothing on that scale. Norwich might have long been the second city of the kingdom, until recently surpassed in size and wealth by Bristol, but its rulers automatically resisted anything that might result in them paying greater taxes. Thanks to them, the city's income was already barely sufficient to cover its existing obligations. There could be no question of taking on any more.

Foxe, these rich merchants told one another, was obviously wealthy. He had turned the day-to-day running of his bookselling business over to a partner, Mrs Crombie, and lived like a gentleman. In such a case, it must be assumed he had at least as much time to devote to pursuits away from business matters as any local squire or minor aristocrat. By this reckoning, he offered the city two obvious advantages: he would require no payment and he could make himself available whenever he was needed.

Greatly satisfied by such thoughts, the leading merchants, who formed the mayor's innermost circle, had reached the unsurprising conclusion that he was the ideal candidate for the job they had in mind.

Foxe, whose mind moved a great deal faster than the ponderous rumination of politicians, had guessed from the beginning that his invitation to one of the regular dinners of the exclusive Mercantile Society was not due to any wish to share his company. Still, the evening had turned out well enough and the meal — and the wines — had been of the finest quality. Maybe one or two of those wealthy merchants present had been too open in their consideration of this unusual attendee; too obviously trying to be certain that his presence would not embarrass them in any way and that he knew how to conduct himself in their company. It was no matter. Foxe had suffered such scrutiny several times before. He understood their concern; it was their awkwardness which amused him.

He must have passed muster, since three of the members of the society, all politicians as well as merchants, had now come to call on him at his home. Their speaker was Mr Henry Humboldt, the premier producer of fine Norwich 'stuffs' — those richly patterned and luxurious woollen fabrics essential for expensive gowns and court attire. With him were Mr Lancelot Gregg, the leading grocer, mercer and tea merchant, and Mr Nathaniel Farmer, grain merchant, maltster and brewer. All three were ushered into Foxe's library and offered suitable refreshment. All refused, explaining they needed to return to their businesses as soon as they could. It was time, Humboldt said, to make clear the reason for the Mercantile Society's recent invitation. They were willing to offer him membership.

Foxe knew he was meant to be flattered. In reality, he was instantly on his guard. These men thought too highly of themselves to ask a mere bookseller — and a young one at that — to drink and dine with them regularly on terms of equality for no better reason than sociability. That must be the carrot to draw him in, so whatever it was they wanted in return was going to be substantial. He had a shrewd notion he knew what it was, but he was determined not to make the process of obtaining it easy for them.

Having dropped their expensive lure into the water, the senior members of the society sat back and waited for the fish to gulp down the bait, hook and all.

Foxe smiled, thanked them kindly for their generous offer — and said no more. The bait hung in the water untouched. This fish clearly knew what it contained and was not to be taken without a good deal more cunning than the fishermen had shown so far.

The three politicians waited. Foxe smiled and stayed silent. He could see their uncertainty mounting. The sidelong glances they gave one another, each hoping a colleague knew what to do next. As the moments passed and the silence lengthened, puzzlement slid into anxiety, then bewilderment. In all the discussions that had taken place before the Society's invitation to Ashmole Foxe, bookseller, some-time dandy and noted favourite of several ladies of dubious repute, it had crossed nobody's mind that he would do anything other than grab what it had cost them so much heart-searching to offer.

Gregg, the grocer, broke the silence.

'For heaven's sake, Humboldt,' he said. 'Tell him the whole story.'

'But we all agreed —'

'And were fools to do so. I can see that now. We agreed we wanted someone sharp and clever. Someone who would be at home in situations where we would find ourselves lost. For my money, Mr Foxe here has proved that description fits him like a glove. Now we treat him like an idiot. Why? Because we're too full of our own importance.'

'But —' Mr Humboldt was the kind of person who stuck grimly to his instructions, whatever the outcome.

Nathaniel Farmer tipped the balance. 'I agree with Gregg,' he said. 'What would you think of the businessman who accepted whatever you were offering and only asked the price afterwards? One or other of you would have to be a fool; either him for paying an inflated price, or you for offering the goods to someone who knew their worth better than you did. Stop blustering, Humboldt! If you won't tell him the whole truth, I will.'

With the other two against him, Humboldt had to give way or lose his position as spokesman.

'I still think we should consult the others —'

'We need him more than he needs us,' Gregg said. 'If I judge the man correctly, trying to hold out on him will have only one result. He'll decline our offer — most politely, I'm sure — and walk away without a second thought. Am I right, Mr Foxe?'

'Quite right, Mr Gregg,' Foxe replied. 'I'll no more buy a pig in a poke than any of you would.' Even Humboldt had to laugh at that.

Step-by-step, they explained the situation; interrupting one another, going back to explain bits they'd missed out and sometimes disagreeing on the details. Foxe listened and said nothing, too busy trying to disentangle what they were saying.

Eventually, he had it clear. From time to time, the business climate in Norwich suffered an upheaval. An important businessman got into trouble and his undertaking wobbled on the brink of bankruptcy. He might be caught doctoring the books, either as an act of embezzlement or to cover up some embarrassing failure. He might be found to have some shameful secret in his private life. He might even, God forbid, decide to free himself of an unloved wife by means of arsenic, or help a rich relative into the unknown by the same means. Not for nothing was arsenic known popularly as "inheritance powder". In all such cases, the impact spread far beyond a single business, however large. It affected suppliers, customers and anyone else involved, from carters and shippers to lawyers and bankers. Whenever this happened, all the other significant businessmen in the city did their best to limit the damage. Too often, they failed. It took too long for merchants to agree on the best course of action. Indeed, in most cases disaster had come about while they were still trying to disentangle exactly what was going on and who was involved.

For some time, they explained, Alderman Halloran had been singing Foxe's praises as a confidential investigator. That was why the membership had agreed to ask him to join the Mercantile Society: to act for them — unofficially, of course — in situations where speed, cunning and, above all, secrecy, were vital if embarrassment and financial loss were to be avoided. They would give him the freedom to investigate as he saw fit, asking him only to present his findings to certain designated senior members before taking any further action.

'Yet Alderman Halloran is not with you,' Foxe said. 'Nor was he present when I attended your meeting. I guessed he must be a member so his absence puzzled me.'

'We thought it best to ask him to stay away,' Humboldt said. 'Conflicts of interest and all that.'

'You would have been better served by encouraging him to be present. The fact that he wasn't there put me on my guard at once.'

'That's the problem, Mr Foxe,' Nathaniel Farmer said. 'We're all experts in our own businesses and quicker than most to size up commercial opportunities. Take any of us onto unfamiliar ground and you can see the result. That's why we need you.'

'And the benefit to me?'

There was a shocked silence. 'Are you demanding payment?' Gregg ventured.

Foxe laughed. 'I ought to, but that wasn't what I meant. I don't need your money. I simply wondered why you imagined I would accept your offer.'

'But... Membership of the Society... Not everyone gets the opportunity...'

'As you said yourself, Mr Gregg, you need me far more than I need membership of your society, however prestigious. My bookselling business depends on three things: a plentiful supply of those titles most in fashion, a welcoming shop with space and time to browse, and prices which encourage people to buy one or two more volumes than they had intended. My excellent partner, Mrs Crombie, takes care of all three. I look after the finances. Tell me what you can add that I do not have already.'

By this time, all three were completely bewildered. They stared at one another, not only lost for words but lost for ideas as well. After a moment or two, Foxe took pity on them.

'Don't be downhearted, gentlemen. I shouldn't be tormenting you like this, but I couldn't resist it. Please forgive me. I mean neither disrespect to any of you nor to your society. I truly am most sensible of the honour you do me by inviting me to become a member. To be entirely honest, I had guessed what you had in mind some time ago. I had also made up my mind to take on the role you have outlined.'

'You're accepting?'

'The role as your unofficial investigator, Mr Humboldt, but not your kind offer of membership in the Mercantile Society. I am well fitted for the first and totally unsuitable for the second. You may return to your colleagues and tell them that you have succeeded in the task they laid upon you and they can relax, knowing they do not have to suffer my attendance at their confidential discussions. Now, tell me what has happened that has caused you to seek me out. I know there must be something specific, despite all you have said. The ups and downs of the marketplace, the mistakes and sins of business owners, and the risk to everyone's prosperity when a prominent business gets into trouble, are well known to anyone involved in commerce. No, sirs, something specific has happened, something recent and concerning to all, which has made you seek me out in this way. Please tell me what it is, and I will do my best to help you.'

'I swear to you, Mr Foxe, you make us all look like babes in arms.' Mr Farmer's eyes were wide with admiration. 'You're the man we want, right enough.' He turned to the others. 'Isn't he? I don't know whether to laugh at our foolishness or cry at our naivety. Very well, Mr Foxe. We'll tell you all we know, little as it is. A man like you will see the seriousness of the matter in an instant.'

This time, the other two stayed silent while Nathaniel Farmer began to explain the crisis now facing not only them, but the commerce of the city as a whole.

'You will doubtless know Mr Samuel Melanus, the goldsmith,' he began.

'Know of him. I don't believe we have ever met.'

'Like many goldsmiths, he also acts as a banker in the city —'

That was as far as he got when they heard the sound of shouting outside, followed by Molly's ineffectual protests. Then the door to the library was thrown open by a wild-eyed man muffled up in a heavy greatcoat.

'Is His Worship here? The mayor? I need the mayor right away.'

Foxe's distinguished visitors started up from their chairs in outrage at the interruption, adding to the confusion and noise by a tangle of oaths, all the while demanding to know who was disturbing their meeting and why, and threatening to see whoever it was thrown into the street. Oddly enough, only Foxe had the presence of mind to step forward and deal with the situation in a rational manner.

'The mayor isn't present, I'm afraid. Ah, you're one of the constables, I believe. Tell me what has brought you here in such haste and I'll try to help you.'

'Mr Foxe? Thank God you're here, sir. It's Mrs Melanus, the goldsmith's wife. She's been murdered.'

2

Early next morning, Foxe received an unexpected visitor. He was still lingering over his morning rolls and coffee, when Molly came in, her face a mass of smiles.

'Captain Brock to see you, master,' she announced.

'Brock? Send him in, girl! At once!'

A few moments later, Foxe's closest friend, Lemuel Brock, retired naval captain, wherry owner and newly married man, stepped into the room.

'Brock, you old pirate!' Foxe cried. 'What, in the name of all that's holy, are you doing back already! I thought you would have to spend weeks and weeks struggling over the Alps and through Bavaria on your way home. No easy route through France, thanks to the war.'

'As for coming home early — as you imagine it — you forget I'm a sailor. Came by sea, via Gibraltar, thanks to His Majesty's Navy. Much more comfortable — for me at least. First real sea journey my dear wife has ever made. It'll be a long time before she undertakes another one too, if I'm any judge.'

'Come, sit and tell me all your news.'

'Yours first,' Brock said. 'I gather you're off on another one of your investigations.'

'I am, Brock, mostly thanks to Messers Humboldt, Farmer and Gregg.'

'There are three names to conjure with in this city, Foxe. What's a humble bookseller doing getting mixed up with a parcel of powerful merchants, bankers and politicians, eh? Don't tell me they've all become book-lovers.'

As soon as the news of Mrs Melanus's death reached him, Brock had hurried round to Foxe's house. He was certain his friend would be involved in an investigation into the unexplained death of the wife of such a prominent citizen as Mr Melanus. He could have tried to catch Foxe in the coffeehouse, but conversation there would not be private. Foxe might well refuse to explain any of the details of the killing. Here, in Foxe's home as always, they could relax and speak openly.

Foxe, always willing to show himself in a good light, explained the visit of the previous afternoon and the background of his invitation to a meeting of the Mercantile Society.

'They were about to explain what had brought them to see me,' he said, 'when one of the constables brought the news of Mrs Melanus's murder. Seems she was killed the previous night.'

'Why did it take so long for someone to call the constables?'

'Her husband has gone missing. That was what Humboldt and his cronies came to talk to me about. A servant found her when she failed to rise at the normal time. According to the constable, she was never an early riser, so no one bothered to enter her room until after noon. I went to the house at once, along with the constable, but found the butler there haughty and uncooperative. He wouldn't even give me any details, claiming he was waiting for instructions from his master.'

'But didn't you say his master was absent?' Brock said.

'Missing was the term I used. Gone, having left no word of his destination. Seeing the butler to be adamant, I returned home, then went to see the alderman — only to find my three earlier guests had preceded me there. By this time, the constables were going back and forth with fresh news. Messages were being sent to the mayor and answers received. None of it added up to more than pointless speculation about the effect Melanus's disappearance and his wife's murder would have on trade. I didn't return home until after midnight. You knew Melanus was a banker as well as a goldsmith?'

'I didn't. Don't move in those circles. That explains the worries about the effect on trade. A disappearing banker is followed by a run on the banks and a collapse of credit.'

'So far, no one except a select few — now including you, Brock — know he's gone. Our mercantile elite mean to keep it that way as long as they can.'

'You must have had quite an afternoon and night,' Brock said. 'If I'd known what you'd been doing, I would have delayed my visit until tomorrow. Given you time to sort yourself out and make up for the sleep you'd lost.'

'I've lost sleep before.' Foxe was making light of it.

'Usually through bedding some pretty woman. This was different. Did you manage to make any headway?'

'Very little. Everybody kept going around in circles, interrupting one another. They were getting in quite a state about what would happen when the news got out — as it's bound to do.'

'Why are they still plotting how to keep Melanus's disappearance a secret? That must be useless, I would think.'

'Of course. They're determined to try though, at least for a time. The smallest breath of scandal or uncertainty about a bank and a crowd arrives within the hour, demanding their money in cash. At this very moment our civic elite are agreeing on stratagems to cope when the news breaks. I was happy to leave them to it.'

'I may have met that goldsmith sometime,' Brock said, 'but I can't remember him. What was his wife like — the poor woman who was killed? How was it done, by the way?'

'Strangled,' Foxe said, 'according to the constable. She was his third wife, you know. A good deal younger than him. Said to be very desirable, if you like your women both lush and painted. That's about all I can tell you about her.'

'You didn't get to see the body for yourself?'

'No chance! That butler wouldn't let me over the threshold. Not much point in going to the scene anyway. She was found by her maid.

The maid called the butler. He summoned the housekeeper. Then — only after some considerable delay — they summoned a constable. When the constable arrived, he doubtless contributed his own dirty shoes and fumbling fingers to the scene. If there had been any sign of who committed the crime — which I doubt — it would have gone long before I could get there.'

'And I thought my arrival would have been the greatest surprise you would have this month.' Brock sounded disappointed.

'I wouldn't call Mrs Melanus's death a surprise. Until last night, I knew nothing of her. Besides, people die all the time.'

'Not by being strangled in their own homes.'

'More often than you imagine. Jealous husbands or lovers. Arguments that get out of hand. Some of the more peculiar types of sexual arousal.'

'Trust you to know about that!'

'Thinking of matters marital, how is Lady Julia? Still coping with the terrible task of being your wife?'

'I still find the notion of being married odd, you know,' Brock said. 'Delightful, but somewhat extraordinary.'

'But you've been married before, Brock, haven't you?'

'Married to the sea. I was never selfish enough to put any woman through the misery of being wed to a sailor. To someone absent most of the time and quite likely never to return. The sea is a jealous mistress.'

'Did you say your wife has been unwell? Is she recovered?'

'My wife is now in excellent health, thank you. Quite recovered from the rigours of the long journey by sea. She's gone to announce her return to her scapegrace brother-in-law, the earl, and see what problems he's got himself into in her absence.'

'She didn't much enjoy the sea journey then.'

'We had decided it was time to come home a month or so ago, when we were back in Leghorn after our second visit to Rome. At first, we'd intended to travel via Geneva and through the southern German lands to the Low Countries. That would mean retracing our outward journey, in fact. France, as you pointed out, is still best avoided. The war may be in its final stages, but their recent defeats are bound to rankle. All that changed when I chanced to meet an old shipmate of mine. He's now a fresh-minted Post-Captain, but he was once Second Lieutenant on my ship. He was about to return to Portsmouth with despatches for their Lordships of the Admiralty and offered to carry us home as well. Much better than a long, jolting journey over wretched roads, staying in inns infested with bugs and mice.'

'Ah! That was how you managed to come back so quickly. How was the voyage?'

'Pretty uneventful. However, I did learn something along the way. Lady Julia turns out to be loyal, determined and courageous, but a long way from being a natural sailor. When we docked in Portsmouth, I thought she would get down on her knees and kiss the ground.'

'And yet you put her through that misery?'

'Neither of us knew how it would turn out. When we did, she refused to turn back or be put ashore.'

'Where are you going to live?'

'We're using my house at present though it's hardly suitable. I thought you might know of somewhere better we can rent.'

'I'm sure I can find you somewhere.'

'You didn't get around to telling me what these grand merchants now want you to do for them. I suppose it's about this murder and its impact on the bank. By the way, was Mr Melanus in the house while someone was choking the life out of his wife?'

'I'll answer your last question first. The answer to the other is obvious. Melanus seems to have disappeared on the day before the murder. One minute everything is normal. The next, the owner of the original goldsmith's business — and now the major shareholder in the associated bank — is nowhere to be found. His chief clerk went to see him with urgent papers for his signature and discovered the bird had flown.'

'So, the husband departs and his wife gets killed the next night! Looks suspicious, doesn't it? Are they sure that's when he went?'

'As certain as they can be. The chief clerk meets with him at least once on every day, usually at eleven. No problem had arisen until the day I mentioned.'

'I suppose they want you to find him.'

'Just that. Their first thought on hearing of his disappearance has been to keep the whole matter secret. They hoped he'd reappear of his own accord. Now that hasn't happened, I am to find him, working as secretly as possible. Now Mrs Melanus's murder has ruled that out too. Everyone will ask the same question you did, expecting Mr Melanus to have been the murderer. When they hold the inquest, his disappearance will become public knowledge. Unanswered questions and speculation about the principal partner and shareholder in any bank is bad. Not just for the bank, but for business in the city as a whole.'

'Even I can work that out. You'd expect there to be a run on the bank, followed by collapse. What's the name of this bank, by the way?'

'The Norwich City Bank.'

'I don't use it, but I've heard of it. Quite a large concern, if I'm not mistaken.'

'Large enough to cause considerable problems if it fails.' Foxe shook his head. 'Two thirds or more of the trade in this city depends on credit, a good part of it placed through that bank.'

'So why hasn't the bank run into immediate trouble?'

'Two reasons,' Foxe said. 'So far, despite the murder, our masters have managed to conceal Melanus's disappearance. Outside the household, only a few people know Melanus has gone. That includes the other directors and the chief cashier, a Mr Paul Richards, according to my visitors — plus the mayor, of course. His Worship immediately summoned his chief supporters amongst the merchant princes of the city —'

'Including Alderman Halloran.'

'Certainly. Halloran, Gregg, Farmer and Humboldt —'

'All those same leading members of the Mercantile Society?'

'Don't keep interrupting me, Brock, or we'll be here all day. Now, where was I?'

'His wife must have known he was gone.' Brock couldn't help himself and received an angry stare from Foxe in return. 'Sorry. Slipped out.'

'Don't let it happen again. The mayor and the others have discussed how to cope with Melanus's disappearance. They agreed Mrs

Melanus's death changes little in the short term. Aside from starting enquiries into her death —'

'You again.'

That earned a still fiercer glare.

'— everything should appear to continue as normal. Those in the know have been sworn to silence. If anyone wonders where Mr Melanus is, they are to be told he has been called away to the bedside of a sick relative.

'The second reason for everyone acting as they have is this. According to the chief cashier, there is no obvious problem at the bank. Nothing is missing. The bank vaults are full of gold and silver — more than enough to cover all normal obligations. The bank's ledgers show no sign of fraud. At least, that's what Mr Richards claims. Despite being the managing partner, Mr Melanus has taken less of an active role in the business of the bank since he married again. His absence makes little or no difference in practical terms. The mayor and his cronies have now agreed to ask Mr Sedgefield —'

'Reuben Sedgefield, the Quaker? He's a partner in a banking business too, isn't he?'

This time, Foxe confined his response to a deep sigh.

'Sorry. Sorry,' Brock said. 'Bad habit of mine.'

'Perhaps your new wife will be able to cure you of it,' Foxe replied in a weary voice. 'In all the years I've known you, it's been beyond my powers to do so. Yes, Mr Sedgefield is a partner in the Cawston & Sedgefield Bank. A highly respected man in the city. Many Quakers turn to banking, as you know. The law bans them from the universities. That in turn means they cannot take up those professions which demand a university education, like medicine and the law. Their religion forbids them to deal in anything associated with violence or killing. That leaves them limited alternatives. Some become merchant ship-owners or brewers or start making sweetmeats and chocolates. Since their religion also requires them to speak honestly, honour their promises and exhibit the highest moral standards, people trust them. Hence many bankers are Quakers. Sedgefield has agreed to go through the books of The Norwich City Bank to make quite certain there hasn't been anything untoward going on. It doesn't appear so, but it will be as well to be sure. If Mr Melanus fails to return, the other directors hope the affairs of the bank can remain a going concern.'

Brock had the sense to wait until he was sure Foxe had finished.

'Do the mayor and his fellows think he killed his wife in a quarrel and fled to avoid the gallows?' he asked.

'That would be a satisfactory explanation, but the facts so far are against it. Mr Melanus seems to have left many hours before the murder took place. There's nothing to suggest he's been back.'

'A prowler or a burglar?'

'The houses and business premises of goldsmiths and bankers are locked up tighter at night than the castle prison,' Foxe said. 'Several locks on the doors. Bars and heavy shutters on the lowest windows and all the rest. There is, I'm told, a separate front door for the house, but I'm sure it must have been locked at night. The back door opens into a yard completely surrounded by a high wall. Even delivery boys have to use the front entrance.'

'How many servants live in?'

'The butler and the housekeeper, who are husband and wife, Mrs Melanus's personal maid and one housemaid. The rest go home when they finish work, usually between seven and nine. Nothing was different on that night.'

'One man and three women. Do you know anything about the butler?'

'If you're thinking about hanky-panky with the mistress, forget it. He's in his fifties, I gather, aside from the fact his wife lives in as well. According to Mr Humboldt, Mrs Melanus was in her late twenties and a noted flirt and coquette. She was Melanus's third wife. No children by either previous marriage.'

'Lovers?'

'Almost certainly, but none admitted to so far. Not that denial proves anything, other than suggesting it's either true or the servants are loyal.'

'Or well paid. Or terrified.'

'I'll find out in time.'

'I can see why our revered mayor and corporation want to keep quiet about Melanus's disappearance. Most people will jump to the idea he's been involved in some kind of embezzlement. Then they'll rush to withdraw their money from the bank. But, why let you in on the secret right away? Why expect you to investigate? I suppose you'd already been to one of their exclusive club dinners.'

'That was to look me over and see whether I knew how to behave properly. Could I hold my knife and fork in the right way and stay upright after their normal ration of wine, port and brandy. They knew nothing about the Melanus affair at the time. I gather Halloran had been pressing them to sound me out in general terms. After some of them discovered Melanus had gone, it became more pressing. You have to remember Brock, they're all grand merchants and the like. Caution is second nature to them. Besides, take them away from their counting-houses and workshops and they're lost. They can only act decisively when they're on familiar ground. Faced with the unexpected, they argue and bicker and try to avoid being blamed if things go wrong.'

'Like politicians.'

'That's what most of them are as well. They try to sound impressive, while making sure there's someone else who can be held responsible when things don't turn out as they'd hoped. Unless things go well, of course. Then it was entirely their idea.'

'What are you going to do next?'

'Send you home to your delightful new wife, bearing my warmest regards as always. After that, I will go through to the bookshop to ask Mrs Crombie what rumours are circulating about Mrs Melanus's murder. I hope they may contain comments on the woman's background and previous life. I need to do as much homework as I can, before seeing what I can wring out of Richards at the bank. I'll also need to question those who work in the shop and the servants in the household itself.'

Foxe retired to his library soon after taking dinner that evening. Despite his brave words to Brock, he felt his lack of sleep the night before catching up with him. He would sit and read a little, to quieten his mind, then retire to bed early. When his housemaid, Molly, knocked on the door an hour later, he had fallen asleep.

'What d'you want!' he snapped, his mind still groggy from sleeping.

'I said I was not to be disturbed.' Feeling so heavy and sluggish was making him bad tempered too. The realisation that he, still a few weeks short of his thirtieth birthday, could fall asleep in his chair like an old man upset him a good deal.

'Beg pardon, master,' the poor girl said. It was obvious she was on the verge of tears. Now Foxe felt angry with himself, as well as with her and the world in general. Dear God, why couldn't he be left in peace sometimes?

'You startled me,' he said. 'I am sorry if I spoke roughly.' It was a poor apology in the circumstances, but it would have to do.

'Alderman Halloran's man is here, sir, asking to speak with you. He says it's awful important. He's not to return to the alderman's house until he delivers his message to you in person. That's what his master told him, sir, and that's what he says he must do.'

Foxe had never known Halloran act this way before. His tiredness and confusion fell away in an instant and he sprang up from his chair, causing Molly to squeak in alarm and cower away from him.

'For heaven's sake, girl! You can't imagine I would hit you, surely? I've never done such a thing in my life and I don't intend to now — or ever. Stop shaking and fetch the man in. Then go to Mrs Whitbread and tell her she's to give you a glass of good brandy to calm your nerves. Go on. You've done nothing wrong.' Other than being a ninny, he added inside his head.

Halloran's man was made of sterner stuff. He apologised for demanding to see Foxe, but explained that an emergency had arisen in connection with Mr Melanus. The alderman was most desirous of seeing Mr Foxe the next morning, immediately after breakfast. Pressed for details, the valet said he knew no more than he had said already. Mr Farmer and Mr Gregg had called on the alderman barely half an hour since, bringing with them another man he did not know. Whatever they had told the alderman greatly upset him. The moment they left, his master sent for him and told him to bring this message to Mr Foxe and to make sure to deliver it in person. He had been most insistent on that point.

'He does not wish me to attend on him at once?' Foxe said.

'No, sir. He said nothing could be done until the morning anyway.

Oh, and he said you should keep my visit secret. Something about a collapse of confidence. To be honest, sir, I didn't quite follow him. When I tried to ask for an explanation, he told me to be on my way and to stop bothering him. I thought it best to leave at once, before he became angry.'

3

Saturday morning and another day of cold, harsh winds from the east. News was spreading through the city that upwards of twenty ships had foundered on the shoals and sandbanks that edged almost the entire coast of the county. The German Ocean was a cruel and dangerous place for mariners; never more so than when, like now, easterly gales were combined with surging tides. Caught against a lee shore — the anchor dragging and no safe harbour to be found for many leagues about — there was little any aboard could do besides praying for a miracle. Many a sailor's wife would be a widow by now. By nightfall, many more would join them, though the news of a husband's death would take days to reach his family ashore.

Foxe had left his home as early as he dared, not knowing when the alderman and his wife took their breakfasts. Once again, his path took him along the western side of the marketplace. After that, he turned eastward into the full force of the gale, before at last turning northwards away from the wind. His way now took him down the slope that edged the castle mound, past the great gates which led into the cathedral close and across the Fye Bridge. At length, he came to Colegate and the alderman's house. Now the two men were sitting in Alderman Halloran's library, with Foxe trying to bring some feeling back into his cheeks and ears.

After the normal exchange of polite greetings, Halloran poured Foxe a cup of wonderfully hot and fragrant coffee and began.

'I must thank you for coming so quickly, Foxe,' he said 'When I thought about it again this morning, there was no reason to send you quite such an urgent message. The truth is, I was badly startled and more than a little confused. I hope I did not disturb your rest.'

'Perhaps a little,' Foxe said. It was barely nine o'clock in the morning. Most days he would not have begun to eat his breakfast by then. For the second night in a row, he'd had far too little sleep, going over and over in his mind the few facts he knew concerning Mrs Melanus's murder. Why had the alderman's message only mentioned Mr Melanus? It was that inconsistency which had bothered him so that he had been awake until the early hours. Finally, still finding no answer to his problem, he had fallen into a heavy sleep. The kind typical of exhaustion that left you feeling sluggish and out of sorts all the next day. To be told that none of it was necessary did not make him feel any better.

'More coffee?' Halloran said, holding up the pot. As he poured Foxe a second cup, he began an explanation of the events of the previous evening.

'Mr Richards, the chief cashier of the Norwich City Bank, and Mr Gregg, whom you have met, came to my house at around half-past nine in the evening yesterday. They had gone to the mayor's house first, only to find he had gone to Lynn for a few days on business. I was their next thought. What they told me was so strange — so inexplicable even — that I knew I was far out of my depth. I also knew they wouldn't leave until I had taken some action. That was why I sent John, my valet, with an urgent message for you. That contented them, for the moment at any rate.'

Foxe waited, but Halloran said no more. He seemed far away, reliving his surprise and bewilderment at whatever his two visitors had told him.

'Your message mentioned only Mr Melanus,' Fox said at length. 'Has he returned?'

'I only wish he had. Then he could explain what this is all about. For the life of me, I can make neither head nor tail of it.'

'Perhaps if you told me what it was?'

'Of course, of course. This is the nub of the matter. At the end of that day, Mr Richards thought he ought to make sure nothing was amiss with the goldsmith's business. He generally has nothing to do with that, though it's housed in part of Mr Melanus's house next door to the bank itself. It has its own shop front, workroom, and the rest. The manager is — or rather was — a man called Isaac Gurtheim.'

'And was all well?'

'No one knows. The butler said he had instructions never to concern himself with anything other than the household. He possessed no keys to the shop, the workroom or the counting-house. Indeed, he swears he has never even entered any of those parts of the house. What he was able to tell Mr Richards was that Mr Gurtheim hadn't been there for several days past. The shop, and everything else, had been shut up at least two days before his master went missing.'

'Mr Melanus has closed the business down?'

'It appears so.'

'Hmm,' Foxe said. 'Are you thinking that whatever persuaded Mr Melanus to disappear has more to do with his original business than the bank? This Mr Gurtheim might know, I suppose. Does anyone know where he is?'

'Richards had his home address written down in case of emergencies. I sent one of the constables to the house straightaway. Mr Gurtheim was there, fit and well, but as bewildered as the rest of us. According to his account, Mr Melanus told him at the end of last week — that's two or three days before the murder of his wife — that he had decided to close the business down. Gurtheim's services would no longer be required.'

'Just like that, with no further explanation?'

'Only that he had no more time to devote to it. According to the story Gurtheim gave the constable, Melanus handed him the wages due to him, plus a few pounds extra to "tide him over". Those were his exact words. Then he asked for the return of Gurtheim's keys to the shop and workshop. His explanation was that he had to leave Norwich shortly. He took the keys, locked them in the shop safe and ushered Gurtheim out of the door. Gurtheim hasn't seen him since.'

'What time was this?'

'Soon after nine in the morning.'

'There was no suggestion earlier of any problems with the business?'

'Gurtheim told the constable he was flabbergasted. It's true Mr Melanus had been running the business down of late. For example, he'd been turning away new orders and laying off craftsmen. Before that, they had a full order book. The business was making significant profits.'

'The books are in order?'

'Who can tell? I imagine they're locked away somewhere. No one knows — except, presumably, Melanus. Only he has the necessary keys to the shop, the workshop or the counting house. If we can find those keys, it may be possible to find the account books. That's presuming Melanus kept them in his personal possession. We aren't even sure of that.'

'Did Mr Gurtheim see Melanus leave?'

'He says he did not. All he can say is that he was standing outside the shop, too stunned to do anything else, when Melanus came out. He saw him lock the door and walk off towards the marketplace. That, you'll recall, was a day or two before Melanus disappeared.'

'The marketplace is where most of the stagecoaches pick up passengers.'

'Precisely. According to Gurtheim, Melanus was carrying a small carpet bag.'

'Yet that was not the day on which he left and did not return — so far as we can tell, at any rate.'

'It was not. He was at home the rest of that weekend, behaving as he usually did.'

'How very odd. Our man closes down what seems to be a thriving and profitable concern and leaves nothing behind to show the reason. He remains at his house for two more days, then leaves — exactly when, nobody knows. It might have been at almost any time that day — or even the night before. We cannot ask his wife, since she's dead. That same night or the next, his wife is murdered in her bedroom. Her assailant enters and leaves the house undetected. Those two events — disappearance and murder — must surely be connected, even if there's nothing to prove as much ... you're certain nothing is missing from the bank and all its accounts are in proper order?'

'Not certain. That's what Mr Sedgefield has been asked to verify. All I can tell you for the moment is that there is nothing obviously amiss.'

'How deucedly curious!'

Foxe sat in silence for a while, running through the problem in his own mind. As they stood, these events made little sense.

'If I try, I suppose I can think of a few explanations for what has happened,' he said slowly. 'None of them are in the least satisfactory. For a start, there's kidnapping. We're assuming Mr Melanus left of his own accord. He might have been going to meet someone. That person might have kidnapped him — though kidnappers usually demand a ransom, and none has yet been sought. Maybe he's dead. He could have met someone away from his house and been murdered, like his wife. But there's no body and nothing to offer any reason for killing the man. Theft? He could have run away to avoid being found out for theft or embezzlement. Yet nothing seems amiss at the bank and we can't get into the shop to find out what, if anything, may have gone from there. So far as the bank is concerned, we can only wait for the report from Mr Sedgefield. For the rest, whatever time he left for the last time, no one claims to have seen Melanus on the day his wife was killed. If we accept that, he cannot have fled after murdering his wife. She was alive, not just for the whole of that day, but for part of the night as well.'

'Do you think he returned in secret and murdered her?'

'That must be a possibility, though it's hard to imagine why he should do so. Why not kill her first and then run?'

'Could he have paid someone to kill her? He might have left intending to return after establishing his presence elsewhere at the time of her death. What if he did that, then could not return. Maybe he fell ill or had an accident?'

They went backwards and forwards like that, raising possibilities only to dismiss them, for another twenty minutes. At the end of the time, however, they were no wiser than they had been at the start.

'My head is aching and I'm only becoming more confused,' Alderman Halloran said at last. 'I've had enough.'

'So have I,' Foxe agreed. 'This is getting us nowhere. My suggestion is that you focus your attention on a single point. Something strange is going on and it concerns the principal partner in the Norwich City Bank. It may or may not be connected to his disappearance and the subsequent murder of his wife. I'm going to begin my investigation by concentrating on the murder. Maybe discovering who did it and why will reveal the answers to the other puzzles as well.'

'Very well, Foxe, I leave the investigation in your hands, as usual. We're all indebted to you for helping us in this way. About the bank — I should hear something from Mr Sedgefield in a day or so and I'll be in touch with you then. We can't hide the fact of Mrs Melanus's death, but we're still trying to keep everything else a secret. That is, at least until Sedgefield has finished his investigation. No point in provoking a panic, especially if her death and Melanus's disappearance prove to be unconnected with the bank after all. By all means let people know you're after her killer. Just don't allow them to suspect you're interested in anything else.'

'I'll also begin an investigation into the goldsmith business,' Foxe said. 'That might distract attention from the bank. People will jump to the conclusion that the murder — or murders, if Mr Melanus's corpse turns up — were a simple matter of robbery.'

'Excellent idea! If word then leaks out that Melanus left of his own volition, the rumour-mongers will decide he killed his wife and ran off with the gold and silver from his shop.'

'You couldn't run with that, Halloran. You'd need a strong carriage — maybe two.'

'Don't be a nitpicker, Foxe! He might have been sneaking small amounts out for weeks before. It doesn't matter, does it? Just so long as nobody begins wondering about the stability of the Norwich City Bank.'

❀❀❀

FOXE DECIDED THERE WAS STILL TIME TO CALL INTO THE BOOKSHOP. He wanted to ask Mrs Crombie if the gossips had shared anything of interest about Mrs Melanus.

He usually entered the shop through the door which connected it to the hallway of his house next door. This time, since he was approaching from the street outside, he entered through the shop door itself, setting the bell above it jangling to announce the presence of a customer. At first glance, the bookshop seemed quiet. Once inside, however, he noticed a finely dressed, handsome woman of mature years standing at the far end of the counter. She was accompanied by two children on that perilous boundary between being girls and becoming young ladies. All three turned at once to see who had entered, and Foxe greeted them effusively.

'Mrs Halloran! Good day to you, ma'am. How delightful it is to see you. Miss Maria, Miss Lucy. It is a pleasure to see you too, of course. I cannot recall when I last did so.'

Miss Lucy Halloran, the younger of the two sisters, was already developing that terrifying honesty and strength of character, which was to be her lot through life. Since, at present, it was accompanied by a total lack of tact, the resultant plain speaking could be off-putting to lesser mortals.

'That's because you never come to see us, Mr Foxe,' she said. 'I expect it is because we are either too respectable or not beautiful enough.'

'But I was at your house only this morning,' Foxe protested. Lucy was not to be deflected.

'Seeing our uncle, not us. Uncle says all the ladies you take an interest in are beautiful, and few of them are any better than they ought to be. That is why my sister and I are ignored.'

The snort that came from their aunt might have been either indignation or suppressed laughter. Poor Maria's face was deep pink from embarrassment.

'Hush, Lucy!' she said. 'You will shame yourself and the rest of us along with you. How can you be so impolite to dear Mr Foxe?'

'You and your sister are both beautiful,' Foxe said, trying to calm the situation.

'Then it must be you that avoid us because we are too respectable to match the second part of uncle's description.'

This was finally too much for Mrs Halloran. 'Lucy! Behave yourself this minute. If you do not, I shall take your new books from you and see they are returned to Mr Foxe's library. You should be ashamed of yourself to speak in such a manner to Mr Foxe.'

'But I can see from his eyes he knows I am only teasing him, Aunt.'

'Some ways of teasing are acceptable, and some are not,' her aunt said. 'Apologise this instant.'

'There is no need, Mrs Halloran, I assure you. I have taken no offence, since none was intended. It is true that your nieces have grown into lovely young women, both of them. It is also true that, as the alderman has obviously suggested, some of my female acquaintances would not be welcomed into polite society. I would rather have Miss Lucy tease me about that than profess herself shocked. As for not calling upon you earlier, Miss Lucy, it was my loss and not yours. Now, are we friends again?'

'Of course,' Lucy said. 'You know how fond we all are of you, even if you are somewhat disreputable.'

'Lucy!' her sister and aunt cried at the same instant. Even Mrs Crombie gasped. Foxe burst out laughing, as much at the sight of the open mouths of the others as at Lucy's irrepressible impertinence.

'Sadly, that is true,' he said. 'Yet I would not have it any other way. Now, let us behave politely towards one another, please. If we do not, your aunt will feel impelled to punish you and your poor sister will die of mortification. I see you have a large pile of books between you. It would be unforgivable to make you carry them home yourself. I will call Charlie and send him as your escort and book bearer. Mrs Crombie? Do you know where the young reprobate is?'

'In the stockroom, I believe, Mr Foxe. Cousin Eleanor? Perhaps you would be good enough to tell him his master wants him.' Mrs Crombie's older cousin, Miss Eleanor Benfield, served as her assistant.

Charlie Dillon, former street child, now Foxe's apprentice, was duly summoned. His master then instructed him to accompany the ladies to their home to carry their books for them.

'Would you mind if I called on Mistress Tabby on the way back, master?' the boy said to Foxe. 'I got word she has a message for you.'

'By all means,' Foxe said.

Lucy was too curious to stay silent. 'Is this Mistress Tabby another of your beautiful ladies?' she asked.

'Mistress Tabby is indeed a very handsome woman, Miss Lucy, though my relationship with her is not of the kind you are hinting at. Miss Tabitha Studwell lives close to the river. Not far from your own home. I have known her for many years and she was my father's friend long before then. She is a kind, generous and intelligent lady, as well as being a skilled herbalist and healer.'

'You are too indulgent towards Lucy,' Mrs Halloran scolded him. 'My husband is the same. As a result, her behaviour does not improve as it should. Miss Studwell, Lucy, is what the local people call a Cunning Woman.'

'A witch?'

'Not a witch, child. Never call her that — nor any other woman either, however old and fearsome in appearance. Witches are only for stories. A Cunning Woman is a person who helps people cope with illnesses and life's other problems. Note what Mr Foxe said of Mistress Tabby: kind, generous and intelligent. Does your lack of tact and politeness suggest you are any of those?'

Lucy hung her head. 'No, aunt.'

'Learn your lesson then. I am greatly displeased with you, miss. I shall withhold your new library books for two days as punishment. Now, let us depart and allow Mr Foxe and Mrs Crombie some peace.'

'Please do not punish your niece on my account, Mrs Halloran,' Foxe said. 'It is true she presently lacks tact or a sense of time and place, but such lively curiosity should never be suppressed. Better judgement will come in time, I am sure. Your aunt's description of Miss Studwell is precise and accurate, Miss Lucy. Mistress Tabby is a lady I am proud to know, even if those who are ignorant and superstitious still look upon her askance. Now, I pray you, listen to your aunt and take greater care with your speech. Understand this also. If you do not learn to behave as society demands — at least outside the circle of your own family and closest friends — your curiosity is doomed to remain unsatisfied. If a person is afraid of you, or thinks you rude, you can hardly expect them to speak openly. I am the most curious person I can think of in this city, but I have found the best way to discover things is to cultivate proper politeness and try always to appear harmless. Remember Aesop's tale of the fox and the crow. The fox stole the crow's bread by using polite conversation and flattery, not by trying to make the crow drop it out of astonishment.'

'An apt comparison, sir,' Mrs Halloran said. 'For yourself as well as my scapegrace niece. Now we must bid you good-day and be upon our way. Come and see us soon. Maybe you will be able to teach Lucy some manners where I have failed.

🙟 4 🙝

T he next day, being Sunday, brought a temporary halt to investigations. The great and the good made their way to churches or chapels, then settled down to a day of solemn indolence. Mr Foxe, who didn't consider himself great in any way and was determined to avoid being good for as long as he could, avoided churches. His Sundays too were spent in indolence, just not of the solemn or holy kind. Whenever he could, he would invite a suitable young lady to his home and his bed on a Saturday night. Then he spent most of the following day luxuriating in feelings of post-coital satisfaction, interspersed with bouts of further lazy love-making.

That Sunday, having had no one to share his bed the night before, he rose late. Then he fretted and fumed at the enforced delay to making a start on discovering who had murdered Mrs Melanus. The weather remained cold and the gales showed no signs of abating. Even so, he wrapped himself in a thick winter cloak and ventured out in the hope that exercise would lessen his frustration. He found the city almost deserted. Those who had attended church or chapel had hurried back to the warmth of their homes as quickly as they could. Even the street children huddled in corners and alleyways, trying to avoid the bitter winds which blew between the buildings. As was his habit, Foxe dispensed kind words and much-needed pennies to them in equal measure. He might care nothing for prayers and hymn-singing, but he tried never to miss those small acts of practical charity. They, to his mind, were worth more than all the pious words of the day's preachers put together.

At length, after enjoying a good dinner, Foxe settled down to make his plans. As agreed with the alderman, he could leave any probing into the affairs of the bank to him and Mr Sedgefield. If the reason for Mr Melanus's disappearance lay there, Mr Sedgefield's report should point the way for the investigation to follow. Meanwhile, he would concentrate on the murder of Mrs Melanus. He would begin by finding out all that he could about the affairs of the Melanus household.

Trying to question the butler would be a waste of time. The same would go for the housekeeper. Senior servants were often most protective of what they saw as the proper levels of privacy due to their employers. The mistress might be dead, but the servants might well believe their master might return at any time. Unless they knew otherwise, which he doubted. If their master found they'd been discussing his affairs with strangers, they would lose their positions. Even a magistrate would find it almost impossible to pierce their unwillingness to speak out, let alone someone with no official standing, like Foxe. Not only would these senior servants preserve their own silence, they would deny him access to the other servants.

Mrs Melanus's personal maid — the one who had found the body — might be another matter. If he could get her on her own, she might be willing to tell him something about the household in general and her mistress's lifestyle in particular. Foxe had an unshakable belief in his ability to charm young women into acts of indiscretion. That is, assuming this maid was young. She might not be. He could sometimes flatter older women into saying more than they should, but many tended to show a stronger resistance to his methods. Still, it would be worth a try. So long as he could find a way to talk to the maid without having to get permission from the butler.

Talking to Mr Richards, the bank's chief cashier, would have to be set aside until Mr Sedgefield had completed his work. Besides, it didn't seem likely that the man would know much about what went on in his employer's private household. That left Mr Gurtheim. He was both the principal craftsman in the gold and silver smithing business and the manager of the shop.

The shop was located on the ground floor of Mr Melanus's house and had no separate entrance. Gurtheim should have at least some idea of what went on in the rest of the house during the day. Questioning Gurtheim might not be very productive, but that was no reason for setting it aside. Foxe thought it wasn't much of a plan, but it was the best he could do for the moment.

He had barely settled himself to eat his breakfast that Monday morning when Molly, his maid, came in with a message. Charlie wanted to tell him what he had learned from Mistress Tabby. Foxe told her to send the lad in at once. To be honest, he'd forgotten about Charlie asking to visit the Cunning Woman on his way back from the alderman's house. That would never do. Mistress Tabby never sent a message which was less than important. This one might be vital.

Charlie must have been waiting outside the door, because he was inside the moment Molly went to fetch him.

'Morning, master,' the apprentice said. 'Sorry to interrupt your breakfast, but Mistress Tabby said I was to give you her message as soon as I could. By the time I got back yesterday, Molly told me you had gone in to take your dinner. I didn't want to spoil your evening, so I decided to wait until now. I hope that turns out to be the right thing.'

'Give me her message and I'll tell you,' Foxe said. He was never at his most welcoming before he'd returned from the coffeehouse.

'Very well, master. I was to tell you that Jack Beeston's back in the area. Seems he never went that far away.'

Foxe swore loudly and at length. So much so that the boy, full of admiration for his master's knowledge of so many foul curses and obscenities, clapped his hands in delight.

'God's teeth, master! I haven't heard cursing like that outside Amos Riddle's grog shop. Where did you learn to swear like that?'

'Never you mind, boy. Just don't let me hear you using such words in this house — and especially not in the bookshop. Mrs Crombie would faint.'

'She wouldn't know what most of 'em meant, I reckon.'

'She'd know enough to give you a damn good hiding. Now, tell me exactly what Mistress Tabby said. I've had to get the better of that evil man Beeston twice before. Last time, I hoped he'd gone for good — preferably to hell, where he belongs.'

'He ain't been in hell, master, according to Mistress Tabby. He's been in Great Yarmouth, trying to work his way in with the free traders there. Seems he intended to run a good part of the smuggling trade up and down the coast for miles in either direction, only they wouldn't have him.'

'Aye, that's exactly the sort of thing he would have in mind, God rot him!'

'Mistress Tabby says you should be sure to keep him in mind. Last time, when you ran him out of the city, he was blackmailing that banker fellow, Mr Morrow, wasn't he? Beeston has also sworn to have his revenge on you, she says.'

'Jack Beeston. Can he be behind this business with Mr and Mrs Melanus? It's not twisted enough to suggest his particular brand of devilry. Not from the outside, anyway. Besides, if he's fully occupied cheating His Majesty out of his taxes and customs duties, I can't see why he'd decide to get up to mischief in Norwich. Where's the profit? Beeston never did anything unless there was a great deal of money involved.'

'Mr Melanus is a banker.'

'True, but no money has been stolen, so far as we know.'

'Beats me then!'

'I can't understand it either. I'd better go and see the alderman. Tell Alfred to go there now to ask whether it would be convenient for Alderman Halloran to receive me. Make sure he says it's urgent. What's the weather like this morning?'

'Wind's dropped a little, but it ain't no warmer. The rumour is most of the colliers managed to anchor safely last night and ride out the storm. One was wrecked on Happisburgh Sands though. The men of the beach company at Cromer are still out acting as pilots to shepherd the rest of the stragglers to safety.'

'Who'd be a sailor, eh? At least we don't have to contend with winds and waves. Just with evil bastards like Beeston. God in heaven!'

This news is going to ruin the alderman's day. Aye, and do the same for a good many other important people in this city, from the mayor downwards. Jack Beeston! If ever a man deserved all the torments hell can provide, it's him.'

Barely twenty minutes later, Alfred was able tell his master that Alderman Halloran would be pleased to receive him as soon as he wished. That was ideal from Foxe's point of view. He had already asked Mrs Crombie to collect all the gossip she could about Mrs Melanus. He particularly wanted to know about her background and activities before marrying the goldsmith. Foxe's nose told him that might prove a rich vein to mine.

Once again, the alderman received him in his library — a room Foxe was beginning to know almost as well as the library in his own house. When Foxe told him about Jack Beeston's return, Halloran went pale, then red, then almost purple with rage. His vocabulary of curses was far inferior to Foxe's, but he more than made up for that in the sheer vehemence of his use of them.

'I thought we were rid of that blasted, blackmailing rogue, Foxe. God damn him to hell! That's where I hope he'll burn for all eternity! Do you think he had something to do with this business of Mrs Melanus? Would he stoop to killing a woman? Don't answer that. You and I both know he'd do it without a second thought. If I had my way, his rotting body would be hanging on a gibbet — though I suspect even the crows and ravens would have better taste than to feast on his flesh. Christ Almighty! The mayor will have an apoplexy!'

'Beeston would kill anyone, if it suited him,' Foxe said, 'but he wouldn't be foolish enough to do it with his own hands. He'd always send someone else to do it for him. As for ordering the killing of Mrs Melanus, he'd do that without a moment's hesitation, if she got in his way, just as you said. How Mrs Melanus might have done such a thing I cannot imagine — if she did it at all. What gossip Mrs Crombie managed to find out by yesterday suggests Melanus's wife was constantly and openly unfaithful. She was also selfish, vain and as greedy as the fattest pig. Aside from those minor faults — and possessing what Mrs Crombie described in her delicate way as "such a prominent bosom people wondered how she managed to stand upright" — nothing seems to be known against her.'

'Did your informant link Beeston with the death of Mrs Melanus in any way?'

'I was told only that I needed to know Beeston was back in business in this area, albeit in Great Yarmouth, and he should not be ignored. So far as I know, there has been no evidence so far — no suggestion even — that he has any part in this particular crime. Until there is, I suggest we don't allow worrying about him to distract us from the main questions. Who got into the house that night and why did they choose to kill Mrs Melanus?'

'Might Melanus himself have returned in secret and caught his wife with a lover?'

'It's possible. He could have caught her *in flagrante* and throttled her in a blind rage. But if he did, what happened to the lover? He'd hardly let the fellow walk out peacefully. On the other hand, nothing suggests Melanus did come back. Why go away without a word to anyone, only to sneak back later, at night, to murder your unfaithful wife? That's something he could have done before he left. Her promiscuity was well known, so it must have come to his notice long before. It's hard to believe he had somehow only just heard of it. Again, according to Mrs Crombie's informants, the woman revelled in the effect she had on certain men. She was also more than willing to take full advantage of it. I'm sorry, Halloran, assuming Melanus returned makes no sense to me. Especially when we don't know where or why he went in the first place. What if he's been killed too? Or fled the country? Or had a heart attack while disporting himself in some tart's arms? Pimps have been known to dispose of inconvenient bodies in secret to avoid awkward questions.'

'Trust you to think of that!'

'How old is Melanus, by the way?'

'Between fifty and sixty, I would guess. Nearer sixty.'

'His wife?'

'Hard to say. Under thirty, some say. Others reckon that's a myth she's put about and she's older. I've only seen her once — maybe twice. Not a woman I found at all attractive, I assure you. Lush and languorous, but rather coarse-featured and reputedly as stupid as a bed-post.'

'How delightful you make her sound!'

'If you'll excuse me for saying so, Foxe, we need to press on. My time is limited, and you've brought me information I need to pass on to the mayor at once. My advice is to turn your attention back to this murder. The inquest is this afternoon, and I suggest you attend, as I cannot. All this about Jack Beeston is important, but it may have nothing to do with Melanus or his wife. Ah yes, before you go, I have some news for you about the Norwich City Bank. Mr Sedgefield sent me a message which arrived shortly before you did. He's had a rapid, preliminary look at the accounts and daily returns and can see nothing amiss. On the face of things, the banking business is in robust health. He's going to delve deeper, but so far all is as it should be.'

'I'm not sure whether that's good news or bad,' Foxe said. 'It's good for the city and the bank's depositors, but it leaves us as much in the dark as we were before.'

'Indeed, it does, Foxe. Now I must be on my way. I have corporation business to attend to and I want to catch the mayor before he starts anything which can't be interrupted.'

'Before I leave, and with your permission, Halloran,' Foxe said, 'I'd like to speak with your two nieces, if they're at home.'

'Of course, of course, my dear fellow. I'll send someone to fetch them. They'll see you out afterwards. My dear wife is getting ready to pay calls this morning.'

When Maria and Lucy arrived, both curtsied in a most decorous fashion and wished Foxe good-day. After that, it was the elder girl, Maria, who spoke first.

'Oh, Mr Foxe! Aunt gave Lucy the most frightful telling-off when we came home on Saturday. If you now intend to upbraid her for her behaviour towards you, it will quite break her heart.'

'Then it's a good job I have no such intention,' Foxe replied, trying to keep a serious expression on his face. 'I have made it my resolve never to break any lady's heart, if I can avoid doing so. I will not stray from that resolve today, you can be sure. What I want to do, Miss

Lucy, if you will agree, is to make an agreement with you. One that I hope will save you from future problems on my account.'

Lucy had been standing looking glum and silent since coming into the library. Now she looked up at Foxe for the first time. Whether it was hope or curiosity, his words had drawn her interest.

'When we are alone, Miss Lucy, you may tease me all you wish. I shall not take offence. Indeed, you may say anything you like to me, short of being rude, and the same will apply. But when others are present — besides your sister of course — let us both obey the conventions demanded by polite society. Will you agree to this?'

'Do you really mean it, Mr Foxe?' Lucy said. 'You are not angry with me?'

'Not in the least.'

'Then you have my solemn promise to do as you ask. I swear it.'

'Will the same agreement apply to me?' her sister asked.

'Certainly.'

'Then I declare for my part that you are the dearest, sweetest person I know. I would swear myself to be quite in love with you, if you were looking for a wife and I were a little older!'

'Shame on you for being such a forward hussy, sister!' Lucy cried. 'Mr Foxe knows he is quite forbidden to marry until I am old enough to become his wife. Besides, I would be more likely than you to overlook his occasional lapses from strict faithfulness. That must argue strongly in my favour.'

'We cannot both marry him. To do so would be bigamy.'

'Then we must toss a coin.'

'Ladies, ladies!' Foxe said, joining in the game. 'Do I not have a choice in the matter?'

'By no means,' Lucy said. 'Whichever one of us you chose, the other would never forgive you. If we leave it to chance, nobody is to blame, and we can all continue to be friends.'

5

The inquest into Mrs Eleanor Melanus's death had been delayed first by the temporary indisposition of the coroner, then by the sabbath. Now it was to be held in the large room at the Red Lion Inn. Once this had been used as for plays and entertainments, but with the building of a fine, modern theatre, now known as The New Concert Hall, it had lost its audience. Even the White Swan Playhouse was struggling to continue, as Foxe knew all too well. A few remnants of the theatre decoration still clung to the walls of the room, along with the gallery at the rear. The stage had been removed and the benches set aside to make more space. For most of the time now, it was simply used as a storeroom for unwanted items from the inn itself.

There were a good many people present to see proceedings. Word of the killing ensured many had come purely from curiosity. From what Foxe had heard, it was unlikely to be from sympathy for Mrs Melanus. Prurient speculation was a far more likely explanation. The unexplained killing of the wife of a wealthy, older husband suggested an abundant source of matters for gossip. Young wives and elderly husbands meant only one thing in the public's mind.

Foxe could see Mr Hirons, editor of the "Norfolk Intelligencer" newspaper, seated in the front row of the public area. For him to come in person meant he also recognised the possible implications of this murder and the interest it must generate. His newspaper would not be printed for several days yet — it was a weekly. When it was, it would doubtless contain a full report of all the inquest had revealed.

Foxe seated himself towards the back of the room and tried to keep out of sight as much as he could. Few ordinary people in Norwich knew of the part he sometimes played in bringing wrongdoers to justice. He wanted to keep it that way. Unfortunately, Mr Hirons was well aware of what he got up to. If he noticed Foxe, it would confirm any suspicions he had that there were other facts about the Melanus household worth seeking out.

The coroner's jury were already assembled when Foxe arrived. They were sitting on the right of the place set aside for the coroner himself. One or two were whispering to their neighbours on the jury benches. The rest were content to wait in silence and enjoy their temporary importance. The law required them to return a verdict on the nature of any unusual death, even though, in this case, their verdict was a foregone conclusion. You cannot strangle yourself — hanging excepted — and Foxe would have known if the finger could be pointed at any specific killer. Only if something totally unexpected happened would they have any real role to play.

The coroner slowly walked to take his place. These chill easterlies caused him such pain from his rheumatism he was sometimes unable to walk at all. Seated at last, he opened proceedings without further fuss, beginning with the usual statement of the reason for an inquest. The victim's death being sudden and unexplained, the matter was grave enough to call a jury to pass verdict on the death. The jury, he told the court, had elected not to view the corpse. That wasn't surprising, given the passage of time. Now the remaining evidence had to be heard.

He called Simmonds first, the butler to the Melanus household. He gave evidence on the identity of the victim. No mention was made of the absence of Mr Melanus. That would be the mayor's doing, of course.

After that, the coroner asked Simmonds if there had been any visitors to the house on the evening of Mrs Melanus's death.

'I admitted no one,' Simmonds replied. With his wig and old-fashioned clothing, the man looked more like an undertaker than a butler. When he spoke, his voice was as gloomy and sepulchral as his appearance.

'Could anyone else have done so?' the coroner asked.

'Answering the door is one of my principal duties.'

'It is never done by anyone else?'

'Not when I am in the house, sir.'

The butler measured out his words with such care you could imagine each cost him a week's wages.

'You were there that evening?'

'I was.'

'Were there any signs that someone might have made an unauthorised entry? A broken window? The lock of a door forced?'

'Neither of those.'

'Nothing unusual that you noticed?'

'Nothing I have not seen before.'

'You check all the doors before retiring?'

'I do.'

'Did you hear anything suspicious or unusual?'

'I did not.'

'Nothing of that kind was reported to you by any of the other servants?'

'No.'

'Describe the events of that evening, please.'

'Dinner was served at the appointed time —'

'Mrs Melanus ate alone?'

'She did.'

'At what time?'

'At six o'clock.'

'That is a somewhat late hour, surely?'

'It was the master's habit never to take dinner until after the shop had been closed and all the stock had been returned to the vault.'

'Go on. At what time did the deceased finish her dinner on that day?'

'At seven.'

'And then?' It was like squeezing juice from a dry, withered lemon.

'Mrs Melanus retired to her room.'

'Did you see her after that?'

'She told me I would not be required further that evening.'

'What about the other servants? Her personal maid, for example?'

'The same.'

Slowly and painfully, the coroner established the events of that evening. The butler and the housekeeper, who were husband and wife, had retired to their room near the servants' hall after supervising the meal for the live-in staff. That meal was taken in the servants' hall on the ground floor of the building, behind the shop. It was over and cleared away by half-past seven.

'Where was Mrs Melanus's room?'

'On the second floor, at the front of the house.'

'Mr Melanus's room?'

'On the same floor to the rear.'

'Any other rooms on the same floor as Mr Melanus's room?'

'Two other bedchambers, both for guests and currently unused.'

'The servants' rooms?'

'In the attic above.'

'You found nothing unusual in any of these rooms?'

'Nothing.'

'Save for your mistress lying dead, of course.'

'Indeed.'

'Can you think of any reason why Mrs Melanus should have been attacked in this way?'

'No.'

At last the butler was told to stand down. Next Maria Worden, Mrs Melanus's personal maid, was called to the witness stand. She was of a very different cast to the lugubrious butler. Not only young and extremely pretty, Foxe thought, but so vivacious she'd stand out in any company. Good figure, too. Just the right kind of woman to flirt with, under different circumstances. Maybe even bed. In deference to the solemnity of the circumstances, she was behaving with proper decorousness that day. He doubted if that was always the case.

Miss Worden took the stand and swore on the bible to tell the truth. On the day in question, she said, she had been dismissed for the evening after Mrs Melanus had retired to her room. That must have been soon after seven. After her own meal, she spent an hour or more in the kitchen, sewing up a torn hem on one of Mrs Melanus's skirts and making other minor repairs to various garments.

'Why do that it the kitchen?' the coroner asked.

'It's warmer there. Save in the middle of the summer, our rooms in the attics are freezing.'

'Are you not allowed a fire?'

'Mr Melanus only gave us coals in the winter — and not much then, the old skinflint!'

The coroner glared at her and she had the grace to blush. I was right, Foxe thought. She's no straight-laced miss or I'm a Dutchman. I need to talk to her as soon as I can. If anyone is going to let slip what really went on in that household, it'll be her. A little flattery, a few smiles, some pleasant attention ...

The coroner continued, immune to anything but the job before him. Under his questioning, the maid admitted, she had stayed in the kitchen until late. After eleven she thought. She'd been enjoying the warmth from the range. She had also purloined a good candle from the stock kept for the family's use and used it to allow her to read a novel borrowed from Mrs Melanus's room.

'With your mistress's permission?'

'She wouldn't 'ave minded.'

Miss Worden then stated she was in bed in the 'freezing' attic when she heard noises below. No, she wasn't asleep. It was too cold to do more than doze. She had woken the housemaid — the only other servant who lived in, besides the butler and housekeeper — and they had both listened to the sounds.

'What did you hear?'

'Various noises from the floor below.'

'What kind of noises?'

'Like people trying to be quiet and not doin' it too good. Sort of muffled squeakin' and gruntin'. Then a thumpin', like the bed being moved, followed by groans and big sighs.'

Since what she was describing suggested only one activity, it caused an outburst of chattering in the room. The coroner suppressed it with angry looks and much banging with his gavel.

'You're saying you heard your mistress's bed being moved?'

'I'm saying the noises sounded like that. I'm not saying that's what was 'appening, am I? Anyhow, the next sounds we 'eard was a cry, followed by more squeaks and gurgles. Then nothing.'

Miss Worden explained that the two women had discussed whether one or both of them should go to see what had caused it. Neither was keen to do so. The butler would be in his bed on the ground floor, far below; too far away to help. If it turned out to be a burglar, the women risked being hurt — or worse. She'd started to creep down, but thought she heard whoever it was leaving the house.

'How?'

'By the front door, I thought.'

'Mr Simmonds has already given evidence that he had checked it was locked before he went to bed and he found nothing unusual afterwards.'

'That's what 'e says. What I'm tellin' you is what I thought I 'eard.'

'Could you have been mistaken?'

'Maybe.'

She doesn't believe for a moment she was mistaken, Foxe thought. Like me, she thinks the butler did find the front door unlocked next morning. He isn't certain he checked it before he went to bed, regardless of what he told the coroner. He'll now swear black is white to protect himself from any suggestion his negligence might have let an intruder into the house.

'What did you do after that?'

'We decided it was nothing to do with us and tried to go back to sleep.'

'You didn't go to your mistress's room until later the next morning?'

'No, sir.'

'When you did so, what did you see?'

'My mistress was lyin' on her back on the bed. I thought as 'ow she might be ill until I got closer. Then I could see she was dead. It was plain she'd been choked to death, so I covered 'er face over for decency, like you do with dead folk.'

'At what time was that?'

'About noon, sir. The mistress was what you might call a late riser.'

Next to give evidence was the constable, but Foxe had already heard his story. The coroner didn't dwell on it either, since little or none of it was relevant to determining the cause of death. That left only the medical examiner.

With a good deal of pomposity, the physician who had examined Mrs Melanus's corpse took the stand to give his evidence. He had been summoned by a young maidservant, he said. That was soon after one o'clock in the afternoon. His house was near that of the goldsmith, so he had arrived within fifteen minutes. He had then examined the corpse in situ.

'What did you find?'

'The body was completely undressed. That seemed unusual, given how cold the previous night had been.'

'You mean the lady was naked?'

'Entirely so. She was covered by a sheet, but I was informed that was due to the action of the maid. I removed it and found she was lying across the bed, laterally.'

'Laterally?'

'Not with her head on the pillow. Lying across the bed, side to side, her lower legs hanging down over the edge of the mattress. One look was enough to tell me she had been killed by manual strangulation. There were finger marks on her throat and her face was mottled and suffused. That is typical in cases of people choked to death. As far as I could see, she had suffered no other wounds or blows. There were no signs she had tried to defend herself. In my opinion, she had been taken by surprise and throttled. As I said, the cause of death was manual strangulation.'

'She did not try to defend herself, so far as you could see. That is correct?'

'That is so, sir, in my opinion. She would have lost consciousness anyway within a minute or less.'

'Did you find any reason to alter your opinion of the cause of death after making further examinations later?'

'I did not. The cause of death was plain from the start.'

At that point, the coroner clearly thought the physician's evidence was complete. He began to tell him he could stand down, but the doctor interrupted him with a loud clearing of his throat.

'I feel bound to add certain other findings, sir, if you will permit me.' The coroner nodded; somewhat reluctantly, in Foxe's opinion. Still, he could hardly do otherwise than agree.

'I have already explained that the general state of the victim struck me as unusual,' the physician continued. 'Given the strong, cold winds we have suffered these past few days, no one would want to sleep naked, uncovered and lying across the bed.'

The coroner winced and was seen to rub one of his knees.

'I therefore examined the victim's whole body carefully to see if there was anything which might account for such behaviour. In the genital area, I found significant bruising about the labia and perineum.'

That set the courtroom abuzz in earnest. Once again, the coroner banged his gavel energetically on the table, calling for silence and turning redder and redder in the face as he did so.

'If those on the public benches cannot restrain themselves,' he said, when quiet had been restored, 'I will have the room cleared.' The poor man was beside himself with irritation. 'Now, doctor, if you please. Continue with your evidence. What do these findings signify?'

'In my professional opinion, shortly before her death the lady had engaged in more than one bout of vigorous, even rough, sexual intercourse. I also noted many signs of the presence of male semen.'

'You say more than one incident of sexual congress?'

'I do. There was too much semen present to have come from a single ejaculation.'

'These signs couldn't indicate a series of assaults? Perhaps after she had been killed?'

'Not in my view. Such extensive bruising would not have occurred after the heart had ceased to beat.'

'How long before death did these ... err... multiple events take place?'

Despite whatever instructions the coroner had received on how the hearing was to be conducted to avoid unwanted matters being discussed, his curiosity had taken over.

'Less than an hour, I would say. The bruises were fresh and some were still developing when death intervened. Once the heart ceases beating, no further blood would flow to cause bruises to develop or spread in such a way.'

There was something for Hirons' newspaper! There would be no keeping the story of the murder quiet after this evidence. Here was proof Mrs Melanus had a lover — at least, for those who knew Melanus himself was absent that evening. For those who did not, the finger of suspicion would now point at the husband.

Foxe smiled to himself. This was better than even he could have contrived. No one would be interested in affairs at the bank now. With a single person's evidence, the murder had been established as a domestic matter. Nothing to do with either of the husband's businesses.

The foreman of the jury set the seal on that view of the case the moment the doctor had been allowed to stand down. Clearing his throat, he asked the coroner why Mr Melanus had not been present at the hearing or asked to give evidence.

'Mr Melanus is not in the city,' the coroner said. Out came the prepared falsehood. 'He is said to be away visiting a relative who is seriously ill.'

'Was he present in the house that night?'

'It seems he was not.'

'Could he have returned in secret?'

'No evidence has been presented to show he did so. Since the relative lives a good distance away, I doubt that Mr Melanus even knows of his wife's death yet.'

The coroner did his best to wrap proceedings up at that point, but the foreman of the jury was not to be silenced.

'Why has no evidence been given of the date when Mr Melanus left?'

'None is available, sir. Mr Melanus came and went as he wished, rarely telling the servants in advance. He may well have left some days before. Whenever he went, he has not yet returned.'

'So, no one knows precisely when Mr Melanus left and whether he might have returned on the night of the murder?'

'That is correct.'

Even then, the jury foreman had the last word muttering that the jurors ought to have been told that earlier, not have to find it out at the last minute. That stung the coroner into a fit of righteous anger. He now directed the jury to find a verdict, suggested it should be that Mrs Melanus had been murdered by a person or persons unknown, glared at them until they did so, then banged down his gavel and declared the inquest closed. All within a couple of minutes.

Foxe was puzzled. Halloran had told him Mr Gurtheim claimed to have talked with Melanus the Friday before the killing. He had also been told the shop and business was to be closed at once, since Mr Melanus had to leave the city shortly. That was three days before the day of Mrs Melanus's death. Surely, he should have been summoned by the coroner to give evidence to that effect? Had someone felt that his evidence, both about the closure of the shop and Mr Melanus's departure, would fuel the idea that Melanus had planned the death of his wife? Did they want to keep the fact of the sudden and final closure of Melanus's shop before he disappeared a secret? It pointed too obviously towards odd dealings connected with that part of his business. That might also produce speculation about the bank. Better to allow the inquest to reach its inevitable verdict without drawing in business matters at all. Whoever had briefed the coroner had not known the doctor was set on giving the jury all the evidence he had found, not just the cause of death.

Still, whether that was what had been intended from the start or not, people would now go away without considering the businesses at all. Most would be sure that Mrs Melanus's husband could not have been the one pleasuring Mrs Melanus. If that was the right word for what had been described as 'vigorous, even rough intercourse'. That must have been what caused the bruises the physician had described. Elderly husband, young wife, you could hear them telling one another. When the cat's away, the mice will play. The old story. Find the lover and you'll have the one who killed her. Simple.

In all the confusion and hubbub now filling the room, Foxe was able to slip out unnoticed.

6

The walk back from the inquest gave Foxe time to ponder and decide what his next course of action should be. Halloran was right. However angry he was at the thought that Jack Beeston had come out of hiding, there was not the slightest evidence he'd had any hand in Melanus's disappearance. Or his wife's murder, come to that. Beeston was in Great Yarmouth, a good twenty miles from Norwich by road. It was time to put Beeston out of his mind and concentrate on the task in hand.

Unfortunately, Foxe still had nothing to help him direct his search for answers. He knew from past experience it was rarely profitable to talk with potential witnesses unless you had a clear strategy in mind. He still knew too little about the victim or her husband. So far as he could recall, he had never met either. All the silverware in his house had been inherited from his father. He had never yet found the need to purchase any more. He didn't even bank with the Norwich City Bank.

Surely someone would be able to tell him — of course! Mrs Crombie! He doubted whether she would know either Melanus personally, any more than he did. However, the sensational news from the inquest on Mrs Melanus's must be spread all around the city soon. His own bookshop was known to be the best place in Norwich to catch up on whatever news or rumours were currently circulating. Mrs Crombie must hear people talking about the evidence given and what it might well imply. He would leave it until she had closed up for the day and then find out what they were saying.

'I'm not sure where to begin,' Mrs Crombie said, when she and Foxe had at last made their way into the workroom; their usual place to talk privately. The apprentice, Charlie Dillon, was still in there, clearing up after doing book repairs, but that didn't matter. The boy was usually party to whatever investigation his master was engaged in. He was able to enlist the help of the street children in the city when it was needed. He also had a good mind, honed by years of living on the streets himself. His contributions were always worth listening to.

'The trouble is,' Fox replied, 'I'm certain I never met either Mr Melanus or his wife. Nor did I go into his shop or bank. Did you ever meet them, Mrs Crombie?'

'Not as far as I can remember. Buying fine gold and silverware is well beyond my means. The only thing I do know is that the lady who has just been murdered was Mr Melanus's third wife. The other two women whom he married both died without bearing him any children. People are saying the man was desperate to have a son to whom he could leave his business and his wealth. That's supposed to be why he married a woman so much younger than himself. He thought a young woman would be more likely to bear children — preferably several of them, so long as they were all male. I imagine it never occurred to him that the inability of his earlier wives to conceive might be down to him.'

'What else are people telling one another?'

'The general view seems to be that this latest Mrs Melanus was a far from suitable wife. The word "trollop" was being banded around a good deal, even before what the inquest revealed about her. There were also several heavy-handed witticisms about a woman obsessed with gold finding her ideal home in a goldsmith's shop.'

'Did anyone know where she came from? Anything about her family?'

'Nothing about her family background. I gather that Mr Melanus went on one of his regular trips to London and stayed there a little longer than usual. When he returned, he had already married this third wife. Where he met her and what her background might be has been a major subject of speculation since her death. Some of the suggestions were wilder than others. One group were adamant that she was a distant relation. A young widow who had fallen on hard times and appealed to Mr Melanus for help. Others claim to be certain she had been a courtesan, whom he had turned to for ... for comfort, shall we say? Finding who he was and what he did for a living, the woman decided marriage to a rich, elderly husband was an attractive option. Few courtesans, these people explain, can keep the attentions of the wealthiest young rakes for long.'

'Not a love-match then?'

'Possibly on his side, definitely not on hers. I blush to tell you this, Mr Foxe. There was wide agreement amongst my informants the lady had been unfaithful to her husband almost from the start. And on a considerable scale. According to Mrs Crilly, the grocer's wife, they had to stop sending young errand boys to the house. Two of them were heard boasting about what they got up to with her when they were there. You can imagine what it was.'

'Any idea how long Mr and Mrs Melanus had been married?'

'A little over a year, I believe.'

'And Mrs Melanus's age?'

'She claimed to be nine-and-twenty, though most were sceptical about that. Nevertheless, the word is that she was a handsome woman, if somewhat coarse in her features. She always dressed in the latest London fashions and had a taste for flamboyant jewellery.'

'Handsome? Not beautiful — nor even pretty?'

'No one used those words. From some of the other comments that were made, many of them catty, I gather she relied on fine clothes and cosmetics for her attractions. Not the looks she was born with.'

'Figure?'

'Well developed.'

'I saw her once or twice,' Charlie said. 'Rather a short woman, dressed in the very best clothes, as Mrs Crombie said. Turned a good few men's heads though.'

'Why was that?' Foxe asked.

'The size of her t— I mean ... um ... err ... her bosom.'

That earned him a hard stare from Mrs Crombie. 'Boys of your age shouldn't be looking at ladies' bosoms,' she said. 'It's not seemly.'

'I always did when I was his age,' Foxe said. 'Still do, come to that.'

'Don't encourage him, Mr Foxe. He doesn't need it. Now, let's have no more talk of bosoms from either of you. I think we've finished with that topic, haven't we? I've not told you all I heard today. There's something else which two or three people mentioned, which seems to me rather more important.'

Foxe found it hard to keep a straight face. It was obvious Mrs Crombie had no experience of dealing with boys of Charlie's age. Perhaps that's why she tended to be somewhat puritanical in dealing with him. If the boy hadn't been present, Foxe was certain their conversation would have been less straight-laced. Mrs Crombie's own bosom was shapely enough to have drawn his own attention on several occasions — in a purely detached way, of course.

'So, what's this other matter?' he asked.

'It's about Mr Melanus's shop: the goldsmiths. The word is he started to lose interest in it about twelve months ago, if not earlier. That was when he started letting his workmen go and turning away new orders. Mrs Morgan — you'll remember her husband's a baker with two shops and a market stall — lives next door to a Mr Gurtheim. He managed the shop for Mr Melanus, as well as being his longest-serving craftsman. According to Mrs Morgan, Mr Melanus dismissed Mr Gurtheim only a few days before he disappeared. Told him he was closing the business down completely and there was no more need for Mr Gurtheim's services. The other craftsmen had all gone by then. Mr Gurtheim was the last one.'

Foxe didn't know what to make of that piece of news. He knew about Gurtheim, of course, but not that Melanus had started running down the business so long before his sudden departure. Had he truly lost interest? Was the Norwich City Bank doing so well that he no longer had time to spend on his original type of work? If so, wouldn't the sensible thing be to keep the business going until he could find a buyer? It's true the demand for items made of gold must be limited. Even gold-plated items were too expensive for most buyers. But nearly all so-called goldsmiths worked almost exclusively in silver. Plenty of demand there. The first thing any new wealthy household bought was a selection of fine silverware to display on the dining table when they had guests.

Another thought crossed his mind. Someone closing down a business needed to dispose of any remaining stock. Most would put an advertisement in the newspaper, announcing the closure and inviting people to come and look for bargains. Items made of precious metals had their own value too. Most sold for far more than the cost of the metal from which they were made. If Mr Melanus had offered a discount on the original price he might have sold many pieces — all for more than he would get if he disposed of them for scrap. Yet there had been, to Mr Foxe's recollection, no such advertisement. No advance announcement of the closure of the business either. If this Mrs Morgan hadn't mentioned it when she came to the bookshop, he'd still be in the dark. He would have gone on assuming Melanus had shut down his original business not long before leaving the city. Mr Gurtheim, as he recalled, had told the constable the other craftsmen had been dismissed before he was. Not how long before that process had begun. It made quite a difference.

'Did you say that Mrs Morgan lives next door to Mr Gurtheim? How often does she come into the shop?'

Mrs Crombie smiled. 'I knew you'd ask me that, so I asked her where she lives. It's over the water, in one of the courts off Magdalen Street. I've made a note of it for you.'

'Mrs Crombie,' Fox said, 'you are indeed a gem. Charlie? Leave off what you're doing and go there right away. If Mr Gurtheim is at home, ask him if it would be convenient for me to call upon him tomorrow at noon. If he's out, give the same message to the servant who answers the door, together with this calling card.'

Maybe tomorrow wouldn't be wasted after all.

7

Maria Worden sat on her mistress's bed and thought about her future. The funeral was tomorrow. Once it was over, she would be without a position and in a city where she knew almost no one. Fortunately, she had put a little money by — enough to be able to take the coach back to London. Even there, it might be weeks before she was able to find fresh employment, particularly as she would not have a 'character' from her last employer. The wife was dead and the husband was missing. She didn't fancy the idea of selling herself on the streets or finding a place in the bordello, but it might yet come to that.

She looked around her at the piles of dresses and other clothes. That cow of a housekeeper, Mrs Simmonds, had told her to sort through her mistress's wardrobes — to put everything ready for the inventory that would have to be taken if the master was found dead. It was typical of her to take the darkest possible view. Still, even if he returned he would hardly have any need for his dead wife's clothing. No one suggested she might like any of it, of course. Not that it would fit. She was a good six inches taller than her mistress had been and much more modest about the bust. Even so, most of these dresses were made of the finest material. It was surprising what a good dress-maker could do these days in terms of alterations.

Mrs Simmonds had said she would deal with the mistress's jewellery herself. Of course she will, Maria said to herself. And pilfer a good deal of it too. Mrs Melanus had liked to show off her jewellery. There was little doubt in her mind the housekeeper's piggy little eyes had taken careful note of each piece. If anything was found to be missing before that woman got her hands on it, there was no doubt who would get the blame.

Maria thought back over the two years and more that she had worked for Eleanor Rogers, later to become Mrs Eleanor Melanus. When they first met, Eleanor was still an actress mostly noted for playing the more comic and bawdy roles. It wasn't usual for the orphanage to let girls go as servants to people like Eleanor Rogers. She needed a dresser. The overseers of the orphanage had found Maria such a thorn in their sides they would have sold her into slavery, if it had been possible. She couldn't blame them. There was something about sour-faced people in authority that brought out the worst in her. She could see now it hadn't been a good idea to lead the parish curate on like that, even if it had been amusing. He blushed and trembled every time she smiled at him and she was sure he must be a virgin. She never expected him to confess all his lustful thoughts to the rector and blame her for tempting him.

Working for Eleanor Rogers had certainly been better than that. The woman had been both secretive and heedlessly promiscuous, that was true. Vicious too, when roused. She could still recall the beating she'd been given after her mistress had found her tucked in a dark corner of the theatre one evening. All she was doing was giving conso-lation to a poor, lovesick lad whom her mistress had enjoyed leading on, then rejected, purely from a sense of power. After that, the evil bitch made very sure Maria was never around when one of her lovers was due. No errand had been too trivial to make sure she was occupied elsewhere. The fat cow had been afraid of the competition, of course.

Then there was the woman's vanity. She tried to convince everyone, including her present husband, she was twenty-nine. Maria knew she was at least thirty-five, if she was a day. Maybe even older. You couldn't cheat your personal maid by the copious use of cosmetics. Nor by spending a fortune on clothes designed for younger women. Those tightly laced corsets and all the efforts of an extremely well-paid dressmaker wouldn't be able to preserve her figure for much longer. See her in her shift, and it was obvious the hefty breasts she liked to flaunt had already fallen prey to gravity and slackening muscles. In a few more years, they'd be round her knees. Nowadays, the mistress always made sure her lovers visited her when the light was poor. Shadows could hide a good many things. Especially the little wrinkles round her throat and the fatty, dimpled skin on her thighs and bottom.

Eleanor Rogers' last year in London had proceeded through a series of increasingly greedy demands for jewels or cash. Anything which could be squirrelled away against the time when her looks would no longer command a high price — nor her willingness to indulge foolish but wealthy men in their wilder sexual fantasies. Maria enjoyed sex too, but she rarely got any. Her mistress was in the opposite position. Abundant sex, but mostly reduced to a tedious and loveless activity. Something undertaken to cause men to lose their grasp on common sense and pay royally for the mere appearance of giving pleasure. Eleanor Rogers' stage acting career had never reached above the mediocre. In the bedroom, however, she gave a long string of skilful and convincing performances.

Maria had never been certain what had made her mistress decide to marry Samuel Melanus, the creepy goldsmith from Norwich. The old fool doted on her, of course, and was said to be rich. Eleanor also knew her popularity with audiences was declining. The young blades who hung around the stage door or the actresses' dressing room, like the rowdy mob in the gallery, preferred younger flesh. She hadn't managed to snare a rich London gentleman either, despite all her efforts. She must have realised her time was running out. Better to marry any old fool with money and hope it wouldn't be long before he went to meet his Maker. In the meantime, she would make up for her husband's cold and feeble embraces by looking elsewhere. She met Melanus in London, so was well aware of his frequent trips to the capital on business matters.

What Maria couldn't understand was this. How had Mr Melanus

convinced himself Eleanor Rogers would make him a suitable wife — let alone a good mother for the children he wished for so ardently? She was an actress of dubious reputation, already past her best. You couldn't ask for better proof that men kept their brains in their breeches. At least, on that count, Mr and Mrs Melanus were a good match. Neither, in her opinion, was possessed of anything more than a certain low cunning.

She'd better get on, or that Simmonds woman would be round to see what she was up to. Only yesterday, the housekeeper had screamed at her for being a lazy trollop. Threatened to bar her from having dinner with the other servants. She'd half a mind to think up some trick to play on the old cow before she left this house for good. Something that would give the woman a reason to scream in earnest. At least that might give her some satisfaction. For the rest, she'd come with almost nothing and she'd be leaving with the same.

The maid suddenly sat up straight and slapped her hand on her thigh. Of course! Why hadn't she remembered that before? Eleanor Melanus may have been sly and secretive, but she wasn't nearly as bright as her maid. She hadn't spent all the money she'd wheedled out of her husband. Oh no! Just as she had in London, the woman had set aside a secret store of cash in case of need. What's more, despite all Eleanor's efforts, Maria knew exactly where it was.

In a moment, she was off the bed, out through the door and heading up the stairs into the attics. There were four rooms up there. Once, two of them had been dormitories for male and female servants, while the other two had been used for storage. There were no male servants now and only her and Bessie, the housemaid, living in. The dormitory for the female servants had been divided in two by a rough partition, giving each of them their own small space. Dear Bessie! She was the only person in this house Maria would miss. Except in the middle of summer, it was so cold up here the two of them had taken to snuggling up together in the same bed. There was no harm in it, was there? Bessie was so pathetically grateful for anything in the way of help or affection. Sleeping with her was more like sharing your bed with a timid child than a grown woman. Mr and Mrs Simmonds, the butler and housekeeper, had their room on the ground floor. With just the two of them up here in the attics, nobody else knew — or most likely cared — what they did.

Nobody would imagine the mistress of the house would ever come to the attics either. If she wanted anything, a servant would be dispatched to find it. That was what had made Maria suspicious. One afternoon, shortly after she had come to this house in Norwich, she'd been sitting in her own room doing some sewing. First thing she'd heard was someone open the door at the bottom of the attic stairs. At first, she thought it must be Bessie, but a second's recollection ruled that out. The poor girl never had a moment's rest from dawn until late in the evening. Certainly not enough to be able to slip away and come up three flights of stairs to her room in the attic.

Maria had slid off her bed as quietly as she could and eased the door open just a crack. Just enough to see through with one eye. It wasn't Bessie. It was her mistress, creeping up the stairs so furtively you knew she was up to no good. Maria closed the door again. She didn't want to risk being spotted. Besides, she knew the attics well enough to be able to tell, just by listening, roughly where her mistress had gone. Past the first attic, then the second. She was heading for the furthest one, the room where the male servants used to sleep. There was nothing in there but old furniture, so what was she after? A moment later, Maria heard the footsteps returning and then going back down the stairs. That was followed by the sound of someone closing the door to the landing. The bitch was trying to be quiet, but making rather a poor job of it.

She waited a full five minutes to be certain the mistress wasn't coming back. Then she left her own room and tiptoed across to the furthest attic. Inside, as she knew, there was nothing but worn out furniture. Things like a table with a worm-eaten leg, some old chairs, a sofa whose upholstery had been attacked by the moths, several old bedsteads, and a desk that had seen better days. The desk then. Maria opened the cupboards and the drawers, but found them all empty. For a moment, she was baffled. Finally, she felt under the edge of the desk at the front and sides and in the space where your knees went. Still nothing. She tried pushing and pulling the knobs on the drawers, but to no effect. Merely by chance, she opened the right-hand draw, felt underneath it, moving her fingers to the left side and then to the right. At last! She pushed the hidden catch and the draw slid open a further six inches. The space revealed held a piece of cloth, carefully folded. When she took it out and opened it, she was rewarded by the sight of gold. Making sure to disturb nothing, she counted the sovereigns. Fifteen. A nice little hoard.

On that occasion, she did no more than re-fold the cloth and leave all exactly as it was. This time, when she opened the folded cloth, she could see at least twenty-five sovereigns. Maybe a few more. With those in her possession, she could look forward to the future with confidence. No bordello for her. She might even be able to set herself up with a market stall.

Maria quickly took the coins from their hiding place, still wrapped in the cloth. Then she carried them back to her own room, clutched tight against her chest. Plenty of time to count the money later, when she was well away from Norwich and this house. In the meantime, she needed to think.

She was wrapping the bundle of coins in her spare shift when she felt something else. Not a coin this time, but a ring with two keys. One obviously from a door somewhere and another smaller, but much more intricate. It didn't look like the kind of key that might fit a lock inside the house. Not a front-door key either. She knew her mistress had a key to the front door, though she had no idea where she kept it. In her jewellery box or at the bottom of a draw? Somewhere unimaginative for sure. It wasn't worth looking for anyhow. Once she was out of this house, there was no way she would ever come back. This was the sort of heavy, complex pattern of a key for a safe.

Maria put the keys back amongst the coins and wrapped the whole bundle in her spare shift. After that, she tucked it in the bottom of the carpet bag holding her few clothes and possessions. She had no time to solve the puzzle of the keys now. I'm not a thief, she told herself. This is compensation for being dragged all the way to Norwich, then dismissed without a character and left to find my own way back to London.

❦   8   ❧

As he walked back from Mr Gurtheim's house, Ashmole Foxe was in an extremely bad mood. The day was both wet and cold. Very wet. Torrents of rain, which poured from the eaves and overflowed everywhere. As a consequence, the streets ran with a foul mixture of mud, horse droppings and human waste thrown from the upper windows. Half-way home, someone drove past him in a chaise, urging the horses on as if all the demons of hell were right behind. The rear wheels sent up a fountain of mud and water, which descended on Foxe and soaked him from head to foot. It was the last straw! He'd wasted several hours of his day on a task which should have taken fifteen minutes, only to be drenched in mud and filth as well.

Gurtheim had proved to be extremely talkative, but most of it to no purpose. It was understandable that he was bitter against his former employer. That wasn't Foxe's concern. All he wanted from the man was to discover something of what went on in the Melanus household. Gurtheim, however, presented with a willing listener, desired nothing more than to repeat his own tale of woe over and over again. Each repetition brought more embellishments and further complaints of ill-treatment. The man had little interest in anything except himself. That meant all that happened outside Melanus's shop. He'd rarely set foot in any other part of the house, save to make his way to the back door and outside to the privy. He probably wouldn't have noticed if the household servants had gone about their work naked. If Mrs Melanus had habitually kept a parrot on top of her head he wouldn't have seen it.

Another carriage now passed, the horses slipping and sliding on the mud and the rear wheel jolting through a pothole. That one too sent up a jet of filth. One that struck Foxe on his hip and ran down his left leg. The cloak he had worn against the rain was now as wet inside as out. The wind blew it open at the front, welcoming the rain. The puddles under his feet sent their splashes upwards to complete the job. He was beyond cursing. He simply trudged on, with no goal beyond reaching home. There, he promised himself, he would strip off all his clothes, down to the skin, and wash as he had never washed before.

A few weeks ago, after he'd been forced to take a public coach to Swaffham and back, Foxe had promised himself that he would buy his own carriage. Now he resolved to make that purchase his highest priority.

As he dragged himself along, Foxe reviewed what few items of interest he had managed to extract from Gurtheim's ranting. Firstly, the shop was kept entirely separate from the bank next door. It had its own counting house and a small strongroom on the first floor of the house, up a small stairway which led off the first half-landing. He could probably have guessed the two businesses would be independent of each other, but it was helpful to be sure. Secondly, Mr Melanus handled everything to do with the finances, the finished work and the supplies of bullion himself. Before the craftsmen had all been laid off, they would sit in the workshop to the rear of the ground floor and concentrate on engraving or other elements of their clients' orders. Only Gurtheim spent any time in the shop itself. Since Mr Melanus had begun to lose interest, he'd said, he had been charged with keeping the shop open for business.

Questioned about what he'd termed his master's 'lack of interest' in the business, Gurtheim said that had begun some eighteen months before. Originally, they had melted their own silver and gold. Mr Melanus had drawn up the designs and the items were cast using a furnace located in a shed in the yard to the rear of the property. Lovely work it had been too. In more recent times, furnace and forge had lain idle. Mr Melanus bought his castings from elsewhere. That left his remaining craftsmen, before they were let go, nothing to do beyond adding the engraved decoration as ordered.

The third point was linked to this change. All the bullion for melting, together with the best of the finished pieces, had always been kept in a safe in the strongroom. Only Mr Melanus had the keys. Gurtheim had no idea how much bullion was still there, if any. In the days of doing their own melting and casting, they had kept substantial stocks of precious metal. Some ingots and some broken and tarnished items that could be melted down. It might be still there, he supposed. He'd not seen anyone come to take it away. You'd hardly walk through the streets of Norwich with a bag of gold and silver bullion, or a sack of copper for the alloys. As he'd said, Mr Melanus handled purchases of bullion personally. It had been delivered to the house in a heavy cart like the one used to take prisoners to the gaol. One with thick bars on the tiny window at the rear, massive locks on the door and two armed guards to travel with the driver.

Why keep the bullion when the business was being run down? Gurtheim didn't know, beyond the fact that it might provide Mr Melanus with a reserve against hard times. Either that, or he might have planned to return to doing his own casting sometime.

Was there nothing of value kept in the shop or work area? Only one or two items of low value to act as examples of their work, Foxe was told. Mr Melanus's habit had been to collect all the pieces his men were working on at the end of each day and take them to the strongroom. Also, the shavings and dust from their work. Each craftsman had two large pieces of cloth, one for gold and one for silver. Whatever item was being engraved, repaired or finished was always kept on the appropriate cloth. At the end of each working day, any dust and bits and pieces of metal were shaken from the cloths into either the gold or the silver bin. Sometimes a few fragments of copper got mixed in, but they didn't bother about small amounts. There was a copper bin too, of course, but only larger fragments went in there. The bins? Taken to the strongroom with the rest. He supposed Mr Melanus had somewhere to empty each one, ready to be re-smelted later. Even after the others had been laid off, leaving only himself, the same procedure was continued.

That was it. Asked about how successful the business was, Gurtheim admitted he had little idea. He and the others never lacked for work, that was certain. Mr Melanus didn't deal much in ready-made items. All their work was done to order. Did Gurtheim have any idea why Mr Melanus had run down the business, then closed it? None. He could only suppose all his time and energy was now taken up with the bank. Either that, or his new wife's demands were wearing him out. Mr Melanus had been a fool to marry such a young woman. Everyone said that. Foxe had asked what else he'd heard about Mrs Melanus, but Gurtheim either knew nothing or refused to disclose what he did know.

A sudden gust of wind snatched Foxe's hat from his head and dropped it in the roadway. Before he could reach it, the wheel of a brewer's dray, laden with barrels, squashed it into the mud. He rarely wore a wig, considering himself too young and without the need to conceal thinning hair. He had his own hair styled and powdered to the requirements of fashion. That day, however, he had put on a wig under his hat. He'd hoped a more formal appearance would persuade Mr Gurtheim of the seriousness of his purpose in coming to talk with him. Now the wig would be ruined as well as the hat. He could already feel the rain down his neck. Soon it would turn into rivulets carrying hair powder to add to the mess on his shirt and jacket. All this and nothing much learned beyond what he might have guessed anyway!

Somehow, he had to get inside Melanus's house and question Mrs Melanus's personal maid. The bank held little interest for him. He could talk with Humboldt, Gregg or Farmer, all of whom were partners in the bank. They would give him permission to question the clerks too, if he so wished. None of that would take him into the goldsmith's private household. Reuben Sedgefield might be examining the bank's books, but no one had any right to pry into Mr Melanus's other affairs. Unless the man was found dead, of course. He may have disappeared, but he hadn't been missing long enough for the law to allow the presumption of his death. That would require years to pass. Was it five years or seven? He couldn't remember, but it was a long time.

Foxe wondered idly who Melanus's heir might be. Not Mrs Melanus anymore, that was for sure. Probably a cousin or a nephew. Foxe wasn't sure of the correct legal steps needed to secure Melanus's affairs until he could be presumed dead and his Will proved. Perhaps the executors and trustees appointed under his Will would take charge. He was assuming Mrs Melanus had no children from a prior marriage, of course. Had she made a Will?

Foxe shook his head in disgust. The only certainty, so far as he could see, was that several lawyers would be rubbing their hands in anticipation. There would be months — probably years — of highly profitable argument and litigation.

He cut across behind St Peter Mancroft Church, grateful for the brief shelter that the massive building gave him from the onslaught of rain and wind. Coming out again, he turned right, then left, then right again, taking the quickest route to his door. Then he paused, conscious of the filth and wet which covered him. As master of the house, he had every right to enter by the front door and leave it to his servants to clear up the mess. The temptation was strong to do just that. Yet if he walked but a further fifty yards or so in the rain, there was an entry through the back gate into the garden. It would take only a little longer and would save him from the sense of guilt he would suffer from causing his household so much trouble.

He therefore turned aside and trudged up the alleyway that led to the rear of his property. There he let himself in through the back gate. Once inside, he called out loudly. That brought first Florence, the kitchen maid, then Mrs Whitbread, the cook, to the back door to see what all the noise was about. The looks of horror they gave him told him his appearance must be even worse that he had imagined.

'Tell Alfred to bring me fresh clothing,' he called out to them, 'and send Charlie out here with two buckets of clean water from the kitchen pump. Then go back inside and don't look. Not unless you want to see a naked man sluicing water over himself in the pouring rain. Everything I'm wearing now is to be thrown out, even the shoes. I'm so soaked in filth from the roads it would take a miracle to get the smell out. I'd rather get rid of them and start again. Now, hurry! It's damned cold standing here like this.'

All was done as he said. Alfred and Charlie helped to sluice the water over him as he washed off all the dirt. Poor Foxe! It took him a long time to live down the disgrace. There he was, standing in the open, stark naked, while his valet and his apprentice poured cold water over him. His female staff, despite his prohibition, peeped through the windows and giggled at his discomfort. Finally, he retreated into the privy, rubbed himself hard with the towels Alfred brought, and dressed in a clean, dry shirt and stockings. Only then, gathering about him such shreds of his dignity as he could, did he hasten to the back door and retreat to his bedroom to make himself fully presentable.

FOXE MADE A POOR DINNER THAT EVENING, PICKING AT HIS FOOD and drinking too much wine. He still felt cold and disheartened. As far as he could see, he had reached a brick wall in his investigation, even though he'd hardly begun. If only he could find some way to question the servants in the Melanus household. Without lighting on some key to unlock the mystery of what Mr Melanus had been about in running down the goldsmith business, he could see no way to advance. Why had the man been closing his business in gold and silver? Exactly who had his wife used to keep her entertained while he was away? What was the real state of Melanus's finances?

Not for the first time, Foxe wished he had someone else living with him with whom he could discuss problems of this nature. Looking back, the weeks that his young cousin Nicholas had spent with him now appeared a golden age of good company and intelligent discussion. Nicholas was away studying the law in Thetford. Brock used to come to dinner and stay talking afterwards, sometimes into the early hours. Brock now had someone else to talk to. He was doubtless enjoying a good dinner and thinking of the comforts provided by his new wife. Foxe could have visited his favourite bagnio and sought consolation in the experienced arms of one of the young ladies. To do so would mean venturing outside again. There was no chance of that. Not while it was still raining and blowing a gale. He could hear the wind driving sheets of water against the windows.

He helped himself to a third glass of brandy. His head would suffer for it in the morning, but he no longer cared. At least it warmed him tonight. Drink enough of it and all his worries would be lost in a haze of alcoholic forgetfulness.

Tomorrow was Mrs Melanus's funeral, according to a note left for him by Mrs Crombie before she shut up the shop and left for home. By God! Even Mrs Crombie had someone waiting for her when she got there. Ever since the affair of the dead man in the church tower, the dumb girl, Jane Thaxter, had made her home with Mrs Crombie. First as a maid, then as her much-loved companion. Emerging from that muddle with an annuity of her own, Jane needed somewhere to live. Mrs Crombie had willingly provided it. From all he heard, it was hard to tell who now earned most from the arrangement. To say the two of them had become close friends was to understate the reality to a considerable degree.

He tried to shake off his gloom by turning again to the matter of Mrs Melanus. Her funeral was tomorrow, he told himself again. Well, he wouldn't go. There was no point, so far as he could see. He presumed members of Melanus's family would attend. That is, if any lived close enough and if the man's third marriage hadn't alienated them all. Mrs Melanus came from London, so it was unlikely any of her relatives would make the journey. They might not even know she was dead. The household servants would be there, of course, including her personal maid, the bewitching Maria Worden. The one whose looks and manner had so attracted him when she gave evidence at the inquest. She was most definitely a person he wanted to be able to question on the topic of her mistress's life. Even so, he could hardly walk up to her in the church or at the graveside and start asking her questions. Besides, he'd little doubt the butler would be keeping a close eye on the other servants. He'd make sure they all went back to Melanus's house the moment the funeral was over. He'd want them home well before the other mourners, ready to serve what Shakespeare had called the funeral baked meats.

After that, the house would be shut up and the servants dismissed. Would the butler and housekeeper stay on to keep the place in order in the hope that Mr Melanus would return some day? Probably not for long, if they did.

Foxe sat up in his chair so sharply his head, already befuddled with too much alcohol, caused the room to spin for a few moments. Fool! Thrice fool! That maid, Maria what's-her-name, would be out of a job. What's more, she'd have little chance of finding another one in a city she'd only come to some twelve months ago. What would she do? Go back to London as soon as she could, of course, provided she had the money for the fare. Whatever happened, he couldn't see the butler allowing her to stay in that house a day longer than necessary. He had to catch her now or lose the chance of talking to her for ever. What better time would there be than when she had left the household and was freed from the oppressive oversight of the butler and his wife.

When would she leave? Early on the day after the funeral was the most likely time. She would be dragooned into helping with the entertainment for the funeral guests, and clearing up after they left. That would leave no time to collect her things and leave before it was dark. Surely even that misery of a butler wouldn't turn a young woman out into the streets of Norwich at night.

Foxe put down the brandy glass and rang for Molly. Coffee was what he needed now. Coffee to clear his head and make him fit for what he planned to do the next day. Please God it wouldn't still be raining!

9

The next morning, much to Foxe's satisfaction, the rain had stopped. The sky was now a watery blue, thickly spread with small clouds. There was still a strong breeze, but it had swung around to the north-west. There was no longer the sharp edge to it he recalled from his solitary and miserable walk home the day before. It wasn't going to be warm — that would be too much to hope for — but at least he wouldn't freeze while he carried out his plan.

As soon as he was up and about, Foxe sent for Charlie Dillon.

'Please apologise to Mrs Crombie for me,' Foxe told the boy, 'but I need you to be with me for an hour or so this morning. We're going to a funeral — well, not exactly to the funeral itself, but somewhere nearby where we can see everyone going in and out of the church. I shall point a young woman out to you and I want you to remember her well enough to describe her in detail to your young friends on the street.'

'What's she done, master?' Charlie asked.

'Nothing, so far as I know. Listen. Her name is Maria Worden and she is — rather, was — Mrs Melanus's personal maid. Now her mistress is dead, there will be no purpose in keeping her on at the house. If my thoughts are right, the housekeeper will turn her out the moment her

WILLIAM SAVAGE

mistress is buried. At least, that's the most likely situation. I haven't set eyes on the housekeeper, but she's the wife of the butler who gave evidence at the inquest. A more miserable, stiff-necked servant you couldn't hope to find. Any woman married to him must be of a similar cast, or she would murder him within a few weeks.'

'You want the street children to watch where she goes? Is that it?'

'I suspect I know that already. The word is Mrs Melanus brought her from London, so she isn't likely to be local. Nor can she have been in the city for more than a year or so. My guess is she'll head back to London, if she can. I very much want to talk to her, but if I go to the house, the butler will send me away with a flea in my ear. I have no official standing, you see. Nothing to lean on to demand entry. If I ask the mayor to lend me a constable, that might get me inside. It will also make the young woman take fright and refuse to tell me anything useful.'

'What do you want my friends to do?

'Young Miss Worden will leave that house, either later today or, more likely, first thing tomorrow morning. She'll need to get a coach to London and she'll be carrying some kind of luggage, like a carpet bag. I want them to keep watch and follow her far enough away from the house to be free from any prying eyes. Then they are to waylay her and tell her I need to talk with her. They can tell her I'll pay her fare to London, if she still wants to go after that. However, I may well know of someone who will give her another position as a lady's maid here. They can tell her anything, so long as they don't let her leave for London. If she goes, I'll never find her again. Do you think they can do that?'

'Of course, master. I'll tell the boys to help watch and only allow the girls to speak to her. She'll trust them more.'

'Very good. There's a whole five shillings waiting for whichever group delivers her, safe and sound and ready to talk, to this house.'

'Five shillings! They'll tie her up and carry her here for that much!'

'I'd prefer her to be walking on her own feet, tell them. Persuasion, not violence. Now, the funeral is, I believe, to take place at eleven o'clock this morning. We'll leave here at ten and find somewhere we can remain inconspicuous while we keep watch. The moment I see Miss Worden, I'll point her out to you.'

'Is she pretty, master?'

'Yes, lad. I'd say she's very pretty.'

'Good figure?'

'Tallish, slender, but with all her curves in the right places.'

'There's no way I'll forget her then!'

THE FUNERAL WAS TO TAKE PLACE AT ST GEORGE'S CHURCH, JUST off Tombland, a small building of flint and stone, now somewhat obscured by later buildings. Why this church had been chosen was not clear. Norwich was full of churches. They were built so closely together you could never imagine any of them found enough parishioners to support their needs. This one must, Foxe assumed, have been the one Mr Melanus had chosen. Many craftsmen who worked in gold and silver came from families who had once been of the Jewish faith. At some time in the past, they converted to Christianity to avoid the waves of persecution which swept through England over the centuries. When they did, they attached themselves to whichever church would receive them.

It wasn't an easy place to find a vantage point with a clear view. One which also offered some element of concealment. Foxe had asked Alfred to lay out his plainest clothing. He hoped to look more like a prosperous artisan or local shopkeeper than a gentleman. It wasn't wholly successful. Even Foxe's dullest garb was made of fine cloth. Still, it was better than the way he usually looked. Charlie had no such problems. The city had more than its fair share of apprentices managing to idle their time away, while running errands for their masters. After some discussion, the two of them decided to wait in the great gateway to the cathedral, up the road a little way from St George's. When the funeral procession arrived, they would leave their place of refuge from the wind and walk down the road. Foxe would mime the part of a man with an injury to his leg. He would hobble along, leaning on his apprentice. That would give Charlie plenty of time to take a good look at Miss Worden.

They almost missed the procession entirely. Foxe had expected the kind of display considered appropriate to the funerals of wealthy merchants and their families. That meant plumed horses with an elaborate bier and a group of professional mourners. Plus, of course, the family members, friends and domestic servants. If Eleanor Melanus had ever thought about her funeral — which Foxe doubted — she would have envisaged something better than this. The group which made its way to St George's was little more than a simple bier, pulled by two small, dark horses, followed by a short line of mourners. This was not the act of laying to rest the wife of one of the wealthiest men in the city. It looked more like the funeral procession of a weaver, or some other simple artisan. If it hadn't been for recognising the remaining directors of the Norwich City Bank amongst the thin gaggle of mourners, Foxe would have wondered if he had selected the right funeral.

Who had arranged this modest affair? Mrs Melanus must have had no relatives in the city or they would have insisted on something more suited to her status. She wasn't likely to have been popular amongst her husband's business associates either. Her funeral stated to the world more plainly than words could have done that this woman's death was a source of sorrow to no one. She was to be given a simple, decent send-off and nothing more.

So far as Foxe could see, the cortege consisted only of the bank's directors and the household servants. Any others were the usual motley gaggle of loungers and beggars. They always attached themselves to any funeral, hoping to receive a few pennies in charity from the embarrassed mourners. None of the lady's supposed hoard of lovers were there — which was hardly surprising. They would deny they ever knew her, if only to avoid the suspicion of being somehow involved in her death.

Foxe bent to point Maria out to his apprentice, though there was no need. Amongst the small group of sombre, middle-aged men and plain, generally hard-faced women, Maria stood out like a gorgeous flower in a patch of cabbages. Even in the plain garb of a servant.

Charlie was already staring at her in much the same way as a man dying of thirst might stare at someone approaching him with a pitcher of water.

THAT EVENING, FOXE HAD BEEN INVITED TO DINE WITH HIS FRIEND Brock and his new wife, together with a few of their mutual acquaintances. Foxe had always like Lady Julia Henfield. She was not a beauty by any means, yet something in her face radiated an unaffected kindness. She could put everyone who met her at their ease in moments. Now, clearly as delighted in her new husband as he was in her, she was the best of hostesses. She made sure everyone was included in the conversation around the dinner table. She also firmly prevented Foxe and Brock from straying onto matters of murder and mayhem.

Once the ladies had withdrawn, leaving the men to smoke cigars and finish the port, Brock and Foxe at last managed to talk to one another discretely. The other two men present seemed wrapped up in their own affairs. One was the cheerful heir to a gentleman possessing a modest estate near Mousehold Heath. The other a clergyman with a worldly nature. They were discussing the prospects for a shooting-party that both were joining the following weekend, which left Foxe and Brock free to talk to one another without appearing impolite.

'What have you been doing since I saw you last, Foxe?' Brock said, keeping his voice down. The other two might feel finding a murderer was more interesting than the best ways of slaughtering pheasants and partridges. 'Still hunting down your murderer?'

'I suppose I have been doing something like that,' Foxe replied. 'At least, I've been trying to discover enough to set a proper hunt in motion. At the moment, I have no idea where to start looking. I went to see Mr Gurtheim yesterday, the man who was in charge of Melanus's goldsmith shop. He made my ears ache with his chatter but ended up telling me nothing of any use. On the way back, I managed to get soaked by the rain and covered in filth from the street. Some madman driving a chaise or a phaeton — I forget which — had his horses going at something close to a gallop. The wretch was veering all over the roadway. Of course, the inevitable happened. His wheels ran over a patch which was nothing but potholes, mud and water, and sent up a fountain of the stuff. It all descended on my head.'

'I heard about that,' Brock said, when his laughter had subsided enough to let him speak. 'It's all about the city. How that insufferable dandy Foxe had to stand naked in his garden, while his servants threw cold water over him. According to the gossip, of course, your lack of clothes hardly mattered. Everyone assumes the female servants in your household are more used to seeing you naked than dressed.'

Foxe spluttered in indignation. 'You know perfectly well, Brock, my behaviour towards my female staff has always been entirely correct. Besides, I instructed them to stay inside and refrain from looking.'

'An instruction which, I imagine, none of them obeyed!'

Foxe could think of no way to refute that suggestion, so he simply glared at his old friend.

'Calm yourself,' Brock said. 'You can't blame me for having a little fun at your expense. To be serious for a moment, I'm glad to see you looking fit and well. I feared your dousing yesterday, at home and abroad, might bring on an ague.'

'I am perfectly well, thank you. Alfred brought me several dry towels and made up a good fire in my bedroom at which I could warm myself. Mrs Whitbread even insisted I drink a copious draught of hot beef tea. That's a potion that I loathe, by the way. Then Mrs Dobbins sent me off to bed early, like a child.'

'I know quite well that you've never sought to take advantage of any of your servants, Foxe. Even so, you have to admit they don't behave towards you as most do towards their masters. They cluck after you like hens after their chicks. They also turn blind eyes to you bedding a succession of young women — even encourage you, so I've been told. They say it makes you sweeter-tempered.'

'To return to Mrs Melanus's death,' Foxe said firmly, 'this morning, Charlie and I took a walk to observe the mourners at Mrs Melanus's funeral —'

'Not hoping to find someone carrying a notice reading something like, "I killed her", were you?'

'Very amusing, Brock. I wanted Charlie to be able to describe her personal maid to those disreputable young friends of his on the street. He's arranging for some of them to watch the house, intercept her when she leaves and bring her to me. I very much need to talk with her before she leaves the city.'

'Bring her bound and gagged?'

'If necessary, but I hope not. I've offered her two incentives: a new position here in Norwich or payment of her fare to London.'

'What do you want with a lady's maid? Or did you have a different "position" in mind for her, as usual? I assume she's young, pretty, good figure — all the rest?'

'You're as bad as Charlie Dillon. I wouldn't be surprised to find he'd found some opportunity to lay hands on her and lead her along personally. No, no and yes are the answers to your questions. I don't find myself lacking a lady's maid, nor do I have designs on her person — well, not more than is usual in my case. I heard a few days ago that Lady Cockerham's personal maid has given in her notice. It seems her father is gravely ill and she needs to return home to nurse him. I've written to Lady Cockerham to tell her I may have the ideal replacement.'

'Lady Cockerham! A most handsome woman. Very fashionable. Frighteningly clever as well, they say. Far too unconventional in her views for the good burgers of Norwich though.'

'Indeed so. I believe she takes pains to fill her house with beautiful things. Beautiful paintings, beautiful furniture and beautiful servants.'

'So, this young woman is beautiful, as I suspected?'

'Strikingly pretty at this stage of her life, believe me. Bound to become still more lovely with a few more years behind her. She's also quick-witted, confident in herself and, hopefully, keen to learn. That's as far as I can judge from the way she gave her evidence to the inquest on her mistress.'

'Now you'll play the pimp and offer her to Lady Cockerham. Some snobbish French maid sounds to be more in her line.'

'That is a crude and inelegant way of putting it, Brock. I simply feel they might be well suited to one another. Lady Cockerham has no need to feel jealous of any pretty servant. She would also be able to give this one some much-needed polish to her speech and manners. If I am right about the young woman — based on what I saw and heard at the inquest — she'll be quite able to deal with Lady Cockerham. You'd be wrong about her ladyship preferring something like a French maid. Lady Cockerham will much prefer a solid, English servant — even if she has to train her somewhat herself. Any foreign woman who thinks she knows it all already and expects her mistress to bow to her expertise would soon be shown the door. Her ladyship is also said to be drawn to people with quick wits and a decided character. That certainly applies to this former personal maid to Mrs Melanus.'

'I can see you're as taken with the girl as Charlie.'

'I admit she intrigues me. Nothing more.'

Brock had to laugh at that. 'If you say so. Still, it's not like you, Foxe, to miss the chance of adding another lame duck to your household.'

'This one is very far from lame, believe me, Brock. I also have more servants than I need already.' He turned to the others. They were showing signs of having exhausted the topic of the weekend's shooting prospects and begun to listen in to what else was taking place. 'Since Brock here has forgotten his duties as host, gentlemen, maybe I can suggest it's time we re-joined the ladies?'

'Damn you, Foxe! The conversation was just becoming interesting.'

Maria Worden didn't leave that evening, so the watching children had a cold night of it. They were used to that. Some managed to sleep a little. The rest kept their eyes and ears open. That was as well, since the young woman slipped out of the front door, carpetbag in hand, very soon after dawn the next day.

Around fifteen minutes later, Charlie was woken by gravel thrown against the window of his room over the stables. Maria Worden, completely baffled by what was happening to her, was standing by the back gate to Foxe's garden, surrounded by a crowd of dirty children.

❧ 10 ❧

It was a measure of Maria Worden's strength of character that she
had eaten a light breakfast and drunk several cups of tea by the
time Molly knocked on Foxe's bedroom door. Once he had
woken sufficiently to listen, the maid told him 'those ragamuffins of
Charlie's' had delivered a confused young woman to the house. What's
more, she said indignantly, Charlie maintained he'd been instructed to
arrange her kidnap by the master himself.

Working for Mr Foxe had long ago freed Molly from any puritanical tendencies. It was nothing to tap on his bedroom door, carrying
hot water for him to wash and shave, and, on entering, find another
head alongside his on the pillow. There had been times, indeed, when
she hoped one day it might be hers. Sadly, she knew her master was
scrupulous at avoiding any suggestion of taking advantage of his own
servants. About his only principle when it came to intimate relations
was that there should never be any hint of coercion or deception. No
master could avoid that charge, if he enjoyed the favours of women in
his employment. Molly, like the other women in Foxe's household, was
in the unusual position of being entirely safe from Mr Foxe's attentions. That was why she was puzzled now. The young woman waiting
in the kitchen downstairs seemed to have no idea why she had been

brought there — and no knowledge of Mr Foxe either. The general belief in the city was that women queued up to be invited into Mr Foxe's house. All would be well aware of his reputation as an accomplished seducer and eager to prove it for themselves. Why was this particular invitee so different?

'Bring me water and soap, so I can wash and shave, girl, and tell Alfred I need him right away,' Foxe said. 'Quickly! I don't want to keep our visitor waiting longer than I must. I'll see her in the dining room as soon as I'm ready. You'd better bring my coffee at the same time — and invite her to take some with me.'

'She's already had tea, master.'

'Bring more tea then.'

Foxe normally took his breakfast wearing a simple morning gown over his shirt and breeches. That day was different. He dressed in a fine jacket of plum-coloured velvet, richly embroidered on collar and cuffs. Under this he wore a waistcoat of silver silk cloth, decorated all over with tiny golden flowers. Then a fine linen shirt with thick ruffles of lace at the cuffs. Buff breeches of the best moleskin, white silk hose and plum-coloured shoes with golden buckles. When Foxe wished to impress, he spared no pains.

What Maria thought of this amazing spectacle, she never admitted. After what had already happened that morning, Mr Foxe could have been an eight-foot-tall Chinaman with a pig-tail. She would still have thought nothing of it. She entered, sat down as instructed, and prepared to discover what on earth was going on.

Foxe explained who he was, what he was doing and by whose request and authority it was done. Maria remained silent, her face betraying no feelings at all. At the end, Foxe was beginning to become unnerved by the maidservant's silence.

'Do you understand?' he asked her.

'Yes.'

'Will you answer my questions?'

'Why did you 'ave those children kidnap me and bring me 'ere?' Maria said. 'Couldn't you 'ave come to the 'ouse and asked to talk to me?'

'I thought the butler — what's his name?'

'Mr Simmonds.'

'I believed he'd turn me away. Probably never even tell you I'd been.'

The young woman considered this. She had a habit of twitching her nose like a rabbit while she did so. Foxe thought it was endearing. Her clothes were plain and had seen better days, but that hardly mattered to him. The girl was so very, very pretty. Given a better dress, with her hair dressed in a more becoming manner ...

'You're right. That's what the old misery would have done. He 'ates me. His wife 'ates me too. Couldn't wait to throw me out. I'll answer your questions, sir. My mistress was a self-centred, greedy, scheming bitch, with the morals of a desperate old tart. Even so, she didn't deserve to be murdered like she was. ... The children said you'd pay me fare to London.'

'When you've answered my questions, I'll give you two options. You can stay here in Norwich a day or so, until I've heard from the person I believe will hire you — and you've decided whether you'll accept the position. Or you can go to London on tomorrow's coach. Either way, if you choose to leave, I'll pay the fare.'

'Why? What do I 'ave to do first? What's your price?'

Oh dear, Foxe thought. She thinks I expect her to do much more than answer a few questions. I wonder what that tells me about her past. Other than the obvious fact that any pretty, young servant girl in London expects to be propositioned on a regular basis.

'Miss Worden,' Foxe said. 'I need to be plain with you. I have a certain reputation in this city when it comes to women. Most of it is true. I like them a good deal and I've slept with quite a few. However, I have several unbreakable rules. Especially in dealing with ladies as attractive as you are — or any ladies, come to that. I always tell them the truth about my intentions. I never, ever, use force, bribery or deceit to get what I want. I won't ask those in my employment to do more for me than their regular work. And I never do anything a woman doesn't want me to do. That way, I can enjoy my pleasures with a clear conscience and, if I can, give each lady as much pleasure as she gives me. I want you to answer my questions, openly and honestly. Nothing more than that. It would be a lie to suggest I wouldn't like to enjoy your favours. I would, very much. But that wish forms no part of the deal I am offering you. I'll pay your fare to London in recompense for delaying you here. There's no other price.'

All the time Foxe had been speaking, Maria's eyes had been growing larger and larger and her little nose had been twitching furiously. At the end, she sat back in her chair and smiled for the first time since she had come into the room.

'Bleedin' hell!' she said. 'Pardon my language, sir, but you've given me the shock of me life. I've never 'ad anyone talk to me straight like you did then. I don't wonder you don't lack for bedfellows, if you treats 'em all like that. Right! Ask me your questions and I'll stop me mouth and listen.'

For the next hour, it was Foxe who did most of the listening. It was clear Maria had a great deal of pent-up anger and frustration to release. Foxe was wise enough to hold his peace and let her tell her story in her own way. He heard about her lonely childhood in the orphanage. About her first position as a skivvy for a landlady who let rooms to troops of actors. How listening to their stories whenever she could had left her stage-struck at fifteen. How she'd finally landed what she believed would be her dream job as an actress's dresser and maid. That actress, of course, was Eleanor Rogers, later to become Mrs Melanus.

From the start, it was clear that Eleanor's acting talent was no more than mediocre. What kept her in work was the ability to sing in tune. That and the willingness to kick up her legs for the enjoyment of the gallery. She did have some talent for broad comedy. She also possessed the largest bosom on the smallest body most had ever seen. Off-stage, she was secretive and sly. She dedicated herself to getting whatever she could from the foolish young men who crowded round the actresses' dressing room, hoping for glimpses of female flesh. Those whom she favoured — that meant those most willing to ply her with gifts — got occasional tastes of what her body could offer them. The rest were required to fawn over her for little more than rare pecks on the cheek and a closer look at those amazing breasts. Only the richest ever got to touch.

'She was a jealous cow,' Maria said. 'She might not want the fools who flocked around 'er, but no one else was to 'ave even one of 'em.

One time, I felt so sorry for an 'andsome young fellow, I let 'im tell me all 'is troubles. I found 'im crying, see, after she'd taken an expensive brooch 'e'd brought her. She'd kicked 'im out to dally with some brute who looked like 'e'd knock 'er down as soon as kiss her. That was 'er type, I discovered. Men who treated 'er rough. It was the polite, adoring coves she couldn't stand.'

'You found this rejected suitor crying?'

'I did, sir, and I 'ates to see a man cry, even if this one looked as if 'e weren't much older than me at the time. About sixteen or seventeen, I'd say. First I gave 'im a cuddle. You know, just to cheer 'im up and show sympathy, as you might say. Then one thing led to another. It weren't more'n ten minutes before 'is breeches was round 'is ankles and me skirts was up round me waist. We were on the job, good and proper, when madam pushes her bloke out the door and spots us. You never 'eard such screeching! The poor bloke tottered off, still trying to pull up 'is breeches as he did, and I gets a real pummelling and kicking. The names she called me! All the time, she was the one who'd up 'er skirts ten times a day, if she thought it would get 'er what she wanted.'

'Why did you stay with her?'

'You've never been a servant, sir, 'ave you? If I'd left without a character, it would've gone 'ard with me to find another position, even as a skivvy. I'd 'ave been forced into a bordello, or made to walk the streets, selling meself for sixpence a fumble. And I still dreamed of going' on the stage meself, didn't I?'

'How long did you stay at the theatre?'

'Not long. Just over a year, I suppose. Madam's star was well an' truly waning' by then. There's no shortage of women willing' to flaunt themselves for an audience, even if few of them 'ad a figure like 'ers. At least they had better voices, could dance proper and could play parts other than in bawdy comedies. She knew she 'ad to get out, so she set 'erself to finding some fool to keep 'er. Along comes that old ninny Melanus and marries 'er. Gawd knows why. Anyone could 'ave told him she wasn't much more'n an expensive tart. So, she's off to Norwich an' pleading with me to come with her.'

'And you did.'

'I could see by then I weren't ever going to make a proper actress.

Not enough talent, you see. Not willing to make a spectacle of meself to get the audience laughing and the men clutching their groins. There weren't no reason to stay, though I'd never been out of London. I'll also admit I fancied the title of lady's maid. Sounds a good deal better than dresser, don't it?'

For the first month or so, Maria explained, her mistress concentrated on playing the part of the wealthy merchant's wife and mistress of a grand house. It didn't last, of course. In a rare moment of shared confidence, she told her maid her husband was desperate for a child, but could rarely manage to do what it required. Besides, he'd been married twice before without fathering any children, so she didn't think he had it in him. Just like he usually failed to get it in her. He doted on her though. She repaid him by sleeping with his younger, coarser customers. She'd also entertained a young groom, several of his craftsmen, a workman hired to make interior alterations to the house, and finally with two bank messengers. There was a yard behind the bank next door, where a carriage and horses were kept. Messengers had to go almost every day to the other banks in the city, taking various papers — even sometimes a bag of coins. They had to ride, of course, to avoid thieves along the way. From time to time, they were also sent to banks in some of the towns round about the city, even as far distant as King's Lynn or Great Yarmouth. For the sake of prestige, the bank also provided its directors with a carriage to use on official business. As well as their other work, the messengers were expected to act as grooms and live in rooms above the stables.

'How many messengers are there?' Fox asked.

'Two, sir, so far as I knows. I ain't ever seen more.

'Were they both her regular lovers?'

'Only recently. She thought no one else in the 'ouse knew what she was up to, but I made sure to keep meself informed of 'er goings on. Aye, she 'ad it down to a fine art. Ol' Melanus suffered bad from rheumatics and gout. It used to keep 'im awake at night, she told me. She'd come over all solicitous for 'is welfare when it suited 'er. Go to the apothecary to fetch 'im medicine to help 'im sleep. Give the poor ol' fool a hefty dose an' all.'

Laudanum, I expect, Foxe thought to himself, or something containing a large amount of it. Making sure he slept.

'She used to wait until 'er husband was asleep in 'is room — listened for 'is snores, which was loud enough to wake the dead. Then she crept down to lift the bar across a particular window on the landin', open the shutters and unlatch the bottom part of the window. Back to bed then an' wait. It wouldn't be long afore I'd 'ear one or other of them messengers creepin' in and tiptoin' up the stairs to her room. Sometimes both of 'em came together. Then you'd hear a rare creakin' of 'er bed and all on 'em gaspin' and groanin' fit to burst. When they was done, they crept back down the stairs and out the same way. Once madam 'ad got 'er breath back, she'd go down 'erself, latch the window, close the shutters and put up the bar again.'

'How do you know all this?'

'I spied on 'er, didn't I? Knew what she was up to but couldn't work out 'ow she got the blokes inside and back out again. I'd forgotten part of the roof of the bank next door would let 'em climb in through that window, provided it was opened inside first.'

'Did she do that on the night she was killed?'

Maria blushed. 'I don't know. I was ... in bed in me room.'

Foxe wondered at the blush and the hesitation. She was where she ought to have been — unless there was someone with her. However, it was no business of his to enquire into Maria's behaviour.

There the questioning ended. The young woman knew no more than she'd already told him. Now she had a question for Foxe.

'If I waits 'ere to find out about this other position, where am I goin' to sleep? I can't go back to the goldsmith's house, can I? Can you give me a bed 'ere? I'd feel safe under your roof. I'd work in the 'ouse for you — or in your shop — 'onest I would. I'm a good worker. I can sew pretty well and I'm not afraid of washin' or scrubbin' or anything like that. Please!'

Despite Foxe's resolve to avoid being seen as hopelessly susceptible to any pretty face, he barely hesitated. Mrs Dobbins was sent for and told the situation. Maria was to stay, but only for a few days, until she either found a new position locally or left for London. Imperturbable as ever, the housekeeper agreed she could find a suitable bed in the servants' quarters for Miss Worden. In return, Maria would undertake such work in the household as Mrs Dobbins asked of her. If nothing was available, she should be sent to Mrs Crombie, who would find her suitable things to do in the bookshop.

It was only afterwards Foxe wondered what effect this temporary visitor might have on young Charlie.

❦ 11 ❧

M aria might have been safely caught and questioned, but Foxe hadn't got over the humiliation and discomfort of his visit to Mr Gurtheim's house. The weather was more seasonable at the moment, but it could never be trusted. He therefore decided it was time to turn his attention to obtaining a suitable small carriage. Then he could go where he needed, safe and dry, in the worst of weather. He'd also need a horse and a groom to look after them. The same fellow could serve to drive him about. Foxe had seen some of the fools who careered around Norwich trying to control their horses on their own, and he had no wish to add to their number.

Unfortunately, he had no idea how best to set about getting what he wanted. Perhaps he could find someone to advise him? Halloran, he was sure, had some kind of conveyance. Unfortunately, the alderman would know as little about the practicalities of horses and carriages as Foxe did himself. Foxe seemed to recall he'd obtained his vehicle and its horse in payment of a debt. Halloran had hardly ever been known to use a carriage anyway, save when his wife was accompanying him. Maybe he'd only acquired the thing to provide his wife with a suitable means of transport. One she could also tell her friends was their own. Poorer folk would have to hire something for each occasion. That would never do for an alderman's lady, would it? Politicians — and their wives — were most sensitive to appearances.

After running through a mental list of his wealthier friends, Foxe finally settled on one. He chose the Earl of Pentelow, spendthrift nobleman and brother to Lady Julia's first husband. He was bound to know about horseflesh — if only the kind which comes in last at Newmarket. If Foxe could find him at his home, he could combine his enquiry with business matters. The earl was bound to be short of money again. Foxe had helped him out many times by purchasing choice volumes from the earl's library. He could sell them later, at a significant profit, to wealthy collectors like Halloran. The earl's father had been a noted connoisseur and collector of rare books and manuscripts. For much of his life, he'd devoted the bulk of his time and money to amassing his collection. When he bequeathed it to his son, it was what any member of the greatest families in the land would be proud to own. Now that son, doubly afflicted with philistinism and gambling, was busy realising the collection's cash worth. Selling it off to sustain his extravagant and feckless ways.

The difficulty would be to find the earl at home. Still, it was something worth trying. He would send Alfred to the earl's town house in Norwich at once to enquire his whereabouts.

Luck proved to be with him. The earl was there, but only for the rest of that day. As soon as he had completed his breakfast the next morning, he intended to leave Norwich. It was time to head for Newmarket and the race meeting there in two days' time. Alfred returned with a message that Foxe could call on the earl that afternoon. The earl, he was told, was eager to see him, being, as usual, in need of the bookseller's expertise. From previous experience, the earl knew he could tell Foxe the amount of money he needed and rely on Foxe to raise it for him. This time, he needed a goodly amount of money within the next two or three weeks. After that, matters would become far too pressing for comfort.

The earl greeted Foxe warmly — as he usually did when he needed ready money — and began right away to explain the sum he required. Foxe listened and said nothing. You got nowhere with the Earl of Pentelow until you had allowed him to deal with his own business ahead of yours. If you attempted to tell him anything before then, he wouldn't pay the slightest attention. Despite his expensive education, the fellow was capable of dealing only with one matter at a time. His concerns also took precedence over all else. Now he explained he needed five hundred pounds as a matter of urgency. Could Foxe oblige him as he had done in the past?

Foxe was nothing if not cunning. Seeing the earl's distress, he decided on a little stratagem. If it worked, it might get him most of what he needed in return for getting the earl out of his present difficulty.

'I'll need to proceed with care to raise a sum such as that, my lord,' Foxe said. 'Of course, I know your father's collection well. There's no doubt it still contains a number of volumes which will fetch a significant price. Three or four of those, properly chosen and presented, might well raise the sum you mention. The problems arise in the selling of them. If we appear too eager, potential purchasers will assume they can use your haste to drive a hard bargain. I wouldn't like to be a party to anything which involved letting go of valuable items at less than they are worth.'

'See that, Foxe. Trouble is, I can't wait too long for these collecting fellows to make up their minds and offer what you ask. Bit hard-pressed for cash at the moment, you see. One or two quite large debts are about to fall due. I'll be deuced embarrassed if I can't pay on the nail.'

'I'll do what I can, but I doubt I can have so much money in that timescale by selling some more books. However, before you become too down-hearted, I do have another suggestion. I've decided I need a small carriage, plus a suitable horse and groom to look after them. Nothing ostentatious or too expensive.'

'Running a carriage is going it a bit for a mere bookseller, isn't it Foxe? Can't imagine what's got into your mind.'

'Simple, my lord. Some of my best customers for books, such as you can offer them, live on estates well away from the city. Hiring a carriage each time I need to visit them is becoming expensive. Unfortunately, I have no other option. Over time, owning my own carriage would prove cheaper I am sure. It would also be far more convenient.

A business expense, you see, not an indulgence. I wondered, therefore, if you could advise me on the best way of obtaining such a vehicle at a price I might be able to afford?'

The bait was set. Would the fish bite?

For a moment, the earl looked bewildered, then his face cleared and he ventured a slight smile. Hooked!

'You know, Foxe, I might be in a position to help you a good deal. My wife's in London at present. Rarely comes to Norwich nowadays either. Can't stand that rambling mausoleum of a house that goes with the Pentelow estate. I have to spend a little time there — pleases the tenants and such, you understand. Trouble is it's cold and gloomy and costs far too much to keep in any kind of repair. Can't sell it, of course. Thanks to my grandfather's Will, the place — and this house too — is entailed on the male heir. All I can have is the income. Most of that gets swallowed up in estate expenses. I'm considering staying in London most of the year, you see. Maybe renting parts of the place out to someone might help. I'd never be able to get anyone to take a lease on the main house. Too large and inconvenient. Stuck with that.'

Foxe nodded, trying not to show his impatience at being told things he knew already.

'As I said,' the earl went on, 'my wife rarely comes north. That being said, there's quite a good brougham that I bought for my wife to use. You know, a small, four-wheeled closed carriage, easy to handle and with a single seat outside for a driver. Ideal for a chap like you who doesn't want to race about the place. Not showy like a curricle or a phaeton. Damn sight more useful in the rain as well. There's even a neat little mare we taught to pull it. You'd need a groom to look after the horse and act as your driver, of course. I might even be able to help you there as well. Look, I'll send someone to drive the mare and carriage to your house, so you see if they'll suit. If you like the look of the groom who brings them, don't hesitate to ask him if he'd like to come and work for you. I'm sure I must have more grooms than I need. Losing one or two would save me some much-needed cash.'

'You'd be willing to sell this brougham and the horse, my lord?'

'To you, Foxe, certainly. Not worth five hundred pounds, unfortunately. Two hundred more likely. Still, if you could raise the money quickly, it would be damned useful. Might be hard for a chap like you, I suppose.'

Foxe had long ago decided never to let the earl have an inkling of his true wealth. If he did, the man would be pestering him over and over again for loans, none of which would ever be repaid. He therefore assumed a grave face and allowed a significant pause before replying.

'That's uncommonly good of you, your lordship. As it happens, I have recently received a small inheritance from my great-uncle. I hadn't seen him for many years. Indeed, I'd almost forgotten he existed.' Have only this moment invented him would be the truer explanation. 'Nevertheless, he must have remembered me for he included me in his Will. If your brougham looks suitable, I could use some of that money to buy the horse and vehicle from you. Might I then offer you the rest as an advance against the book sales you have asked me to undertake?'

'How much in total?'

'A little over five hundred pounds, my lord.'

'You're a fine fellow, Foxe. Always said as much. If you could see your way to agreeing this deal between us, I'd be most obliged to you.'

'When could you send the brougham, my lord?'

'I'll write to my steward this very day. Depend upon it, Foxe, you'll find it ideal for your needs. The advance?'

'I'll talk to my banker in the morning, my lord, and ask him for a bill of exchange for three hundred pounds, shall we say. Where should I send it?'

'My London address, Foxe. Number Six, Golden Square. And the rest?'

'Assuming I purchase the vehicle and horse you are offering, you will have the balance within the week.'

'Splendid chap! I'm sure it'll suit. Then you can use your new carriage to go to Pentelow Hall and get started on choosing the books you need. You've no idea what a weight you've just taken off my mind.'

Flushed with a mixture of relief and pride in his own cleverness at making a deal he imagined to be in his favour, the earl became quite expansive. Foxe, well aware the horse and brougham were almost certainly worth somewhat less than two hundred pounds, could still afford to smile. The five hundred pounds the man needed would indeed be paid. The exact amount of profit Foxe would be able to make by selling a suitable number of books need never be disclosed.

'Bad business about Mrs Melanus, Foxe, wasn't it?' the earl said. 'Did you ever see the woman? Didn't come from the right level of society, of course. Definitely common. Still, she had the most remarkable pair of bubbies you could imagine. Huge! Couldn't have seen her feet in years. Not afraid to show 'em off, either. Once I managed to stand quite close to her. Could see everything — nipples too, you understand — just by looking down the neck of her dress. Shortish woman, see? Good foot smaller than I am.'

Foxe smiled. 'I don't recall ever seeing her, my lord. From your description, I'm sure I can't have forgotten.'

'You would remember her if you had, Foxe. Not a beauty, by any description. Too coarse in her features. Much too bold in her ways as well. Reminded me of actresses I've known. Not difficult to understand what Melanus saw in her, though. He was such a dry old stick. I suppose, at his age, he needed something extreme to spur him on to do the business, if you know what I mean?'

Foxe indicated that he did. Then a thought came to him — something he should have considered from the start — and he hastened to put it into action right away.

'Have you ever bought any gold or silverware from Mr Melanus in the past, my lord?'

The earl burst out laughing. 'My God, Foxe! Why would you think I needed to buy such things? Thanks to my ancestors, especially my great-grandfather, I've inherited more than enough of the stuff. Great-grandfather was something of a favourite of Queen Anne towards the end of her life, d'you see? She kept giving him bits of plate and he kept making up to her, trying to get something more useful. Had his eye on becoming the first marquis, I imagine. Never happened, of course. I did try selling some of the stuff to Melanus, but he wouldn't bite. Odd fellow altogether. Had a curious desire to buy old silver spoons and other oddments of no great value. Turned away the best stuff — said he couldn't afford it and no one else would be able to either. Then started buying trash. I was more than happy to oblige when I could, of course.'

'Can you recall when he started asking for these oddments?'

'Began about eighteen months or two years ago, I'd say. Only bought a very few bits and pieces at first. Later, he couldn't seem to get enough of it. The attics at the Hall are full of such rubbish. I had the servants rummage through them to come up with anything he could be tempted to take. The butler did the same amongst the canteens, knife boxes and cupboards in his pantry. Now I think about it, Melanus bought a parcel of mismatched, tarnished candlesticks, snuffers and silver buttons only a few weeks ago. More or less the last my people could find for him. I wished I'd had more. The amount he'd pay for the stuff you'd scarcely believe. To my mind, none of it was worth more than the weight of silver it contained. I've heard recently the fellow has gone away to attend some sick relative or other. Bit of a shame, to my way of thinking.'

Walking back to his house — mercifully still dry this time, if not especially warm — Foxe turned over in his mind what he had learned from the earl. The logical explanation must be that Melanus was collecting items to be melted down into bullion. Yet, why do it, especially recently? He was closing down his business at the same time, according to Gurtheim. Moreover, they were no longer casting any items themselves. What few things they did provide to customers used castings bought in, then engraved and decorated to order. Assuming Melanus sold no bullion to other dealers — and Gurtheim never mentioned him doing so — his strongroom must have held a fair amount still unused. Why buy more? Why pay more than the scrap metal was worth too? Foxe could find no answer to either of these questions.

❧ 12 ❧

Next morning — another dry day, praise be! — Foxe decided to bear what fresh information he had to Alderman Halloran. The coffeehouse and the London papers would have to be passed over again. Telling everything to the alderman was the simplest way to make sure the other city grandees were kept up to date with his progress. They, in turn, had chosen the same means to send Foxe details of anything they considered relevant to his investigation. Not much, in practice.

He told Halloran what he had gleaned both from Maria Worden and the Earl of Pentelow. The alderman shook his head in disgust and wonderment at the brazen behaviour of Mrs Melanus.

'Did one or other of these bank messengers kill Mrs Melanus?' Halloran asked. 'Is it as simple as that?'

'It might be,' Foxe said, 'but I can't believe it. What reason would they have? They were getting free fun and games on a regular basis, sometimes even both of them together. Why spoil it?'

'It doesn't ring true to me either. We'd never prove it to a jury anyway. All our jurors would be thinking is what you just said. Why spoil a good thing? The only other emotion in their minds would be envy. Without any more definite evidence than you have, it would be a waste of time trying to bring a case.'

'That's my conclusion too.'

Foxe tried asking Halloran what he thought her husband's continued purchases of scrap silver and gold might mean. It was no use. Alderman Halloran was not a man at home with speculation of that kind, especially when he was not in a good mood. Foxe's explanation of the late Mrs Melanus's dubious background and moral failures had clearly upset him a good deal. He might laugh at the dubious behaviour of some young, London buck. To find a substantial merchant, one of the city's mercantile elite, had married an second-rate actress with the morals of a courtesan was a different matter. That reflected badly on his beloved Norwich.

'Your efforts so far seem to have produced little of use, Foxe,' he said, scowling. 'Pity about that. Still, I have some new information to give you, which may prove more useful. Mr Sedgefield has made certain discoveries at the Norwich City Bank, which I believe may suggest a more profitable area of enquiry for you than erring wives and fleeing maidservants.'

Balderdash! Foxe thought. Halloran's only trying to suggest he's above petty matters like Mrs Melanus's taste for rough lovers and her multiple infidelities. Not a profitable area of enquiry. Nonsense! He's letting his moral prejudices stand in his way. The type of lover she preferred explains the bruises the physician found about her private parts. It also suggests a plausible reason for her death. One of the ruffians she favoured could have throttled her out of jealousy or during some lovers' tiff. Even if she had enjoyed regular partners for her adultery lately, as her maid said, that needn't imply she was any more faithful to them than she had been to others in the past.

Halloran cleared his throat. 'I find this difficult to accept, Foxe, but Mr Sedgefield has found evidence that Mr Melanus was engaged in defrauding his own bank in a way only a banker would think up.'

No wonder the alderman had lost interest in Mrs Melanus's marital failings. None of that would affect anyone other than the couple themselves. Fraud at a bank must prove a serious matter for everyone engaged in commerce in the city. For a grand merchant like Alderman

Halloran — and the others who managed Norwich's affairs — money was more important than morals any day of the week.

'As you can imagine, Foxe, banks keep careful records of all bills of exchange and bank notes given to their customers. In the case of the bills, each has to bear the name of the person to whom it was issued. Bank notes are not made personal in this way, but a clerk records the serial number, written on each note as it is issued, in a ledger. To be valid, notes and bills must bear also the signature of an approved bank official. Generally speaking, this is the Chief Cashier, Mr Paul Richards. However, in case of illness or accident, several other persons may also sign the bank's financial instruments. One of them is Mr Melanus himself, in his position as senior partner.'

The alderman paused for breath and Foxe slipped in a question. 'Does the customer asking for such instruments have to deposit an equivalent amount in cash, do you know?'

'Of course. Otherwise the bank would be giving money away. Paper money of this kind is a substitute for cash. It's more convenient in most cases than bags of gold or silver coins.'

'Does the payment have to be in coins of the realm?'

'By no means. You'll be well aware that Spanish, Portuguese, French and other coins circulate freely in this land. All that matters is the weight of gold or silver they contain.'

'So all the coins are weighed as they are received?'

'That would be a dreadfully slow business! As I recall, English coins are weighed only when there is some reason to suspect counterfeits. Perhaps the person handing them over isn't a regular customer. Maybe the amount is unusually large, or the cashier's experience makes him think certain coins feel far too light for their face value. Foreign coins are different. They're more likely to be checked.'

'Someone hands over the required amount of cash — preferably in coins of the realm — and receives paper money in exchange. Where's the scope for fraud in that?'

'If you'll stop asking questions, I'll tell you how Mr Sedgefield explained it to us. He has noticed a significant number of bills and notes for larger than usual sums. All were issued over the past two months and all were signed by Mr Melanus in person. There should have been no need for Mr Melanus to sign any, save when he dealt personally with specially favoured customers. Richards was neither ill nor absent in that period. The other point is this. The amounts recorded as paid over by the customer — the same customer on every occasion, you understand — included, in one case, two small bars of gold. In another, some French and Spanish currency.'

'Does Mr Sedgefield think these supposed payments never happened?'

'He doesn't know. All appears above board. However, the oddities invite suspicion.'

'Is there any way to find out?'

'Perhaps. Anything like a bar of gold would have been deposited in the vault, pending conversion into usable coinage. Foreign coins are used in certain transactions, but — as I just said — usually have to be weighed before being accepted. Only thus can their proper value in English money be established. It often turns out to be an odd sum, like twenty-six or twenty-seven shillings for a Portuguese moidore. A slow, cumbersome process, as you can imagine. Where English coins are available, they will always be preferred. It's rarely a problem unless the customer brings, say, pieces of eight from a customer abroad.'

'What do they do with the foreign coins?'

'Keep them in the vault until they're either needed or can be exchanged for English money elsewhere. Mr Sedgefield will now look through the money stored in the bank's vault to see if he can find the items indicated in the ledger. In his experience, what may look correct on paper may not turn out to be so, when you seek physical evidence to back it up.'

'So, Mr Melanus might have issued himself paper money and falsely recorded the receipt of matching funds?'

'Precisely. He would not, of course, have recorded that the bills and notes were issued to him. He would use a false name. After that, he could take the paper elsewhere, claim to be this other person, sign his name accordingly, and walk away with English coins again.'

'Do we know if the paper money was issued in this way?'

'Two aspects are suspicious. All the notes and bills were recorded against the name of a Mr Joseph Smith — a suitably common name, you'll agree. None, as yet, have been returned to the bank after being redeemed for their face value. What does that suggest to you, Foxe?'

'Our Mr Melanus is not dead. He's gone elsewhere and is calling himself Mr Joseph Smith. Not just anywhere either. I imagine the Norwich City Bank will quickly notify neighbouring banks of a possible fraud. To remain safe, Mr Melanus will have to present his paper money somewhere distant from Norwich and Norfolk. A place from where it would take some time for those pieces of paper to find their way through the banks' clearing system and back to the issuer. London, perhaps?'

'Exactly!'

'Do you think he was relying on his dealings remaining undiscovered for long enough for him to be able to escape overseas? Or did he plan to cash in his fraudulent paper so quickly he could have the cash before anyone could catch up with him? Either way, it rules out him being the murderer of his wife. His disappearance alone would sound the alarm — as indeed it did. The murder of his wife would cause an even more pressing investigation to be set in hand.'

'Who did kill her, Foxe?'

'Heaven only knows!'

Foxe had already thought of at least one other explanation for Mr Melanus's actions and the delay in those bills and notes being presented. What if Mr Joseph Smith was a real person extorting money from Melanus by some means? Melanus might want the bills and notes to be found and cancelled as fraudulently issued. That would deprive the blackmailer of his reward. Meanwhile, to avoid any revenge, he'd dispose of his other source of realisable wealth — the stocks of bullion and scrap in his shop. Only after that would he make a run for it. He must have known his disappearance would cause the affairs of the bank to be investigated at once. The oddity of the paper money issued to Mr Smith would come to light at once. If this Smith were not a local man, there would be a delay before he tried to redeem what Melanus had given him. With luck, the bills and notes would then be refused.

What if the name of Mr Smith concealed a foreigner? That might explain the foreign currency used at least on one occasion. Was Smith an enemy spy, newly arrived and needing to turn funds from overseas into English money? Was Mr Melanus perhaps in league with those with whom this country was at war?

Foxe's mind churned around and around, coming up with ever more outlandish explanations for what might be going on. Fortunately, he had learned to keep his mouth shut on such occasions. He had made a complete fool of himself several times in the past. Usually by jumping to conclusions based on nothing but his own imagination. Once his excitement was given time to subside, he always saw how unlikely many of these explanations of events must be.

By the time Foxe returned to his house after seeing the alderman, he felt totally confused. He even considered going to his room to lie down. All he had were little snippets of information, none of which fitted together to form a comprehensible pattern. Indeed, most of it scarcely deserved the name of information. It was nothing but partial facts, possibilities, guesses, imagination and broad assumptions.

What he needed most was someone to whom he could expound what he thought he knew. Doing this helped him sort things out in his mind. The need to explain to another person always identified gaps in the information and suggested links. Then he might glimpse the beginnings of a pattern which would give his investigation a much-needed direction.

He therefore stopped short of his front door and entered his shop. He could always rely on Mrs Crombie to provide a sympathetic ear when he needed to talk. Better still, she had a sharp mind and abundant common sense. Her grasp of practicalities, and her ability to spot irrelevant items, might save him from wasting his time with illusory notions.

To his amazement, he found Maria Worden standing behind the counter. Mrs Crombie herself was busy rearranging books customers had taken from the shelves and put back in the wrong places. Of Mrs

Crombie's cousin and assistant, Miss Eleanor Benfield, there was no sign.

'Mrs Dobbins said I was to see if Mrs Crombie had any work for me, sir,' Maria said. 'Seein' as 'ow I'd finished what she'd given me. I 'ope that's alright.'

'Maria has been most helpful, Mr Foxe,' Mrs Crombie added from across the shop. 'Poor cousin Eleanor has been struggling since early this morning with one of her sick headaches. She needed to go home and rest, but refused to leave me on my own. As soon as Maria appeared, I overruled Eleanor's objections and packed her off at once. Fortunately, it has been quiet for the past hour or so. Maria has, however, made a most positive impression on some of our customers —'

The male ones, I'm sure, Foxe thought. She really is damnably pretty.

'— and as long as I am close by, I can handle difficult questions. Most want only to be pointed to the correct shelves for the type of book they want, you see. Maria has picked that up surprisingly quickly. I sent Charlie to work in the stockroom, by the way. He seemed somewhat distracted by Maria's presence.'

Damn! Foxe wanted Mrs Crombie to retreat with him to the stockroom, where he could talk with her without interruptions. That would leave Maria alone in the shop. She could hardly be expected to cope with only a few minutes casual instruction. Charlie? Foxe had to agree with Mrs Crombie that sending his apprentice into the shop to be with Maria would not be a good idea.

'I had hoped to be able to talk with you privately for a while, Mrs Crombie,' Foxe said. 'I suppose it will wait until another day.'

'Not at all. The circulating library is due to close in five minutes. I can ask Miss Gravener to come downstairs. She usually spends time at the end of each day tidying up and restocking the shelves. She can do that in the morning before the library opens. Maria, please go upstairs and ask Miss Gravener to close up at once and come down to take over the shop while I speak with Mr Foxe.'

'May I stay, Mrs Crombie?' Maria asked. 'I've found being in 'ere real enjoyable. So different from what I does normally.'

'Of course. Miss Gravener will look after you. Charlie will stay with us in the stockroom — unless you wish to speak with me without him, Mr Foxe.'

'As it turns out,' Foxe said, 'I've remembered a suitable task for the boy that will keep him occupied and out of the shop.'

'That will be most useful. He will stand and stare at Maria as if he's never seen a pretty young woman before. I went through to the servants' hall for a light meal at midday. The servants told me relations between that young man and Florence, the kitchen maid, have become very tense. At one point, she had to be restrained from tipping a pan of water over his head.'

'It's not my fault,' Maria said. 'Honest it isn't. I never encouraged 'im. It's ever so embarrassing. Unless I'm real strict, 'e follows me about like a gormless puppy.'

'I'll speak to him,' Foxe said. 'It's his age, I suspect. Still, he needs to learn that being infatuated is no excuse for silly, bad-mannered behaviour. Now, Miss Worden, go and fetch Miss Gravener. Mrs Crombie won't be far away if anything arises that Miss Gravener and you aren't able to deal with.'

Charlie, suitably chastened after a severe telling off, was sent away to bear a message from Mr Foxe to the street children. They were to report any instances of seeing Mr Melanus coming or going from his house late at night in the past few months. After he had done that, the boy was to go to Mistress Tabby's house. His master, he was to say, would be grateful for anything more she could tell him about the gold-smith and his household. The Cunning Woman had lived in the city all her life. Thanks to the steady stream of people, rich and poor, who sought her advice and the healing herbs she grew, little happened in Norwich she was not told about. Charlie was to note what she could tell him and repeat it to Mr Foxe next morning. If there was too much for him to recall in detail, he was to tell Mistress Tabby his master would call on her whenever it was convenient.

With the decks cleared, so to speak, Mrs Crombie sat down and prepared to listen. Foxe followed his usual habit of walking up and down, emphasising various points by the waving of his arms and hands.

It took almost five-and-forty minutes for him to acquaint Mrs

Crombie with all he now knew about Mrs Melanus's murder and the affairs of her husband's bank. He still understood almost nothing of the reasons for Mr Melanus's disappearance. Even less about where he might have gone. What he said on those subjects was no more than the product of his imagination — a point Mrs Crombie leapt upon at once.

'It seems to me, Mr Foxe,' she began, 'that, for the present, you have gone as far as you can on the subject of the murder. Without more material, you can only speculate. That is rarely productive. I should set that part of the mystery aside for the moment.'

'Until Mr Sedgefield produces any more information, there's no more progress I can make with what has been going on at the bank either. Are you suggesting I sit back, forget the whole matter of Mr Melanus and his wife, and watch the flowers grow?'

Mrs Crombie grinned. 'I would like to see you doing that, but I doubt I ever will. I am merely pointing out that knowing Mrs Melanus was a person of loose morals, with a series of lovers, gets you little further. Until you have a better sense of the priorities in this case, all you will find yourself doing is collecting a list of her amours.'

'But one of those lovers could be her murderer.'

'Of course, but which one? According to Maria, her mistress changed lovers as often as she changed her clothes. How she could have imagined her husband would remain ignorant of her behaviour is beyond me. Perhaps she thought him so besotted he would overlook what she was doing. Perhaps she didn't care. You see what I mean? Every statement begins with "perhaps". Perhaps one of her lovers killed her. Perhaps it was someone else. I say set her aside and try to find more solid ground.'

'The bank?'

'You've ruled that out yourself. Don't you see what you have overlooked? The goldsmith's shop.'

'But I spoke to the senior craftsman. He said Melanus had been taking on less and less business for over a year. During that time, the workshop had been gradually closed down. For a time, one or two of the other craftsmen had been kept on to complete outstanding orders.

After that, Gurtheim was there on his own. Finally, he was discharged a day or so before Mr Melanus went missing.'

'Precisely. Why was such a flourishing business closed?'

'Mr Melanus was too busy with the affairs of the bank.'

'That's what he told his craftsman. Was it true? Wouldn't it have been more sensible to sell the business? Why close it down over such a long period? Could the outstanding orders not have been handled with more expedition?'

Foxe stared, his mouth hanging open. What a blind nincompoop he had been! Gurtheim, the leading craftsman, might have been fool enough to swallow Melanus's story wholesale. He should have been far less naive and trusting.

'Of course!' Foxe cried, coming to a sudden halt and clapping his hands in excitement. 'Mrs Crombie, you're a marvel! You should be the investigator and I should confine myself to handing out books. How could I have been such a dim-witted idiot? The man was a goldsmith!'

Foxe spun on his heel and commenced marching to and fro at high speed.

'Melanus must have been planning whatever he was going to do months and months ago. Probably soon after his marriage, when he realised Mrs Melanus was the worst choice for a wife he could have made. If I'm right, he must have made up his mind to disappear some eighteen months past. First, he makes a detailed plan. Next, say around a year ago, he starts putting his plan into action, using the one area of his life over which he had total control — his original business. Everything must be done secretly. He therefore proceeds slowly and methodically, one step at a time, making sure to draw no attention to what he is doing. Selling the business would have been a public act, so he closes it down instead. He also feigns blindness to his wife's infidelities. In part, that's because because he no longer cares; in part, it's because he wants no fuss, since that might attract an unwelcome interest into his affairs in general. He's playing the role of a dull-witted, besotted old fool — save in the bank, where he acts normally.'

'My guess is that he had a timetable to follow,' Mrs Crombie added. 'See how neatly he arranged the final act of closing the business and dismissing the last employee to take place only a day or so before he disappeared. The paper money he amassed in the name of Mr Joseph Smith represented whatever funds he needed for his new life. He could hardly leave stealthily, if he was weighed down with bags of coins. Understand what Mr Melanus was doing, and you'll have the key to unlock the whole mystery.'

'But was Mrs Melanus's death connected to her husband's action?' Foxe said. 'I don't know that for certain.'

'Once you know why he disappeared, it will become clear, I'm sure. You need to focus, Mr Foxe. You're like a hound trying to follow three or four trails at the same time. That's an excellent way to lose them all.'

❧ 13 ❧

The next day was the eighth since the murder of Mrs Melanus and the ninth since her husband had last been seen. Despite his excitement when he had talked with Mrs Crombie, Foxe was frustrated with his slow progress. He felt he knew precious little more now than he had at the start. Worse, he was still without a clear sense of how best to direct his efforts going forward.

Maybe the street children could come up with something? Charlie had managed to assemble about a dozen and told them his master was willing to pay for certain information. They would pass the word on to the rest. In no time at all, they would be thinking over the past few weeks and months, searching their memories for what Mr Foxe needed.

Most people would assume such an offer would produce a torrent of imaginary sightings, just to get the money. Foxe was not one of them. The street children might be pickpockets and petty thieves, as well as whores of both genders, but the poor creatures had to live somehow. They'd tell lies to most adults without a moment's hesitation. With Foxe it was different. He was almost alone in the city in neither cursing nor despising them. He didn't hand out kicks and blows if they came too close. He didn't treat the girls as mere outlets for momentary sexual urges. He treated them kindly, gave them money for food and showed concern for their welfare. You didn't survive long on the streets without friends, and Mr Foxe was the best — and by far the most generous — friend they had. He was their god. Any amongst them found to have lied to Mr Foxe, or tried to cheat him in any way, would be driven away by all the rest. In their world, that meant condemnation to a future of exploitation, misery and starvation, followed by a lonely death in some gutter. None would dream of taking such a risk.

Foxe had heeded Mrs Crombie's injunction to focus on one matter at a time, so he now framed his instructions carefully. All he wanted to hear about were definite sightings of Mr Melanus coming and going from his house very late at night. If he was behaving in a furtive way, so much the better. He needed to know when the goldsmith left and returned. If possible, Foxe also needed information on where he went. Each sighting would be worth at least a penny. If anyone could tell him, with certainty, where the goldsmith had been going, that would earn thruppence. Foxe was only interested in Mr Melanus, no one else. If Maria was right in saying Mrs Melanus had entertained a string of lovers, it was probable that some of them had visited her in the hours of darkness. He wasn't interested in them. If one of them had murdered her, it would be almost impossible to prove. The street children made poor witnesses, even if he could drag them into court. Most would not even be certain about the night when any particular man had been seen. Besides, if word got out that Foxe had paid for the information, no jury in Norwich would convict.

All Foxe could do now was wait. He was not a patient man. He went to the coffeehouse, as usual. Looked at the sky, filled with heavy clouds which promised rain yet again. Took his habitual walk around the vast Market Place. Roamed about the shop, getting under Mrs Crombie's feet. Cursed and fretted. Annoyed his servants by upsetting their routine. Finally, he found himself banished to his library until it was time to prepare for dinner.

The only bright spot in his day was the arrival of a reply to his letter to Lady Cockerham. In his letter, he'd stressed both Maria's history as an actress's dresser, as well as her more recent experience as a lady's maid. Now her ladyship wrote that she would be most interested to meet the person he suggested. So far, her attempts to replace the maid who had now left had been fruitless. For the past week, she had been forced to rely on the fumbling efforts of a well-meaning, but clumsy housemaid. With some polishing of her speech and manners to fit her for aristocratic society, she thought Maria Worden might suit her very well. Perhaps Mr Foxe would be able to spare the time to bring the young woman to her house himself? He knew he was always welcome. If that proved impossible, he should send the young woman any day save Friday. Noon would be an excellent time.

Foxe's satisfaction was mingled with a certain amount of curiosity. Lady Cockerham was the daughter of an earl and an elegant, cultured and well-educated woman. At eighteen, she had married Baron Cockerham, heir to the Marquis of Leominster. Five years later, he died, leaving her a wealthy widow, still well short of her thirtieth birthday. Now, she was generally described as 'something of a difficult character'. Despite her wealth, background and connections, she was not welcomed into local society. Her wit was too sharp. She was too outspoken, too independent, too clever, too wayward in her mode of life. In sum, she displayed far too many attitudes quite unsuitable in a woman. Worst of all, she gloried in them.

For example, she made it abundantly clear she had no intention of remarrying. Suitors should not waste their time on her. She'd escaped once from male domination and she was not going to invite it a second time. As a widow, she controlled her own money. She could live as she wished, without needing to consider a husband's demands and prejudices — or those of his family. Children were of no interest to her. They spoiled your figure and bearing them was too often the cause of an early death.

Foxe, so far, had resisted her attempts to draw him into her small circle of friends. It wasn't in any way due to her looks, her lifestyle or other peoples' opinions of her. A good many so-called respectable members of society disapproved quite as much of him. Without wrapping it in excuses and weasel words, Foxe admitted he was more than a little afraid of her. She was too sharp and forceful, especially with certain men. Maybe her manner was a defence against male attempts to control her. Maybe she would discover his fear and make fun of him. Foxe wasn't at all used to women who said openly what they wanted and expected to get it. He was far more at home with those who relied on the softer arts of feminine persuasion. In short, he liked to feel he was the one in charge. In her company, he suspected that would not necessarily be the case.

He would send Maria soon and on her own. Charlie could show her the way. No! That was a bad idea. Alfred should be her guide. He was well into his fifties and had never revealed any tendency to be affected by a pretty face, female or male. Alfred would be ideal. They should go that Monday without fail. The quicker he could get Maria out of his house, the better. He could feel his resolve weakening each time he caught sight of her.

FORTUNATELY FOR FOXE'S PEACE OF MIND, THAT EVENING HE WAS again due to take dinner with Captain Brock and his new wife, Lady Julia. It proved to be a great success. Contrary to custom, this time no other guests had been invited and Lady Julia did not retire at the end of the meal to leave the two men on their own. Neither Brock nor Foxe were heavy drinkers, so they contented themselves with no more than two glasses of brandy each. Lady Julia took a small glass of port 'to keep them company'.

Most of the talk, naturally, was about Italy and the sights Brock and his lady had seen in the course of their Grand Tour. They had visited all the usual places. they'd been to Pisa, Florence, Verona, Bologna, Rome and Naples. They had viewed the excavations now underway at Herculaneum and Pompeii and inspected the ruins of Rome. Again and again, they marvelled at grand mansions and magnificent churches. They had admired more fine paintings and sculptures than either of them could recall in any detail. All in all, it had been the experience of a lifetime, but both were somewhat relieved to be back at home in Norwich. Italy, Lady Julia said, was like eating a vast banquet of rich food. Each dish might be exquisite, but in time you began to feel unable to consider another mouthful. You longed instead for a good, plain piece of beef and a simple cup of tea.

Having, at length, exhausted the wonders of Italy, the conversation turned to Foxe's doings while they were away. He had kept Brock informed of most things by letter, but writing always missed out a good deal of the detail. Both the Brock's were fascinated by his account of the death that had taken place in the ringing chamber of St Peter Mancroft and all it had revealed. Foxe's description of the killings in the White Swan Playhouse, and especially the character of the murderer, caused Lady Julia to shudder in horror. Even Brock expressed the opinion that there were times when the depravity of humankind was hard to credit.

Right at the end of the evening, seeking some lighter topic than crime and criminals, they somehow found themselves swapping tales about Lady Julia's feckless and spendthrift brother-in-law from her first marriage, the Earl of Pentelow. He had inherited a sizeable fortune and a grand house filled with works of art. Since then, he'd spent his time dissipating that wealth in drinking and gambling.

'I know he's a fool,' Lady Julia said, 'But I can't help liking him. His parents spoilt him dreadfully, indulging his every whim. Now he's like an overgrown baby, unable to pass a sweet shop without wanting all he can see. He's bored too, of course. No taste for country pursuits, none for politics and too lazy for scholarship. Fortunately for his wife, he hasn't the taste for adultery either. Gambling is all there is left.'

'I like him too,' Foxe said. 'He sends for me whenever he's pressed for ready cash to meet some gambling debt or other. Asks me to sell enough books from that magnificent library his grandfather put together to raise the sum required. I saw him only the other day on the same business. Now he's also selling me a carriage and a horse to go with it. A small brougham. Have you seen it, Lady Julia?'

'Many times. His wife used it a good deal at one time. Of course, she hardly ever leaves London these days and probably has something else suitable there. I can't say I blame her. Pentelow Hall is such a gloomy place. I believe most of it dates from the time of the last King Henry, so you can imagine how inconvenient that makes it as a place to live. You've been there often I imagine, Mr Foxe. The library collection used to be outstanding, I understand.'

'The present earl's grandfather was a noted collector of books,' Foxe said. 'My father always believed him to be the cleverest man in England when it came to his collection. It pains me to assist your former brother-in-law in selling what his grandfather held so dear, but if I didn't do it, someone else would. At least I try to make sure each volume finds its way into the hands of someone who will appreciate and care for it properly.'

'To be honest,' Lady Julia said, 'I doubt if my brother-in-law has looked at a single book since he left the university. Nor, I imagine, did he open many then either. His father had to take him away after two years, without obtaining his degree, to avoid a scandal. His poor wife is at her wits' end with him. Her own fortune is sorely depleted, along with his. At least the estate is entailed. If it were not, their son would inherit little or nothing and her two daughters would lack suitable dowries when they reach a marriageable age. If it wasn't for you, Mr Foxe, his creditors would be even more abundant and demanding than they are. I swear he thinks of that wonderful collection of books as little more than one of those clay jars people call 'pigs' in which they keep their spare coins. Each time he needs money, he raids the store pot represented by his library. To his mind, since he rarely reads, the place has no other use.'

If Lady Julia had slapped him across the face, Foxe could not have looked more startled. Of course! Why hadn't that idea occurred to him? That must be what it was about. He forgot where he was and what the conversation was about in a moment. Instead, his mind raced away, fitting hitherto inconsequential remarks and details into a sensible pattern.

It was the silence that brought him back to the present and made him aware at last of the worried looks of Lady Julia, coupled with Brock's amusement.

'Are you quite well, Mr Foxe?' she was asking with the greatest anxiety. 'Shall my husband summon a physician?'

'He's well enough, Julia,' Brock said. 'Just got an idea. I've seen this happen before. Give him a few moments to work it out in that weird brain of his and he'll be right as ninepence again.'

'I am perfectly well, Lady Julia,' Foxe said, shaking his head and having the grace to look ashamed of his discourtesy. 'Thank you for your concern. Your husband is correct. Something you said acted to spur my mind into action. I am working at present on a most baffling investigation, as I'm sure your husband has told you. You gave me an idea which makes sense of several things I have hitherto failed to understand.'

Nothing would then dissuade his hosts from demanding to know — in detail — what those things were and how they should now be understood. Since he had not thought everything through fully in his own mind, Foxe was unwilling to say too much.

'It's about the missing goldsmith, Mr Melanus. I learned that he decided, on a sudden, to close down his original business. Since it was, by all accounts, doing well, it was hard to make sense of this action. I spoke with the senior craftsman, the last to be retained, and he could make no sense of it either. All he was told was that his employer was too much taken up with the affairs of the Norwich City Bank. He no longer had time or energy to conduct another business as well.'

'That's plausible, surely?' Brock said.

'Of course. What doesn't make sense — or didn't until now — was Melanus's failure to seek a buyer. If you had a prosperous business and felt you could no longer pursue it, wouldn't you try to sell it? Would you simply close it down and walk away? Wouldn't you try to get a good price, if only as a reward for all you had done in the past?'

Brock shook his head. 'Put like that, the man's choice seems impossible to credit.'

'It makes even less sense when you know that Melanus must have been holding significant stocks of scrap and bullion to be melted down and cast into new pieces. And that he'd been buying more scrap almost up until the time he disappeared.'

'I suppose bullion could be sold to bullion brokers.'

'It could, but there is, as yet, no evidence that it was. It's heavy, Brock. You couldn't put a vault full of bullion in a bag and take it to a broker. It would have to be transported in a large cart, armoured against thieves along the way. No one has mentioned seeing such a conveyance at Melanus's premises. The senior craftsman never mentioned seeing anything of that type and he was present every working day. Nor would that explain why he bought more.'

'Is it still there, then?'

'Some of it, maybe. Thanks to your wife's words, I now believe Melanus was using it as the earl uses his library: as a convenient source of the cash he needed. He couldn't sell the business itself. Not only would that reveal all the bullion had already gone, but he wished to keep his plans to leave a secret.'

'Did he need so much money?' Lady Julia asked.

'Apparently he did. Where it went is still a mystery. Now Mr Sedge-field has found Melanus issued a whole series of bank notes and bills of exchange over his own signature during the past two months. That was something he had rarely done before. All were made out to a Mr Joseph Smith.'

'A false name?'

'I believe so.'

'The bullion wasn't enough, so he turned to embezzlement too?' Brock said. 'It's unbelievable!'

'If it was embezzlement, it was theft of a most peculiar nature. Mr Sedgefield said earlier the bank's holdings are precisely what he would expect from its transactions as recorded in the ledgers. The vaults contain all they should. Those notes were paid for, Brock! Paid for in proper, legal currency. Mr Melanus is certainly up to something but stealing from his own bank doesn't seem to be it.'

'What was he doing?' Lady Julia said. 'How exciting this is, dear Mr Foxe! Have you worked it out?'

'I believe he wanted to be able to convert the wealth locked in the items in his safe into a form which made it portable. As I said before, he also wanted to do it secretly. Somehow, he slowly turned his scrap and bullion into coins, probably by selling it over time in small amounts that wouldn't attract attention. When he'd got what he needed, he then used his position at the bank to turn those coins into paper. As managing partner, he had every right to sign the documents.

Again, if he issued them at intervals over several months, no one would comment.'

'But they have.'

'Only because Mr Sedgefield was looking for anything that might suggest fraud. In the ordinary course of events, Mr Melanus's actions would have passed unnoticed. No fraud was committed, no rules of the bank broken, no sudden large and unusual transactions took place. I'm informed Mr Melanus always dealt with the most important customers in person. If anyone noticed he had signed more notes himself than was usual, they would have assumed he had been handling the business of an important customer. Maybe a merchant with a need to make frequent payments to distant suppliers. You wouldn't pay a supplier in, say, London, by sending someone on the coach carrying a large bag of guineas.'

'Do you know who he was paying — other than this Mr Joseph Smith, who you think is fictitious?'

'No. So far, not a single one of the notes or bills has been returned to the bank after being cashed.'

'What has he done with them?'

'No more speculations, my friends. I have not had any time to think the matter through properly. You'll have to excuse me until then. Besides, it's late. Time I took my leave after a truly delightful evening. Next time, I insist that you come to my house. Mrs Whitbread, my cook, rarely has any occasion to prepare more than food for myself and the servants. It will gladden her heart to have the opportunity to show off her skills in the kitchen. I can assure you they are considerable. No, Brock. No more. You will have to be patient for once in your life.'

FOXE RETIRED THAT NIGHT FEELING SURE HE NOW UNDERSTOOD exactly what Mr Melanus had been doing in the weeks before his disappearance. He also believed he knew how he had bought the paper money without defrauding his own bank. When he awoke next morning, however, this mood of elation had evaporated. The idea seemed sound enough, but the details would not support it. Put bluntly, Melanus's safe must be too small. Unless it was of gargantuan proportions, it could not have held enough bullion to meet all he needed to start his new life in any comfort. Not even if he'd emptied it, filled it again with scrap and emptied it again. Besides, where had the money to buy the scrap been found? The earl had said he usually paid more than it was worth, purely as metal.

While he still lay in bed, Foxe went over it again and again, but could find no solution. In the end, he rose in a bad humour, washed and dressed quickly, and went down to his study. There he took pen and paper and wrote down every expense Melanus would need to meet before setting aside a single penny for his escape from Norwich. That must have been in his mind all along. Freedom from a life rendered miserable by a wife whose extravagances must lead him into increasing debt. A wife who made him a cuckold almost daily. A wife whose children, should she bear any, would almost certainly not be his. A wife he must have come to loathe and despise.

As he consumed the fresh bread rolls, butter and jam provided for his breakfast by his cook, Foxe went over his problem again and again. He was so engrossed he hardly tasted the food. It could as well have been sawdust, smeared with pig fat and soap.

That Mr Melanus intended to escape to a new life, he felt was certain. His wife was much younger than he was and would surely outlive him. While others might see her murder as representing her husband's bid for freedom, Foxe did not. The man might have returned that night, believing everyone would think him still absent, but killing his wife made no sense. Not in light of what he was known to have done in the preceding months. Assuming he escaped justice, his wife's death required nothing in the way of preparation. Once she was dead, all his problems would end. He could go on as before. In the unlikely event both preparations and disappearance were intended to prove his innocence, why go to such lengths? Foxe had no cause to doubt his previous view that someone else was responsible for Mrs Melanus's death, not her husband.

The most serious drawback to his earlier notion of how the gold-smith planned to fund himself after his escape was simple. The bulk of the bullion Mr Melanus had held would be silver, not gold. As he recalled it, even the painted sign over the door to the goldsmith's shop described him as "Goldsmith & Silversmith". Anything other than jewellery, if cast in pure gold, would cost more than most wealthy gentlemen and aristocrats could afford. Mr Melanus was not a jeweller. The objects he made and sold were large. Things like serving dishes, candlesticks and candelabra, cruets, and tankards. Even the silver ones were luxury items. Melanus might have held enough gold for gilding and occasional plating, but little more. If a rare order arrived for something in solid gold, he would buy what he needed then, not rely on long-held stocks.

Silver was far less valuable, ounce for ounce, than gold. Foxe guessed silver to the value of one hundred pounds must weigh as much or more than a man could lift. A hundred pounds' worth of gold could be carried in two hands.

Think of the expenses Mr Melanus still had to meet, while running down his business and declining new orders. Aside from the normal daily expenses of his shop, there were his craftsmen's wages — even if they were gradually being dismissed. He would hold outstanding invoices from which to expect payment, but many of Melanus's customers were wealthy landowners. Such people were notorious for their reluctance to discharge their debts. He might well be forced to wait six to twelve months to get his money, with no means of hastening payment. These people acted as if having them as customers was sufficient reward in itself. Foxe knew that from his own experience.

To this must be added Mrs Melanus's extravagance. Her constant demands for jewellery, new gowns and hats, and all the rest. Maria Worden said her mistress was more than vain and greedy. Dressing in the latest fashions and showing off before the world were compulsions to her. What she already had was nothing to her after a week. All her attention was fixed on the next purchase, the next desire, the very latest in London fashions. Keeping her even partly satisfied must have been like carrying wood to a roaring furnace. However much you threw onto the flames, it would be consumed in an instant, leaving you hurrying for more.

It didn't add up. All that to pay for, with a declining income from his shop and only silver bullion to sell beyond the few outstanding orders. That brought him back to what the earl had said. Melanus was still buying scrap. And at prices that must have produced a loss when it was sold as bullion. It was senseless!

Of course, Foxe had no idea what Melanus could draw from his position at the bank. Whatever it was, he doubted it was enough to pay for those bank notes and bills of exchange. Several thousand pounds' worth at least, Halloran had told him. If even that paltry sum represented all his future funds, where had he got the money? Especially if he'd obtained the bills legally.

Give up, Foxe told himself. You're no closer to solving either Melanus's disappearance or his wife's murder than you were at the start. It's hopeless.

The rest of the morning passed in a haze of depression and misery. Instead of visiting his usual haunts, Foxe sat slumped in a chair in his library. Outside, another day of gales, northerly this time, drove sheets of rain along the street and sent the few pedestrians brave enough to venture out scurrying to find shelter. The morning's post brought a letter from the Earl of Pentelow promising that the brougham Foxe was to purchase would be with him next morning. That should have pleased him. Instead, he grunted and tossed the missive aside. He hadn't even taken steps to make sure the carriage house and stable at the end of his garden were clean and dry enough to receive their new occupants. If he did make the purchase, that was. He was already starting to regret speaking to the earl on the matter. As it was, horse and carriage would have to be stabled at one of the inns until the preparations were complete. The groom could have the room next to the one Charlie occupied above the stable.

As the hours passed, Foxe's disappointment began to subside, and his normal optimism reasserted itself. It had all been an overreaction. A return to reality after imagining a breakthrough in the case. His theory that Melanus had been cashing in his stock of bullion, and setting aside the funds received to use later, was still sound. It might not supply a complete answer, but it was surely part of the explanation. There must have been other sources of funds, that was all. There was no reason to give up all attempts to understand. He simply needed to find what those sources were.

What if he assumed Mr Melanus wasn't a thief? What if he didn't want to set out on a new life based on destroying all he had laboured to build up in the past? That might be a better explanation. It certainly fitted the few facts he had just as well.

Melanus's shop was closed down in an orderly fashion. Those who had worked there were paid off one-by-one and received what was due to them. That and 'a little more' in his case, Gurtheim had said. So far as he knew no outstanding debts were left unpaid. The notes and bills made out to Mr Joseph Smith had been properly paid for, Mr Sedge-field believed. If so, the Norwich City Bank would continue to be the stable, successful operation Melanus had made it. There was no actual evidence of fraud, corruption or any other wrongdoing. Assuming Mr Melanus wished to be remembered as a successful merchant and an honest man, there was no reason to challenge this view. Not even his sudden disappearance. Nothing except Mrs Melanus's murder, of course. What if that was no more than a coincidence? Foxe didn't like coincidences, but he had to admit they happened. It was quite likely Mr Melanus intended no harm to his wife and had left believing her to be fit and well and likely to continue being so.

Foxe couldn't imagine how young Charlie managed to be so clear-eyed and enthusiastic so early in the day. He felt as if he needed at least another hour to wake himself fully before facing the world. It would take that long to persuade his mind to free itself from the soft folds of sleep and prepare for whatever was to come. His first question, when Molly had knocked on his door with his shaving water, had been whether it was still raining. She said it wasn't. That the day was fine, the sun was shining, and it felt quite warm when she had ventured outside earlier. He had found it hard to believe her. It took Alfred saying the same to convince him she was telling the truth.

Now he looked at the long-case clock in the corner of the dining room. Barely half-past eight. At least, thanks to Alfred, he was washed, shaved and dressed — after a sort — and had managed to stumble down to the dining room. In a moment, Molly would come in with warm rolls, butter and jam and — most sorely needed of all — a large pot of fresh coffee. When the door opened, however, it was Charlie bursting with news.

'Say that again,' Foxe said to his apprentice. 'Who was here soon after seven o'clock this morning?'

'Two callers, master. Well, one caller and a whole group of them.

First, a man driving a smart carriage, who says he's brought it for you to examine to decide whether you want to buy it. He's in the kitchen, drinking tea and flirting with that little hussy, Florence. She claimed she was angry with me, because she says I've been staring at Miss Worden with sheep's eyes. Next minute, she's fluttering her eyelashes and puffing out her chest for this groom fellow. Women! Can't understand what they want from one minute to the next.'

'Don't try, my boy. That's my advice. Saves a good deal of confusion. Who was this group of callers you mentioned?'

'Some of the street children, master. The ones you asked to come and tell you if they'd seen that Mr Melanus going out and about in the dark. There must be twenty of them by now. They started arriving soon after dawn. I didn't think you'd want to be woken quite so early—'

'I would not, I assure you.'

'— so I asked each one to tell me what they'd seen. Most of them had only seen the same thing. The goldsmith leaving his house in the middle of the night and striding away towards Tombland. Not all of them saw him return, but those who did said he was away less than a quarter of an hour, so far as they could guess.'

'He didn't go far then. Was he carrying anything? A large bag, perhaps?'

'He was always carrying something, master. No one noticed exactly what, so it couldn't have been particularly large. They would have remembered that. Several of them also said he was wearing a heavy coat, but that wouldn't be unusual in the dead of night, would it?'

'That depends on when it was. Could you get any idea of how long these night-time errands have been going on?'

'The first time anyone saw him about in this way was sometime in late December or early January, so far as I could make out.'

'About ten months ago. That fits. How often did he creep out like this?'

'Those who saw him more than once reckoned it was twice or three times a week. Certainly not every night though.'

'So ... Let me count this up. I'll guess at least twice a week since ... when? Let's say mid-December. It's now approaching the end of

September and Melanus disappeared almost ten days ago. Make it ten months or ten-and-a-half. Twenty or thirty trips. Let's say twenty-five, to account for the times he made three such nocturnal excursions —'

'What's "nocturnal", master?'

'Done by night. Damn, I've lost my train of thought now. Yes … twenty-five trips, each time taking only what he could fit in a small bag or in the pockets of a coat. I wonder how much that would be? Guess at five pounds each time. Five times twenty-five is one hundred and twenty-five pounds. I wonder what that weight of silver is worth?'

'Don't ask me, master! I can scarcely imagine it.'

'There's about half an ounce of silver in a half crown, I think. One hundred and twenty-five pounds is 2000 ounces, so that roughly equals 4000 half-crowns. 8,500 shillings … say £425. Not a fortune, is it?'

'It's more than I've ever even thought about having, master. You could live for years on that.'

'Mr Melanus couldn't. He's been used to far greater wealth than that. What in heaven's name has he been doing with it? Even if my calculations are out by a factor of two, it still comes to no more than £850. I was imagining thousands.'

By now, Charlie was speechless. These were sums of money which were far beyond his comprehension.

'Wait a minute! What if sometimes he was carrying gold? Let's assume four times the weight of silver to gold. We know he used two small gold bars to pay for two bills of exchange. Hmm… add about 200 ounces of gold … worth about 600 or 700 sovereigns at three sovereigns or so to an ounce of gold. Six or seven hundred pounds then. Add that to the silver and we've reached more than a thousand at last.'

So much arithmetic so early in the morning was making Foxe's head ache. 'Molly!' he yelled. 'Molly! Where's my breakfast, you wretched girl.'

'Right here, master. And your coffee. Nice and hot, it is.' Molly had entered the room just as Foxe was giving vent to his irritation at being made to think on an empty stomach.

'Right, boy,' he said to Charlie. 'Go away and let me eat my breakfast in peace. I'll deal with anything else afterwards.'

'Shall I tell all the children to wait?'

'What? No. Are there any with more to tell than you've mentioned?'

'Two or three, master. That's all.'

'Here, take this key and open the right-hand cupboard in my desk. You'll find a bag of pennies on the upper shelf. Take it out, lock the cupboard again and bring me back the key. Use what's in the bag to give two pence each to all those who've reported seeing Mr Melanus going or coming from his house. Those with more to tell should wait for me to come. Yes, and ask Mrs Whitbread if she can find them all something to eat.'

'I already did that, master. When I came up here, they were tucking into a second pile of slices of bread and dripping.'

'Good lad.'

Now Foxe's brain had been kicked into action, it started racing away, running through all the reasons he could imagine for Mr Melanus's night-time expeditions. Of course, they might have had nothing to do with disposing of the bullion from his business at all. That was pure supposition on Foxe's part. Maybe he had a woman. Surely not that! He had one already who was making his life a misery. Had to be considered though. Very well. Five minutes to leave his house, reach hers and get started; five minutes to straighten himself afterwards and walk back home. Old men were generally said to have difficulty in reaching the required state even to begin with. He would hardly be able to complete the whole job in around five minutes or less. That sounded more like a young man over-excited by reaching the promised land. Foxe could still recall his own embarrassment. The first time that red-haired girl let him do it with her, he'd been unable to hold himself back more than a few moments. What was it she'd said? Something about him hardly being worth raising her skirts for? What was her name? You're supposed to be able to remember the name of your first love for ever. Well, he didn't exactly love her, he supposed. Lusted after her would be a better description.

To his surprise — and greatly to the detriment of his digestive processes — Foxe found he'd eaten three rolls in less than five minutes, along with two cups of scalding coffee. He'd also burned his mouth by doing so, adding to his general state of irritation.

He hurried into the kitchen. There he found a small group of dirty, poorly-dressed children who had been herded into a corner by his scandalised cook.

'Look at them, master!' she said. 'I'll need to wash the place down after they leave, filthy little brutes that they are. And they and their friends have eaten three of the loaves I baked yesterday. Aye, and emptied the pot of good dripping too! It took me nearly a month to fill it and they empty it again in five minutes.'

It took all Foxe's powers of flattery and persuasion to calm his cook enough to manage to talk to the children at all. When he did, it proved disappointing. He'd hoped they could tell him exactly where Mr Melanus had gone. The best they could do between them was narrow it down to somewhere in one of the streets where the road swung down the hill past the edge of the castle mound. Still, he gave each thruppence and sent them on their way happy. At least it was a start.

By the time he returned to the hallway, Foxe had decided he would dispense with his morning walk yet again. He needed to retire to his library to think everything through for the twentieth time or more. He therefore waved Alfred away and told him to see a fresh pot of coffee was brought to the library. Not quite so hot this time either.

'What about the horse and carriage, master?' Alfred said. 'The groom has been waiting here since soon after seven.'

'Serves him right!' Foxe snapped. 'Shouldn't have come so early, should he.'

That was merely temper, of course. The truth was he'd begun to regret acting quite so precipitately over acquiring a carriage. He'd agreed this deal with the earl before he'd even seen to it that the old stable and carriage house was made ready for new occupants. He'd not bought hay and oats for the horse. There were none of the thousand and one things needed to groom and care for the beast, let alone look after all the bridles and girths and reins and ... Well, all the tackle needed, which he knew was a great deal. As for taking yet another servant into his household ...

He couldn't go back on his deal with the earl. He knew that. He had to buy the brougham and horse. Even if the vehicle had only three wheels and the horse turned out to be a broken-winded old nag scarce fit to send to the knacker's yard. Better go and make the pretence of looking it over, he supposed, even though he knew next to nothing about horses or carriages.

Fortunately, the carriage looked to be in good repair and ideal for what he had in mind. The horse was well-groomed and sturdy looking. It also proved to be calm, standing quietly while he bustled about; even trying to nuzzle his arm when he came close enough. To Foxe's inexpert gaze, all was as it should be.

The groom also solved Foxe's other problems. He told Foxe that, whatever his master had said, he had no wish to come to live in the city. He was prepared to stay a day or two until the horse was settled, but no longer. Another groom would have to be found.

'I doesn't belong in the city,' he told Mr Foxe. 'See, I lives with me old mother in a cottage on 'is lordship's estate. If I left 'is service, where would we live? Mother's more'n seventy years of age, sir. Lived in the fresh air o' the countryside all 'er life. 'Twould fair kill 'er to bring 'er into the city. I ain't just a groom for 'is lordship either. I been 'elping the gamekeeper as well, and 'e's been teachin' me 'is trade. The earl ain't one for country sports, but 'e likes to invite 'is friends to come and shoot from time to time. To be 'onest with you, sir, I likes the keepin' better than I likes bein' a groom. Keeper we got now is going' to need to step down soon. It's 'is rheumaticks, you see. Then I 'opes to persuade 'is lordship to let me 'ave is job. The city's not for me, you see, sir. I needs to go back to the countryside, where I belongs.'

Mr Foxe saw very well. Trust the earl to make a grand gesture without thinking for a moment about the poor devil whose life he would be turning upside down. It would be cruelty to try to make this fellow stay a moment longer.

All the time he'd been talking, Foxe's mind had been working at its usual pace. Now he told the groom he fully understood the situation and would not dream of asking him to leave his cottage or his elderly mother. He should get Charlie and Alfred to help him put the brougham into the carriage house. Then he could ride the horse back to Pentelow Hall and return it to its stable for the time being. Once everything was in place for its comfort and well-being in the stable here, and a new groom had been found, he would be sent to collect it.

Once that business was settled, Foxe returned inside. He was now more determined than ever to shut himself away from domestic responsibilities and similar petty concerns. Alfred, waiting in the hall, took one look at his master's grim expression and clenched fists and made a hasty retreat to a safer location. He also decided to send Molly with the coffee. She needed toughening up. Maybe Florence should do it. That might stop her complaining about the fickleness of certain apprentices and the shamelessness of "that woman" who had turned Charlie's head.

❧ 15 ❧

As it turned out, it was Maria Worden herself who volunteered to take the master his coffee. She'd arrived back late after her meeting with Lady Cockerham the day before; barely in time to take dinner with the other servants. Much to their annoyance, she'd refused to tell them whether her ladyship had offered her a position. Nor if she'd accepted it. All she was willing to talk about was the elegance of Lady Cockerham's house and the stylish, fashionable apparel of the lady herself. Most of them thought she was boasting. As a result, the whole topic had been dropped. After their meal, Maria had pronounced herself worn out by her day and retired to bed as soon as she had helped to clear away. At breakfast that morning, aware of the dissension she had caused, she had wisely left the subject alone.

Volunteering to take Mr Foxe his coffee was not, as some of the servants imagined, an attempt to make amends for the evening before. Maria wanted to talk to Mr Foxe in private. Making that plain to the others would most likely ignite their hostility again. So, she seized on what appeared a heaven-sent chance to achieve her purpose another way. She hadn't been boasting the evening before, only trying to deflect their curiosity. It was surely right that Mr Foxe should be the first to know of her good fortune. She also had another topic to raise with him, which might well cause trouble in the servants' hall. Since she was determined to do it anyway, she thought it best to try to keep it quiet for as long as possible. Most of all, she wanted to ask a favour — and that worried her a great deal.

Foxe had himself been wondering how matters stood between Maria Worden and Lady Cockerham. Now when she came in with his coffee, he thought it an excellent opportunity to ask her. The young maid, however, got her news in first.

'Lady Cockerham 'as given me the position as 'er personal maid, Mr Foxe. She wants me to begin next Monday, if you 'as no objection.'

'None at all,' Foxe said. He thought he could just about hold onto his resolution not to seduce this delightful young woman until then. 'You have no obligation to me. All I did was recall hearing Lady Cockerham needed a personal maid at a time when I discovered you lacked a position. How did you find your new mistress?'

'I liked 'er from the start and she treated me with the greatest kindness and condescension. That was why I didn't return until so late. We fell a'talking. She wanted me to see my quarters and to take me on a tour of the 'ouse, and the time seemed to fly by. Quite early on, she told Alfred 'e needn't wait for me. She'd see me delivered back safely when she was ready.'

'I wondered why I noticed Alfred was back so soon.'

Maria's eyes shone with excitement. 'I came 'ome by carriage! I ain't never done that before.'

'I'm glad it all went so well.' In truth, Foxe had never doubted that it would. Maria was exactly the type of less conventional servant her ladyship favoured. Her new mistress would have found the girl's pert beauty irresistible.

'I was to give you this letter, 'er ladyship said.'

Foxe took the folded sheet, broke the seal and read Lady Cockerham's message. He'd never seen her handwriting before. Now he couldn't help but smile, since it so clearly expressed her character. She wrote in bold, flowing sweeps, the letters elegantly formed, each line neatly parallel to the ones above and below. Even so, there remained something wild and untamed in her penmanship. It looked as if, for all its neatness, the letter had been dashed off in a moment. Foxe was sure he could detect a delicious feminine scent on the paper.

My dear Mr Foxe,

I am most grateful that you thought of my need when you happened upon this young woman. She will, in time, make an excellent addition to my household. At present, she lacks little in skill as a lady's maid, but her speech is shockingly ungrammatical and lazy. I can deal with both of those defects, for she assures me she will let me guide her into better ways of speaking. Given her looks, I am only surprised you did not attempt to keep her for yourself. More surprised still by your behaviour towards her, for she assures me you have treated her with little more than politeness.

Your loss, however, will be my gain. She will ask to come to me on Monday and I trust you will agree to that request. I would suggest you accompany her in person, but I know you will not do so. Why you resist my overtures of friendship I do not know. I will not eat you, nor am I a sorceress to ensnare you in some spell. I admit that you intrigue me a good deal, but I mean you neither harm nor offence. Since neither of us are, I understand, much affected by the sillier conventions of polite society, we ought to find much common ground on which to base a friendship. Still, there it is. Perhaps Maria can somehow persuade you that you will not be compromised in any way by calling upon the two of us from time to time.

I am, sir, your most humble, if bewildered servant,
Arabella, Lady Cockerham

She's laughing at me, Foxe thought. I probably deserve it too. But why does she imagine I would wish to visit her maid? And why is she surprised that I have kept a certain suitable distance between myself and a person who is, after all, both a servant and a kind of guest in my house?

Of course, he knew the answer to his own questions perfectly well. His reputation as a danger to young women was known to everyone in the city. If only her ladyship knew what an effort it was taking to keep up that façade of distant politeness!

He realised Maria was standing watching him.

'Thank you,' he said, folding the letter again. 'Her ladyship confirms that you are to start your duties on Monday. Can you find your way, or shall I tell Alfred to accompany you again? I do not know how heavy your bag is. I can ask young Charlie to carry it for you, if you wish.'

'I'm sure I can manage by meself,' Maria said. Then she paused before adding, 'Can I ask you a question, sir?' Foxe nodded assent. 'I never truly worked for you, did I?'

'No. You were never in my employ.'

'I was a kind of visitor?'

'Let us say I gave you refuge for a short time.'

'Now I'm engaged by Lady Cockerham and will be 'er servant come Monday. Till then, I'm still taking refuge here?'

'I suppose so.'

'You took in Charlie and Florence, didn't you? Took 'em in off the streets, I mean. Gave 'em a place when they had nothin' else.'

'Yes, but I have been well rewarded.'

'You've been very kind to me too, sir, an' you mustn't think you won't 'ave a reward for that too.'

'I didn't take you in with any expectation of reward, Miss Worden. You must never think that. I did only what anyone in my position would do.'

'That's not true. Not true at all. Most gentlemen would 'ave either ignored me or treated me as easy game, to be thrown aside afterwards. No, Mr Foxe. It will never be said Maria Worden takes kindness towards 'er for granted. I just wanted to be clear you don't think of me as one of your servants. You've told me you don't, so I'm now easy in my mind.'

Foxe was quite bemused by the path these questions had taken. Still, the girl seemed satisfied, so he decided it was best to leave it there. Maria hadn't finished though.

'I wants to ask you a last favour, sir. It's not for me. It's for a friend of mine. The 'ousemaid at Mr Melanus's 'ouse, Bessie. They'll throw 'er out onto the street, sir, I knows they will. The 'ouse will be shut up and there'll be no more need for maids. She's an orphan, like me, so she'll 'ave nowhere to go. If I goes an' finds 'er, then brings 'er to this 'ouse, will you give 'er refuge, like you 'ave me? That awful Simmonds pair goes to some dissentin' chapel on Sunday mornings and tries to make her go along with them. Only she was brought up in the proper church, see, and goes to mornin' service in the parish church instead. Them rantin' preachers the Simmonds listen to go on for 'ours and 'ours. Poor Bessie 'as to wait in the church porch after the service till the Simmonds comes along and takes 'er back with them. I could slip along Sunday mornin' — that's tomorrow, ain't it — and catch 'er there. She can't be 'appy in that place all on 'er own every night. Can I bring 'er back with me? We can share my bed Sunday night, sir, and she can 'ave it to 'erself after that.'

'I can't take in every lame duck in Norwich,' Foxe said, 'however much I'd like to, Miss Worden. Nor can I be expected to find work for every servant who's fallen on hard times through no fault of their own.'

'I loves the way you calls me "Miss Worden"! Nobody ever did that before. Makes me feel like a proper lady. No, sir, I knows you can't be expected to find poor Bessie work, but I don't think you'll 'ave to. When I was in your shop those few 'ours the other day, I 'eard Mrs Crombie tellin' 'er cousin that she and the lady who shares a house with 'er are looking to find themselves an 'ousemaid. Bessie would be ideal, sir. She's hardworkin', reliable and as 'onest as the day is long. Quiet too — not like me. I says me piece, even if it gets me into trouble — like it usually does.'

Foxe sighed. One day he'd find a way to say no in cases like this. Until then ...

'Very well, Miss Worden. You may bring Bessie here, as long as that is what she wants. On Monday, Mrs Crombie can meet her and decide if she will suit. If not, the girl can't stay here for ever, mind. I'll do my best for her, but she'll have to find work elsewhere. There are no more positions in this household.'

To Foxe's immense surprise, even shock, Maria darted forward, put a hand on each of his cheeks and planted a soft, warm kiss full on his mouth. He was rendered so breathless by her action that she was away and out of the door before he could utter a single sound. Damn the woman! Simply having her near him caused enough problems. After that kiss, he wouldn't be able to stand up for a while without everyone seeing all too clearly the effect she'd had on him.

✺

SOMEHOW, FOXE RECOVERED ENOUGH PEACE OF MIND TO SEE HIM through the rest of that day. Fortunately, Maria was nowhere to be seen and he took care not to enquire about her whereabouts. It was obvious she'd told the other servants she would be leaving on Monday. There was a certain sense of relief in the air. It wasn't that she had caused them any problems; just that the others had been uncertain of her position in the household. They didn't know whether to treat her as one of them or as the master's visitor. Foxe didn't realise it, but his staff would have been a good deal happier if he'd acted in his usual manner and seduced Maria right away. They knew how to deal with what they referred to as 'the master's pets'.

Only Charlie and Florence showed real emotion over Maria's impending departure. Charlie went about looking as if he'd lost a guinea and found sixpence instead. Florence smiled at everyone and had to be admonished by Mrs Dobbins for whistling. In the end, Charlie took himself off to his room over the stable to nurse his broken heart. Florence was sent to the market to bring back fresh eggs and give the others a rest from her relentless cheerfulness.

When Foxe finally blew out his candle and settled down that night, he was sure he must still be too aroused to find sleep. Instead, he soon slipped into a deep slumber, filled with deliciously wanton dreams. At one point, his dreaming became so realistic he could almost imagine himself awake and enjoying a second long, tender kiss, such as he wished he had secured that morning.

He *was* awake. The gentle pressure on his chest was caused by Maria's breasts as she leaned over him to press her mouth on his. A moment later she slipped a hand under the bedclothes and stretched down to satisfy herself that she was producing the effect she wanted. Then she pulled her nightgown off over her head and urged Foxe to do the same with his.

'I said I was grateful, didn't I?' she whispered. 'Now it's time for you to see just 'ow much.'

When Molly crept in on Sunday morning to pull back the curtains and ask her master if he was ready for his first cup of coffee, she touched nothing and left as quietly as she had come in. Two heads on the pillow. Life in the Foxe household was back to normal.

❧ 16 ❧

Most of Sunday passed quietly. Maria found Bessie sitting miserably in the porch of the parish church and brought her back to Foxe's house. At first, there was some suspicion amongst the other servants. Yet another 'waif and stray' to take in! But once Bessie had recovered her spirits sufficiently, she told them what her treatment had been since Maria's departure. After that, there was general agreement the master had acted rightly in letting Maria bring the girl to stay with them. Bessie, of course, was treated with every kindness. So much so that she gave way to floods of tears at one point and had to be comforted by Mrs Dobbins, the housekeeper. Even Florence seemed to have taken to her — perhaps as much because of her drab, homely appearance as her obvious desire to upset no one.

It wasn't until late in the afternoon that Bessie was introduced to the master of the house. Mrs Dobbins had warned Foxe of the fragile state of Bessie's nerves. He therefore welcomed her warmly, then allowed her to be led away before her emotions could take over again.

After she'd gone, Maria lingered for a private word — and several kisses — with 'her dear Mr Foxe'.

'I'm sorry, Mr Foxe, but I really got to stay with Bessie tonight. You can see the state the poor creature's in. I can't leave her to sleep on 'er own in a strange 'ouse the minute she gets 'ere. Look, Lady Cockerham said, after I join 'er, I can still visit this 'ouse. If that's convenient, of course. That's what she said. You could've knocked me down with a feather, but she insisted she meant it. She also told me she'd invited you to call on 'er several times, but you'd always made excuses to stay away. That doesn't sound like you, Mr Foxe. Not to treat such a well-spoken and elegant lady unkindly. You will call on 'er, won't you? For my sake, if not for 'ers. If people know you're avoiding 'er, it'll look real bad.'

'Lady Cockerham is well known for her unusual, even eccentric attitudes, Maria. Even so, if she says she means something, she almost always does.' Foxe saw he was trapped, but secretly he felt pleased Maria wanted to see him again. 'Yes, I will call on her. I promise.'

I hope she hasn't taken the girl on only to act as bait to get me to call at her house, Foxe thought. To be honest, I can't see why she's so set on making a friend of me. She surely can't be contemplating marriage. She's always been adamant in declaring she'll never marry again. Heaven knows what's going through her mind. Still, she's never been known to do other than speak and act honestly and I have no real reason not to call …

'Just one more thing,' Maria said, 'then I'll leave you in peace. I got somethin' to show you. Somethin' I found in the attic in the gold-smith's 'ouse. I'll just run up to me room and get it, if that's alright.'

What she brought back was a small leather bag, which clinked as she carried it.

She told Foxe about Mrs Melanus's strange behaviour in coming to the attic. That was how she had discovered the secret hiding place for the bag and its contents, she explained. He mustn't think of her as a thief.

'They was going to throw me out, you see. Throw me out with nothing. When I saw the money in the bag, I thought it would be payment for the wages I was due. That's why I took it, Mr Foxe, not for any other reason. They owed it to me. I ain't no thief and never 'ave been.'

Foxe hastened to reassure her — physically and in no uncertain manner — that his good opinion of her was unchanged. She then handed him the bag and he tipped its contents onto his desk.

'Sovereigns! Have you counted them?'

'There's thirty-two of 'em. That's a lot of money, ain't it? I could live well for a year an' more on that.'

'It's certainly a large amount to hide away in your house. Were these keys with the coins when you found them? They were? Do you have any idea what they fit?'

Maria shook her head. She'd never had access to any of the keys in the household.

Foxe examined each key, turning them over in his hands and inspecting the shape. One might be a door key. It looked large enough, though its design was more elaborate than he would have expected. Would the front door to a goldsmith's house have a particularly complex lock? It was possible. The other key was smaller, but the part that fitted into the lock was even more complicated than it was on the other key. If he had to guess, he'd say it was the key to a strongbox or a safe. Why would Mrs Melanus have these keys? Why would she hide them away? He had no idea.

He idly picked up one or two of the coins and looked at them. Gold sovereigns. Odd that they both bore the same date. He picked up another. No, that had a different date, but the fourth one he picked up had the same date as the third. He decided to make an experiment. He sorted through all the coins, putting those bearing the same date into separate piles. By the time he'd come to the end, there were four piles with eight coins in each one.

His suspicions now aroused, Foxe searched in one of the lower drawers of the left-hand pedestal of his desk. From it he drew out a small pair of balances. Then he took his purse and looked for a gold sovereign. Damn! Only a single half-sovereign. He must have a sovereign somewhere.

After a lengthy search, he found two in the small cash-box in which he kept what money he thought he would need during each week. Bringing both of them to his desk, he put one into each scale of the balances and held it up. They matched, or as near as made no differ-ence. Then he left one of his own sovereigns in the right-hand dish and put a coin from those Maria had found into the dish on the left side. When he held the balance up again, the coin on the right hung lower than the one on the left. It was quite a bit heavier.

While Maria looked on, fascinated, Fox tested each coin in turn against his own sovereign. Not once did the beam on the balance show the two coins weighed the same amount.

'They're all counterfeit,' he said. 'Everyone of them.'

'Gawd 'elp me!' Maria squeaked. 'I could've been found with a whole bag o' Spanish brass! Who'd have believed I didn't know? That lot could've got me 'anged!'

Foxe grinned at her. 'Good job you brought them to me then, isn't it? I'm sorry, my dear, but all these sovereigns of yours are worthless.'

'They ain't mine! I wants nothing to do with 'em. Even when I thought they was real, my conscience wouldn't hardly let me sleep at night, telling me I was a thief — which I ain't ever been. You won't tell anyone it was me what brought 'em to you, will you? Please, Mr Foxe!'

'Set your mind at rest, my sweet. I will have to take these to the authorities, but I won't bring your name into it. I'll say they had been in Mrs Melanus's possession, but I'll think up some story to explain how they came to me.' He thought for a moment. 'The people I need to talk to are used to me having contacts with all kinds of strange people. I'll invent a burglar who's broken into the house knowing there's hardly anybody there. He could have found them, realised they were fake, and decided to bring them to me in the hope of a reward. Weak, but it'll do — at least until I can think of something better.'

After Maria had gone, Foxe sat for some while, staring at the piles of coins. Where had Mrs Melanus got them? There were plenty of counterfeit coins in circulation; far more than the authorities could prevent, however hard they tried. Most, he knew, were of relatively low value: shillings, half-crowns and the like. People were less likely to check those and discover they had been duped. Gold sovereigns were a different matter. People who accepted those in payment might well look at them closely.

He picked up one of the counterfeit coins, took up his quizzing-glass and peered at it. For a counterfeit, it was wonderful work. He thought even an expert would find it hard to distinguish it from a genuine coin. If he hadn't noted the oddity that so many coins in the bag Maria had found all bore the same dates, he too would have accepted them as genuine. They were lighter than the genuine coins, but you wouldn't necessarily notice that simply by holding one in your hand. Only when he had placed them on his balances had the discrepancy become obvious.

Had Mrs Melanus been setting aside a small hoard of cash saved from her pin-money? If she had, it would hardly all be in gold sovereigns. The same would be true if she'd sold a few pieces of jewellery or stolen from her husband's purse without him noticing. Nor would all the coins have been counterfeit ones — and certainly not fakes of this quality. Could he really believe that this greedy, heedless, promiscuous former actress was involved in coining? He could not. She wouldn't have the expertise or knowledge of how to adulterate gold or silver, let alone how to get the necessary dies and operate a coining-press.

It would make more sense to assume she and her husband were in it together. He definitely had access to the means of melting metals and creating alloys. Every goldsmith and silversmith did. He would also have the necessary knowledge, as well as skilled engravers. One of them might have been willing to make the dies. Foxe had already established that closing down his business would have left Mr Melanus with unused bullion. Was there a coining-press hidden somewhere in the cellars of that house? If only he could get inside to take a look.

The more Foxe thought about it the more sense it made. The night-time excursions the goldsmith made must have been part of the means he used to put his fake coins into circulation. He had to take great care they could not be traced back to him. Perhaps he had someone close by to distribute the coins to market traders and shopkeepers, who would hand them out in change. He might even know a dishonest bank cashier. The kind who would substitute the fake coins for real ones in the course of his work. Such a clerk could keep a proportion of whatever he swapped as payment for his help, then give the rest to Mr Melanus. It would be a highly profitable business, if you could get away with it. If you were caught, the result would be very different. Making and issuing counterfeit currency counted as treason. Your reward then would be an appointment with the public hangman.

He had to find out what was in Mr Melanus's house. If the gold-smith and his wife had both been involved in coining, it might explain why she was murdered. They may have been too successful and upset some of the others who pursued the same illegal trade. Criminals like these, with everything to lose if they were taken, would be ruthless with unwanted competition. Either Mr Melanus had fled to save his life, or one day someone would find his body.

It all fitted.

Foxe put all the counterfeit coins back into the bag and locked it away in his desk. Tomorrow, he'd show them to Alderman Halloran and ask him to pass them on to the mayor. He felt sure he could convince Halloran with his explanation of what Mr Melanus had been up to. If he could, the alderman would support him in asking the mayor to send constables to demand entry to the goldsmith's house. If the butler and the housekeeper had left the place empty, they would break down the door.

17

'No, Foxe, no. It won't do.' Alderman Halloran shook his head. 'You've done an excellent job by discovering these counterfeits. Even so, you have no solid evidence to link the coins with Mr Melanus. The mayor is hardly going to accept the word of a burglar!'

Foxe opened his mouth to argue, then shut it again. Halloran was right, of course. He couldn't explain the burglar was imaginary and Maria Worden was the source of the coins. He'd given her his promise. Besides, breaking it would make little difference. Mr Melanus had been an important man in the city. A wealthy merchant and banker. A well-respected and upright citizen, at least on the outside. To demand entry to his house to make a search, or — much worse — to force an entry, would cause an enormous scandal. If nothing were found, apologies would be demanded, and legal action threatened. Whoever had authorised such an outrage must then be hounded out of public office. Fox had hurried to the alderman's house full of hope that his investigation had almost reached its end. Now it seemed he was back at the beginning.

'Don't look so glum, Foxe,' the alderman said. 'Your explanation for the death of Mrs Melanus and her husband's disappearance, coupled with finding these coins, makes perfect sense to me. I'm not saying you haven't come upon the truth. It's just that we don't yet have the evidence needed for such a drastic step as demanding to search the house of one of the foremost merchants in this city. Get me that evidence and I'll speak to the mayor right away.'

'If only I could.'

'Look, Foxe. I know you hope to prove Mr Melanus was involved in making these coins. That's why you want access to his house. So far, you don't have the evidence that would persuade the mayor to allow it. Try another approach. See if you can find the person responsible for distributing them and trace it back that way. By the way, I agree with you Mrs Melanus cannot have played any part in the operation. She may have known what was going on. She probably profited from it too. But I cannot believe she had any more than a minor role in the business. She was a singer and a comic actress. You told me so yourself. Not a very good one either. Unless you find something to show she was born and brought up in a household of coiners, how could she have gained the expertise required?'

'Several women have been convicted and hanged for coining.'

'I know they have. It's nothing to do with being a woman, Foxe. It's a matter of knowing what to do, other than get in the way. Most of those women you mentioned knew the trade from birth.' Foxe could see the alderman was becoming exasperated.

Very well, Foxe said to himself. If I can't use legal means, I'll find another way. The burglar I used in my explanation of how these coins came into my hand was invented to protect Maria. I'm sure the street children can find me a real one, if I ask them. I've still got those keys as well.

He took his leave from the alderman and walked home, deep in thought as usual.

At no stage in talking with Alderman Halloran that Monday morning had Foxe mentioned the two keys Maria found in the bag with the coins. They were still locked up in the desk in his library. In the small hours of the morning, lying awake and alone, Foxe had hit upon another explanation for their presence. Suppose Mrs Melanus had 'borrowed" those before her husband had gone. Taken advantage of times he was away. She probably knew where he kept his valuables and had gone there to see what she could find. That's how she had come upon the coins. She couldn't take more than one or two at a time, or he would have noticed. Of course, once he'd disappeared, she might have decided to keep the keys — and the money — for herself.

Let's suppose she knew he had supplies of counterfeit money locked in his strongroom. If he disappeared and didn't return, someone was bound to want the safe opened and the contents inventoried. Then, when the coins were found, she might well be implicated. At the least, she would face some awkward questions from the authorities. Far simpler to take his keys. When she had time, she could remove the coins and hide them together with the keys. Then she could dispose of them as before. What prevented this plan was her murder, but she wouldn't have imagined there was any threat to her life. Immediately before her murder, the medical investigation showed she'd been having vigorous sex. What's more, it had probably involved more than one partner. It was hardly the action of a frightened woman.

Forget Mrs Melanus for the moment. Mr Melanus had somehow been involved with the production of counterfeit coins, unlikely though it seemed. His first notion that Melanus had been taking bullion from his safe and selling it secretly to fund his plan of escape didn't hold together. He could not have collected enough funds in that way. If he had been using the bullion in coining, he'd have turned every pound's worth of pure metal into five or six pounds' worth of false coins — perhaps even more. If so, the thousand pounds Foxe had reckoned as the value of the bullion Melanus had taken from his safe would become five or six thousand. Even allowing for what he would have paid his distributor, a very useful sum would have remained.

Damn and blast! Why hadn't he thought to ask Halloran to find out the total value of the bank notes and bills of exchange Melanus had issued to this Mr Joseph Smith? Did they represent something like the amount he guessed would be the profit from the coining? If they did, it would be a damned useful piece of evidence, though still not conclusive.

Foxe almost turned to go back to Halloran's house, then pressed on homewards. The alderman would not wish to keep those counterfeit sovereigns in his possession a moment longer than necessary. It was quite likely he was already on his way to the mayor's house to shift the burden onto him. The best thing would be to write him a note when he got back home and send Alfred to deliver it.

It looked as if this entire investigation was going to consist of piling up tiny facts and snippets of circumstantial evidence. It wasn't at all how he liked to do things, but it might well be the only way. All Foxe's excitement had faded by this time. It was beginning to rain again too.

As Foxe was about to cross Fye Bridge, he realised a short detour would take him to the house of the Cunning Woman, Mistress Tabitha Studwell. She would let him shelter from the wretched weather until it blew over. Since she knew a great deal of what went on in the city, his visit might provide him with fresh ideas. He needed them even more than he needed to get out of this rain.

Thanks to the weather, the lady was not in her garden when he arrived. Bart, her servant and protector, answered the door and indicated by a wave of his hand that Foxe should go inside. The fellow rarely spoke if he could avoid it. Foxe had learned how to understand what he said, but his speech left most people baffled. Poor Bart suffered from some congenital problem of the brain. It had left him with a bad impediment to his speech and looks which frightened most folk. It had compensated by making him grow tall and develop enormous muscles. The one thing it hadn't affected was his character. Bart was the kindest, most placid and sweet-tempered of men. To see him fussing over a tiny kitten, or cupping a baby bird in his hands, was to see the true Bart behind all the rest. Only if he thought Mistress Tabby was threatened would he ever unleash the monster he appeared to be.

Foxe did as Bart had indicated and went inside. There he found Mistress Tabby busy rubbing some dried herbs between her hands. As she did so, she was catching the small fragments this produced on a sheet of paper. She used this to put each pile she made into an earthenware pot.

'I'm replenishing my stocks,' she explained. 'These are to use when fresh herbs are not available. The dried ones are more powerful and pungent. They're also easier in this form to mix with ingredients such as honey. Sit yourself down, Ash. I won't be long. Then I'll brew you some relaxing tea and you can tell me what you've been doing. Over-exerting yourself for certain, that I can see. Did it involve the mind or the body? Both, I think. What is the young lady's name this time?'

'Maria. You know me too well, Tabby. At least the exertion was enjoyable — extremely so. I hope it was for my partner as well.'

'From what I hear, Ash, you rarely disappoint. Quite the opposite. Most of your conquests hurry back for more of the same.'

'As for my mind,' Foxe said, ignoring the compliment for once, 'my investigation into the death of Mrs Melanus has become mired in uncertainties. I cannot resolve any of them.'

'I will make chamomile tea,' the Cunning Woman said. 'That will help you to relax. I will also give you a salve of lavender and valerian to rub on your temples each night before you sleep. With their help, your slumbers will be calmer and more restorative — at least when you sleep alone.'

If the chamomile tea was not exactly to his taste, Foxe knew enough of Mistress Tabby's skills to drink every drop. While he did so, he set out as clearly as he could everything he knew about his investigation. He ended with his frustration with Alderman Halloran's response to his request for constables to search Melanus's house for signs of counterfeiting equipment.

'I must discover what is inside,' Fox said. 'Until then, I cannot know for certain whether my thoughts about Mr Melanus and the bullion he owned even approximate to the truth. I will have to take matters into my own hands, Tabby. As soon as I return home, I intend to send young Charlie to ask the street children for the name of a suitable burglar.'

'What do you wish this burglar to do?' Mistress Tabby said. She showed no surprise that Foxe intended to break the law, if that was what it would take to satisfy his curiosity.

'Mr Melanus's house is either unoccupied or nearly so. I don't know whether the butler and housekeeper have been asked to remain, or who will be paying them if that is the case. Most likely they will also have departed. Maria told me they sleep on the ground floor at the back of the house. Mr Melanus's counting house and strongroom are both on the first floor. According to her, the floors and walls of the building are substantial. Little noise passes from one room to another. She also gave me two keys that she found. One, from the look of it, must be the key to the door of the strongroom. The other I judge to be the key to a safe. I want my burglar to get inside, find the strongroom, enter it using the key I will give him, and see what is inside. If there is a safe, I am hoping the other key will open it.'

'What will this law breaking tell you?'

'Whether there is still any bullion in the house. If the burglar finds a large amount, my reasoning about Mr Melanus is wrong from start to finish. If he finds little or none, it will prove I am on the right track. He can also conduct a swift search for the equipment needed to press coins from blanks.'

'You need an honest burglar then, Ash, or he will tell you there was nothing and take what he finds for himself. It's no use telling me you will pay him well. Most criminals would take your money and still cheat you.'

'I know finding such a person will be a considerable challenge, but I cannot see any other way. If I could get into that building myself, I would certainly do so. Sadly, I lack the necessary skills to enter and leave without leaving unmistakable signs that I was there.'

'I can see your dilemma,' Mistress Tabby said. 'This is a job for Young Davey. I could not vouch for his honesty on all occasions, but he will not cheat me, of that I am certain. Let me be the one to ask him to do this job, Ash. After he has agreed, as I'm sure he will, you can explain what you would have him do.'

'Who is this fellow? What's even more important: can he do it? Can he enter and leave without any sign he has done so?'

'If he can't, nobody can. He may be only a lad — maybe sixteen or seventeen years old, by my reckoning — but I would wager he is the best burglar in Norwich. He is small of stature, as agile as a monkey, and as cunning as one too. He was trained in his — shall we say his profession — by no less a person than Silas Morton.'

'Morton was definitely the best burglar in Norwich in his day,' Foxe said, his eyes wide with surprise. 'Perhaps the best in the whole of the east of England. He must be an old man by now though, if he is still alive.'

'Yes, he is still alive, though barely so. That's what brings young Davey here. I give him medicines to ease Silas Morton's pain, for the old man's sickness is mortal. He cannot last much longer. Without Davey's devoted care, he would be dead already. He found Davey on the street and took him in as an act of kindness. He has been repaid for his generosity many times over.'

'Young Davey it is then. Does he have another name?'

'If he does, I do not know it,' Mistress Tabby said. 'I will send for him today and ask him to do what you want. If he agrees — and I told you I'm sure he will — I will send you a message to come and explain the rest to him in detail. There is one thing on which I must have your promise, Ash. When you meet Davey, you must not judge him on his appearance. I told you he was small in stature. What I did not say is that, were you to give him the appropriate clothes to wear, you would not doubt that you were being faced with a young woman of striking beauty. Silas Morton rescued Davey from a molly-house, Ash, where he was the star attraction. Davey has suffered too much from the notions of other men. The boy took to being a burglar at once. What other job would allow him to stay inside through most of the hours of daylight, venturing out only after dark? What other would reward him for lurking in the shadows, trying his best not to be seen? He trusts me, because I am a woman and because I welcome him without judgement or comment. If I vouch for you, and you show him the same considera-tion, he may come to trust you. The time is not too far off when Davey's protector must leave this world. Then he will be on his own again. He will need friends.'

'You have my solemn promise, dearest Tabby. What did I do without you? I was the most arrogant fool to avoid you for so long.

Now, it is time that I departed. Let me give you a kiss and take my leave.'

'Not without your salve, Ash. Use it every night when you sleep alone. At other times, you must rely on your companion — or companions — to leave you relaxed.'

'Companions?'

'Wait and see. Come to think of it, there is one thing more. I need another promise from you. You must promise me to send in your card and pay a visit to Lady Cockerham. It is not like you to snub any woman, my dear, let alone one as acute in her mind and as witty as she is. Recently, Ash, she sat where you are and declared herself quite downhearted after you had once more rejected her attempts at friendship. It is only because I told her of your morbid fear of matrimony that she professed herself willing to forgive you. She is as averse to the married state as you are – and with better reason. She tried it once. She's lonely, Ash. Another one who needs a friend. You know as well as I do what passes for polite society in this city is made up of people wholly conservative in their outlook. Even Lady Cockerham's impeccable background and considerable wealth cannot persuade them to overlook the way she thumbs her nose at conventional behaviour. She thought you would be different, Ash. After all, you're the one who took the Catt sisters to the Mayor's Ball — one an actress, the other the madam of a bordello — and both known to be your mistresses. Please try to like her, if only for my sake.'

'I will, Tabby, I promise. But now I really must leave you.'

THE RAIN HAD CEASED AT LAST, ALTHOUGH THE CLOUDS PROMISED more to come. Perhaps he hadn't been as hasty as he feared in buying that carriage. If he hurried, he might get home without a drenching, but not by much. He hadn't intended to stay out for as long as he had. Now he'd missed his midday meal, as his stomach was reminding him, and it was not far off the time for dinner. He wanted to talk to Mrs Crombie, but she would have already closed the shop and be hurrying home to her beloved Jane.

Shortly after, he was proved right. There was Mrs Crombie coming towards him with the girl, Bessie, walking beside her.

'Mr Foxe!' she said. 'Wherever have you been all day? Mrs Dobbins came into the shop looking for you when you had not returned by two o'clock. Young Charlie has been on tenterhooks since well before that. He has told me a dozen times and more that he has something to tell you of the highest importance.'

'I did not intend to be back so late,' Foxe replied. 'I called on the alderman this morning, then decided to visit Mistress Tabby on my way home. In both cases, there was much to discuss.'

'I hope it was useful.'

'Very useful in the second case. Somewhat frustrating in the first one. But I must not delay you, Mrs Crombie. If I can, I will come into the shop tomorrow morning and tell you all. I see you have Bessie with you. You should hurry before the rain begins again, I think.'

'I'm sure we have a few more dry minutes yet, Mr Foxe. Maria brought Bessie to meet me this morning, before she departed for Lady Cockerham's. It seems she overheard me talking about dear Jane and I seeking a maidservant. Bessie has spent the bulk of the day in the shop with me, doing various jobs and being most helpful. I have therefore offered her the position on a three-month trial and she has accepted. If all goes well — and I feel sure it will — she will join our little household permanently. I have told her of Miss Thaxter's small infirmity and she assures me it will be no problem. Maria has been teaching Bessie to read, it seems, and we will continue her lessons. She should soon be able to understand instructions written on Jane's slate. With Bessie to cope with most of the housework, dear Jane will have more time to spend on her painting. I must bring some examples for you to see, Mr Foxe, for she has become most accomplished. I might even set one or two out in the shop for our customers to purchase.'

'It all sounds a most satisfactory arrangement, Mrs Crombie,' Foxe said. 'But let us not tempt the weather further by discussing it now. I'm sure I just felt a raindrop fall on my hand, and you have further to go than I have to reach home before getting wet. I wish you a pleasant evening, Mrs Crombie. Please give my regards to Miss Thaxter.'

I hope Bessie does undertake to work for Mrs Crombie, Foxe said to himself as he hurried the last few yards to his front door. If she does, my household will at last be back to normal. The only cloud on the horizon is my promise to Tabby to call on Lady Cockerham. I only hope that will not be as rash an undertaking as I fear. I have little taste for rich, bored widows, however elegant they may be.

18

Charlie Dillon knew better than to disturb his master's evening, save in the most exceptional circumstances. That's why he waited until the next morning before knocking on the dining room door and delivering his news. The result was even more impressive than he had imagined. Foxe leapt up and began striding up and down the room, muttering to himself. Then he left the rest of his breakfast untouched and rushed out, calling for Alfred to help him dress at once.

It was not very long after when Foxe, suitably attired for visiting, set out once again to walk to Alderman Halloran's home in Colegate. After almost a week of the most meagre progress, the news Charlie had brought had set the whole investigation in a new context. It had also renewed Foxe's energy into the bargain.

Foxe's visits to the alderman's house were becoming almost a daily affair, though he rarely arrived quite so early in the day. That might have been the reason why, this time, Alderman Halloran's greeting was somewhat cool.

'Back again, Foxe? I can't offer you refreshment. You'll need to be brief too. The mayor is holding a meeting of his inner circle this morning. Fifteen minutes is the most I can give you, I'm afraid.'

When Foxe explained why he had come, all that changed. The alderman became as animated as Foxe had ever seen him.

'Harris? Ned Harris? That ruffian who worked for Beeston? Do you think he still does?'

'I'd be surprised if he didn't,' Foxe said. 'He was always Beeston's man.'

'Ned Harris and Jack Beeston. There's an ugly pair and no mistake.' Halloran paused, thinking through the implications of what Foxe had told him. 'On the night Mrs Melanus was murdered?'

'That's what the boy told Charlie. He saw Ned Harris coming out of the front door of Mr Melanus's house, sometime between midnight and one in the morning. Bold as brass, he said.'

'Why have we only heard of this now, Foxe? Why didn't that butler tell the inquest he found the door unlocked the next morning? Do you think Harris had a key and locked the door behind him?'

'Let me answer your first question before tackling the others. The delay was partly my fault. When I asked the street children to report nocturnal comings and goings at Melanus's house, I made sure to stress I was only interested in the goldsmith himself. I was trying to save myself trouble, you see. If they reported every one, I would need to work through many sightings of irrelevant people — mostly Mrs Melanus's various lovers. This boy thought he needn't mention seeing Harris. No, that's not quite true. He knew he'd seen the man's face before, but he couldn't remember where or when; nor could he recall the fellow's name. Once he'd worked out it was Ned Harris, he came along to Charlie at once.'

'Better late than never, I suppose.'

Foxe ignored this minor display of bad temper.

'As for locking the door after him,' he said, 'if Harris had a key, he most likely found it inside as he was looking to leave. Being the arrogant ruffian that he is, locking the door behind him would never have crossed his mind. If he did kill Mrs Melanus — and he's the most likely suspect by a mile — he'd want to get away as soon as he could. I'd also take a large wager that miserable butler did indeed find the front door unlocked. Probably assumed he'd forgotten to lock it the night before. I gathered from both Maria and Bessie, the young women who were servants in the Melanus household until recently, Simmonds the butler was something of an old soak. With the master missing, and madam safe in her bedroom, he'd take the opportunity to make free with the contents of Melanus's cellar. Besides, he wouldn't own up to laxity in security before the coroner, would he? Especially with his mistress murdered that same night. Everyone would have assumed that was how the murderer got inside. He'd be blamed for what happened.'

'Do you think that is how Harris entered? Or was he going there by appointment?'

'I think we would have been told before now if Ned Harris had been one of that woman's regular lovers. I'd take a large wager Harris had been told by Beeston to break into the goldsmith's house for some reason. It's up to us to find out what that was.'

'He gets inside. Then what does he do?' Halloran asked. 'Do you think he found Mrs Melanus *in flagrante delicto*, as they say?'

'Quite possible. Probably took the fellow's place too. If there was a lover with her, he wouldn't come forward either, of course. Especially if it might mean implicating Ned Harris. That would be as good as cutting your own throat. Upset Harris and you upset Beeston.'

'It all makes sense, Foxe. What do you suggest we do next? The mayor would be delighted to see Harris and Beeston dangling from the scaffold — as would every other right-minded citizen of this place.'

'For the present,' Foxe said, 'we should do nothing. If you can bear it, don't mention this to the mayor either. I'm convinced the boy is telling the truth, but he'd not make much of a witness in court. Especially since a local jury would be convinced their own lives were in danger, if they convicted Harris. Beeston would be bound to take revenge on them if his creature, Harris, was hanged. No doubt about it. We need to plan this carefully, so we have time to put pressure on Harris to confess, before Beeston learns he's been arrested.'

'How can we do that?'

'I'll find out exactly where Harris is living. Then we'll arrest him by night, not at his lodging but somewhere in the street close by. We want him in our hands, but we need to do that without any witnesses. No one to pass the word to Beeston — which they surely would. Once we have him safe, we'll tell him we have a witness who saw him leaving

Melanus's house, without saying who that witness was. If I can think of a way, I'll try to suggest Beeston has betrayed him. How would this do, do you think? Beeston realised Harris could lead us to him and decided to get Harris out of the way first. The main thing is to jolt Harris into confessing to the murder. He's never been the cleverest criminal in the city — far from it. Brawn is his stock-in-trade behind that dandyish exterior.'

'Will that work?'

'I expect he'll try to threaten us with Beeston's revenge, if his case comes to court. If he does, we can turn that to our advantage as well. We'll imply Beeston isn't of any relevance in this case. Even claim to be sure we know Beeston no longer has any interest in Harris's future. That might convince Harris that Beeston is trying to distance himself from the killing and leave him to bear the blame.'

Halloran was delighted with Foxe's plan. The alderman was a bluff, straightforward individual, to whom stratagems such as this were foreign. He would have tried to break down Harris's resistance by pressure alone — and probably failed. Foxe's devious solution was, he saw at once, far more likely to succeed.

His message delivered, and a plan formulated, Foxe was keen to return home and set things into action. Then, at the last minute, he recalled the note he'd sent to Halloran after his last visit.

'By the way, Halloran. Did you manage to find out what was the total amount of the bills and notes made out to Mr Joseph Smith?'

'Not yet,' Halloran said. 'Sedgefield's gone to King's Lynn on some business matter and won't be back until Thursday or Friday. I'm going to ask the other directors of the bank — Humboldt, Gregg and Farmer — to tell the chief cashier to get the answer for me. They'll all be at the mayor's meeting, I expect. Some of them anyway. Don't worry, Foxe. I'll not mention a word of what we've been talking about now.'

IT LOOKED AS IF, ONCE AGAIN, FOXE WOULD MISS HIS MORNING VISIT to the coffeehouse. However, he could still make his constitutional around the marketplace if he went home by a longer route. He would cross Fye Bridge, then walk through Tombland and up past the castle. That way, he would come out at one corner of the huge space that held Norwich's thriving market. Then along the northern side of that space, passing the toll house on his way, and past the Fish Market. At least this unseasonably cold weather might lessen its usual stench. On hot days in summer, no one in their right mind walked along the western side of the market where the fish were sold. Those who worked there must have long since lost their sense of smell, he told himself. Either that, or they considered the reek to betoken money, not simply the piles of decaying, fly-infested fish guts. Once past the fish, he would soon reach St Peter Mancroft's churchyard and turn into the streets that led to his house. Only Gentleman's Walk would be missed out.

Foxe was strolling past the old guildhall when he saw Mr Sebastian Hirons. The editor and owner of the "Norfolk Intelligencer" was taking the opposite route and thus coming towards him.

'Morning, Foxe,' Hirons said. 'Haven't seen you at your normal table in the coffeehouse for several days now. Been up to something, I'm sure. Come on, cough it up! Is it still the murder of Mrs Melanus? Stale news these days, of course, unless you care to pass on some fresh snippet you've picked up.'

'Unlike you, Hirons, I spend most of my time minding my own business.'

'What use is a newspaper man who does that? You always were a glib liar, Foxe, even as a boy. Found Mr Melanus yet? In my office, they're giving odds of two to one that all you'll find is a body. Would you care to place a bet yourself?'

'You're wasting your breath, Hirons. You'll have to hope for some interesting news from London to fill up the columns of your rag this week.'

'Which I have, never fear. Know anything about counterfeiting — or is that an embarrassing question?'

Confound it! Did the damned fellow know or guess something? It took all Foxe's nerve to keep his face calm and his expression disinterested. 'No more than the next man,' he said. 'Why?'

'Interesting story from London about some public-spirited citizen handing in a bagful of counterfeit sovereigns. Damned good ones too, the story claims. If the fellow hadn't been a silversmith, he reckons he wouldn't have been able to pick out the fakes.'

'How did he?' Foxe's voice had slowed almost to a drawl, though his whole body felt to be quivering.

'Seems this cove had been collecting on a debt and had received a small bag of sovereigns. He took them back to his lodgings and was about to put them in his baggage, when he took it into his head to count them again. Gloat over them, more likely! According to the story, he noticed a good many of them looked new and unworn, even though they bore two different dates, several years apart. That aroused his suspicions, so he decided to weigh each coin.'

'Weigh them? What with?'

'He's a silversmith, Foxe. I told you that. Always carries a small set of balances in his baggage, just in case.'

'In case of what?' This scepticism was costing Foxe a great deal of nervous energy. Still, it looked to be working. Hirons's irritation was provoking him into giving away far more of his story than he would usually do.

'If you'd stop interrupting in that know-all way, Foxe, you'd find out. I don't know why silversmiths carry such things, but I'm assured they do. This fellow did anyhow. Where was I?'

'He was weighing the coins.'

'Right. As soon as he did, he could see more than half of them were lighter than the rest. He'd been paid in fakes! Guess what he did then.'

'Went back to the man who'd paid him and beat seven bells out of him.'

'Wrong! He went to the Royal Mint and showed them what he'd found. They gave him a substantial reward too. Now the king's ministers are all a-flutter fearing there are hundreds, even thousands, of these fakes in circulation. They're that good, see? Undermines faith in the currency and the Treasury. The word's out that anyone who peaches on the coiner who made them is going to get a fat reward. The coiner himself will make a trip to the gallows, of course, once they can catch him.'

'The fellow who handed these false coins in. Any idea of his name?'

'Always get the name, Foxe. First lesson in the newspaper world. A

Mr Joseph Smith, a silversmith from our American colonies. In England for a short time to attend to various business matters.'

After he'd left Hirons, Foxe abandoned any intention of going home at once. He had to find Brock. With his mind in a whirl of speculation and excitement, what he needed most was someone he could talk to. Someone who'd help him sort it all out and check any wild guesswork. He needed Brock.

It must have been Foxe's lucky day, for he found Brock in the first place he looked: his own favourite coffeehouse. Brock, it turned out, had been looking for him, hoping to enjoy a relaxing chat over a cup or two. When Foxe wasn't there, he decided to stay anyway. Perhaps Foxe would arrive later. Meanwhile he could see if there was anything of interest in the most recent London papers. Moments before Foxe arrived, he'd decided to give up and go back home for a late midday meal. He met Foxe at the door.

Foxe demanded at once that the two of them go to his house and talk there.

'I've got things to tell you that I don't want other ears to hear, Brock. Come along! Stop complaining like some decrepit old man trying to beg a few pennies. You can have your midday meal at my house — along with coffee, punch, wine, or whatever you like. Only do let's get a move on.'

'You're like a nagging fishwife, Foxe. I'm coming. Here's me, enjoying a quiet relaxing time before returning to my wife. Then you come along like a whirlwind and whisk me off before I'd hardly got my backside raised from my chair. I call that damned inconsiderate.'

'Call it what you like, you miserable old pirate, but do hurry up.'

When they got to Foxe's house and were more or less settled in the dining room, Foxe sent poor Molly flying for food and drink. Next Brock had to endure the sight of his friend jigging up and down in his chair with excitement, all the while pouring out the tale he'd got from Hirons.

'Could be more than one Joseph Smith, you know,' Brock said, unimpressed. 'Common enough name.'

'Another one carrying a supply of unusually fine counterfeit sovereigns? Come off it, Brock. This is our man. I can feel it!'

'Well, I suppose if you can feel it ...'

'Do stop criticising and listen. By God, Brock, this Mr Melanus is such a cunning rogue!'

'Could almost be you,' Brock muttered. Foxe ignored him.

'He sneaks out of Norwich and heads for London.'

'Bit risky, isn't it, carrying all these counterfeit coins?' Brock said.

'At last, a sensible remark! Yes, very risky. My guess is something forced him to leave early, before he'd managed to dispose of all the counterfeits he still had. Look! He took some with him and left others with his wife — or she found them after he'd gone. Probably he couldn't carry them all without drawing attention to himself. Right you are, then. He left in a hurry. Why did he do that?'

'Harris?'

Foxe grinned. 'Not Harris. Beeston,' he said. 'Beeston's favourite activity is extortion. How's this for an answer? Somehow, Beeston discovers what Melanus is doing — at least as regards the counterfeits — and demands money. Lots of money.'

'How could he find out?'

'I don't know, do I? Beeston used to be the premier criminal in the city. Back then, he knew about everything illegal or shady. He may be in Great Yarmouth, but he must still have sources in Norwich. Let's not worry how he found out. He did.'

'If you say so.'

'I do. Melanus realises Beeston aims to drain him dry, which would mean the end of his plan for escape. He manages somehow to fob Beeston off — Don't ask, Brock. I don't know yet — gathers as much of the remaining money as he thinks he can carry, and heads for London. He's still working as closely as he can to his original plan. London is where he always intended to be at this stage. Now he can begin the most cunning bit of stratagem. Using his own counterfeit coins to establish his alter ego, Mr Joseph Smith, as an upright citizen from one of our American colonies.'

Despite his attempts at cynicism and disinterest, Brock was engrossed in Foxe's narrative. Even if it all turned out to be fantasy, it still made a gripping tale.

'The moment he reached London,' Foxe went on, 'Melanus became

Mr Joseph Smith. That's the person to whom all those bills and notes had been issued. He takes lodgings in that name, and says he's a silver-smith from the American colonies. Probably chose somewhere like Boston, because that's a town where you might expect to find silver-smiths. He's still got those counterfeit coins, of course, and he needs to get rid of them for genuine ones. What does he do? The brazen fellow uses the Royal Mint itself! Goes to them with a cock-and-bull story of a debt paid partly in Spanish brass. They fall for it, praise his public-spirited gesture and hand him a nice reward. In one fell swoop, he's freed himself of the coins and further established his bona fides as this American silversmith.'

'Now all we need to do is look for Mr Joseph Smith, a silversmith from Boston, and we have Mr Melanus. Is that what you're saying?'

'It won't be that easy, Brock, I assure you. Consider how clever he's been up to now. He must know the story of his so-called discovery will be a small sensation. Even a great city like London won't be big enough to hide in for ever. I wager he left for somewhere else as soon as he could. If I'm right about the extortion, Beeston will be looking for him too. Melanus won't rely on a false name and fresh identity to save him. If I were him, I'd start moving from town to town, perhaps dropping off a few fake sovereigns in each one — if I still had any left — but never staying long in one place. Melanus has some ultimate destination in mind, Brock, I'm sure of that. How about Bristol or Liverpool? Both are ports used by ships crossing the Atlantic. For my money, our Mr Smith is heading either for America or somewhere like Jamaica. He has money, he has a trade. He'll change his name again, once his alias as Mr Joseph Smith has allowed him to turn all that paper money back into cash. Mr Samuel Melanus, goldsmith, has gone, Brock, and we'll never see him again.'

'Maybe.' Brock sounded cynical.

'What do you mean, "maybe?"'

'You do realise all this is based on nothing more than a story in a newspaper? Together, of course, with a gigantic helping of your typical brand of excited speculation. You don't even know for certain yet that Melanus was involved in coining in any way. He might have been the victim of some cunning counterfeiter, not the one responsible for producing bad coins. He might still turn up tomorrow, having visited the tin mines of Cornwall or something like that.'

'What on earth would he want with tin mines?' Foxe asked in exasperation.

'I don't know. It was the first thing which came into my head — like a good deal of the story you've been trying to get me to believe.'

At that moment, Foxe's maid bustled in bearing a tray of dishes heaped with cold meats, pickles and cheeses. Florence came behind her with a jug which might be holding beer or cider.

'Ah, Molly and Florence,' Brock said happily. 'You, my dears, are angels indeed. Food is exactly what I need to stop my stomach being curdled by the furious looks your master keeps giving me. All because I refuse to be carried away by his latest fantasy.'

'I'll give you worse than sour looks, if you go on in that way,' Foxe said. 'What's in that jug, Florence? Cider? Excellent. Pour me a glass. My throat is quite parched. You can leave all else and we'll help ourselves. Captain Brock is eager to be on his way.'

'No hurry, Foxe, I assure you.'

'There is, if I say so. If you don't stop behaving in that insufferably patronising manner or leave soon, I'm going to waste this fine cider by pouring the rest of it over your head. I mean it!'

ᲓᲔ 19 ᲓᲔ

Foxe was always happiest when he could take some action to push an investigation forward. As soon as Brock left to return home, he sent for Charlie and gave him instructions to pass on to the street children. He was to tell them his master needed to know right away where Ned Harris was lodging. Once they found where that was, they shouldn't approach Harris, or let him know he was being watched. All that was needed was to keep an eye on his movements at all times. They must never let him out of their sight. That was vital. If the man showed any sign of trying to leave the city, they should do all they could to obstruct him from doing so. Then they should send for Foxe immediately.

He also received a message from Mistress Tabby to go to her house at three o'clock the following afternoon. Young Davey, the burglar, would be waiting for him. Thanks to these developments, Foxe retired to his library in a cheerful mood. His mood was improved still further by a second message, this time from the alderman, which came soon after. Mr Richards, the Chief Cashier of the Norwich City Bank, had counted up the total value of the bills and notes issued to Mr Joseph Smith. Taken together, they were worth no less than five thousand, two hundred and thirty-five pounds.

Now I'm sure I'm right about what Melanus was doing, Foxe told himself, despite Brock trying to make fun of my deductions. The goldsmith may even have made the dies for stamping out the coins himself. It was known he started out as a skilled engraver. Such a task should have been well within his powers. It might also account for the unusual quality of the counterfeits. Most coiners were not so accomplished.

You might imagine Foxe's present mood of near euphoria would lead him to relax. Such an assumption would have proved wide of the mark. Foxe, pleased and excited, was unable to rest for a moment. He considered making a visit to his favourite bordello that evening, but soon dismissed the idea. With everything that was going on in his head, he wouldn't be able to concentrate. No use going if he couldn't do justice to the skills of his chosen partner to make sure her enjoyment matched his. He needed to be on the hunt; he needed more evidence to convince the sceptics. Fellows like Brock and the mayor, for a start.

Throughout dinner, he kept turning the problem of Mr Melanus and the murder of his wife over and over in his mind. What had he missed? Brock was correct in pointing out the evidence against Ned Harris was meagre to say the least. The case against Jack Beeston was non-existent. They could have them seized and questioned. Then what? Unless Harris could be brought to confess, they didn't have enough to bring him before a judge. If he didn't implicate Beeston, launching any prosecution against that vile rogue was out of the question.

How could he cut through this Gordian knot of assumptions, all without enough supporting facts? As so often before, the idea came to him late at night, as he was blowing out his candle and settling down to sleep. It was so obvious, he couldn't imagine why he hadn't thought of it earlier. Better late than never though. If he set out early the next morning, he could see all done by noon at the latest. That would allow time to enjoy the walk to Mistress Tabby's house to meet his burglar and tell him what was needed.

EARLY — VERY EARLY — NEXT DAY, A CASUAL PASSER-BY MIGHT HAVE noticed Mr Foxe stopping near the entrance to the banking hall of the Norwich City Bank. For several moments, he peered intently into the passageway between the banking hall and the next building in the street. True, there was little to be seen. However, Foxe was not using his eyes but his ears. He was trying to catch the sound of horses in their stables and people moving around to make all ready for the day ahead. Satisfied that all was in order, Foxe walked up the passageway and into the bank's stable yard.

The entrance way was a narrow one. For more than half its length it ran between the banking hall itself and the wall of Mr Melanus's house. At one point, the roof-edge of the banking hall and a window in the house itself were almost on the same level. Once past the end of the banking hall the space widened into a commodious yard. Straight ahead lay a range of brick-built stables with a tack-room, hay loft and quarters for the grooms above. To Foxe's left, at right-angles to the stable block, was the carriage shed. The yard was well kept and mostly covered with cobbles. There was also a large water-trough with a pump to fill it. Finally, Foxe noted an affair of three walls about four feet high, set at right angles to each other. Its purpose was made clear as much by his nose as his eyes. It contained a pile of horse-dung which filled one side of it, and two shovels resting on the other side, ready for use.

There was no one in sight, but the door to one of the stables was open and Foxe could catch distinct sounds of voices within. For a moment he hesitated. Should he go inside or call someone out to him? On balance, he thought a demanding and imperious manner might be the most effective. He took a deep breath and shouted, 'Ho, there!' in a tone he hoped would suggest he was not the sort to brook anything less than immediate obedience.

The young man who came outside in response to Foxe's call was dressed in working clothes, probably a groom from the curry-comb in his hand. The sight of a gentleman in the stable yard at such a time of day must have shocked him, for he darted back and returned with his fellow for support. The second young man wore more formal clothes of the type appropriate to a servant of the bank.

Foxe brushed aside their timorous enquiries with a wave of his hand. Then he stood a long time without speaking, looking them up and down. Fine, strapping lads, he said to himself. Rough, rather than refined, which was the kind Maria said her former mistress preferred. Little finesse, but plenty of staying power. Shame about the strong smell of horses about them. Maybe she liked that as well.

Once Foxe felt his ominous silence had produced a suitable level of nervousness in his victims, he launched into the attack.

'You are both grooms here, I take it?' he snapped.

'Bank messengers, your honour. We looks after the 'orses as well,' one of them said. His voice sounded shaky and uncertain.

'Very well. Take me somewhere we can talk without being seen or overheard. Make haste! I have not all morning to spend on wretches like you.'

'We can't leave the yard, sir,' the other said. 'To do so would be more than our jobs be worth.'

'Somewhere here then, though your jobs will be worth less than nothing unless you tell me what I need to know at once. Come along! Stop staring at me like a pair of village idiots and lead the way.'

They took him up a set of steps built into the side of the stable block and into the tack-room, as he guessed they would. There was no chair for him to sit in, so one of them pulled a small barrel into the middle of the room. Then he folded a couple of sacks over it to make a cushion. They both remained standing.

'Are you sure we won't be disturbed?' Foxe demanded.

'Not for more'n an hour, sir. The bank don't open its doors 'til half-past nine. I reckon it can't be more than half-past seven right now. The cashiers won't put in an appearance till nine. Nor will Mr Richards. There's no one here but you and us.'

'Good,' Foxe said, sitting down. 'Listen! I want you to tell me exactly what you did on the night Mrs Melanus was murdered. No lies or excuses! I know you got into the house through the window she left open for you. I expect you put a plank across the space between the roof of the banking hall and the window ledge. It can't be more than six or seven feet at that point. You've no need to tell me why you did it. I know very well what you and she were up to that night.'

The two lads gaped at Foxe, their faces ashen and their eyes stretched wide with fear. They couldn't have been more than nineteen or twenty years of age, he reckoned. Probably less.

'You ... the window ... 'ow in God's name did you find out?'

'Never mind that. I know that's what you did and that you'd done it several times before. Mrs Melanus liked to entertain young bucks by night and the two of you were close at hand. Let's get back to the night of her murder. Did you go together, or one at a time?'

'It weren't us what killed 'er!' the older of the two gasped. 'Why should we? We give 'er what she wanted. She was right fit and well when we left 'er. You can't pin this on us, sir. I knows it looks bad, but what I said be God's own truth. We both been nervous as kittens these last few days, in case someone found out we was there on the night, as you might say. Now you 'as, though for the life of me I don't know as 'ow you did.'

'We didn't do it! I swear we didn't,' his friend added. 'You got to believe us, sir. It must a'been that Ned 'Arris.'

'Shut yer face, you bloody fool!' the other snapped. 'You'll get us killed, talking like that, even if we manages to escape the noose.'

'Ned Harris,' Foxe said. 'I thought it might have been.' He dropped his voice into a far friendlier tone. 'Very well, lads. The mayor has asked me to find out who killed Mrs Melanus, which is why I'm here. I don't believe you killed the lady, even if there's a good deal of evidence against you both. If you tell me all you know, holding nothing back, I can promise you two things. You won't be charged with murder and I'll do my best to make sure you won't have to give evidence in public against Harris. Your night-time frolics with Mrs Melanus will also be kept from your employers. That will mean you won't lose your jobs.'

'Can you do that, sir? Really?' The same one again, grasping at this unexpected lifeline. Foxe nodded assent.

'What d'you think, Frank? I say we ain't got much choice.'

Before the other could answer, Foxe spoke up. 'None whatsoever. If you don't co-operate with me, I'll inform the magistrate you've admitted you were both in Mrs Melanus's bedroom on the night she was killed. You won't need to worry about much after that. At least, not until the hangman slips the sack over your heads and the noose around your necks.'

'Don't say that, sir, I begs yer. Turns me stomach over, it does. You sit yerself there a while longer, an' we'll tell yer everything. You got us at yer mercy, right enough. I can only 'ope you meant what you said a moment ago about believing we be innocent o' murder.'

It turned out that the two lads had been visiting Mrs Melanus about twice a week, singly or together, for more than six months. As one of them put it, she needed 'a right seeing to' regularly. She also liked the action to be fierce when she got it. Nor was she ever satisfied with less than two bouts, often wanting three or even more in quick succession. Though they were both young and fit, they admitted her demands were often a strain on their capacity. That was why she'd suggested they came to visit her together. One could recover while the other took his place.

Such had been the case the night she was killed. As they put it, they'd both took a turn at the ploughing once and were hoping she'd be content with caresses and 'lewd talk' for a little while longer. That was when the door burst open and Ned Harris stood there, laughing, fit to burst at the sight of them.

'What did he do after that?' Foxe asked.

'Told us to pick up our clothes and get out — fast.'

'Which you both did?'

'You don't argue with a man like 'Arris, sir. A real vicious brute, 'e is. Slit yer throat as soon as look at yer.'

'So, you ran and left the way you came in.'

'That's the nub of it, sure enough. We stopped a moment on the landin' to get dressed, then we was out o'that window fast as we could.'

'Hear anything while you were doing that?' Foxe asked.

'Not much. A bit o' thumpin' an' creakin' from the bed, like, as if 'Arris was takin' advantage of the opportunity to 'ave a bit o' fun, if you understands me. Nothin' else.'

'Did you close the window behind you as you left?'

'Never thought of it, we didn't. All we wanted was to put as much distance as we could between us and that bastard.'

'When did you hear Mrs Melanus had been murdered?'

'Not till the next morning. Then we was terrified almost out of our wits in case someone should find out what we'd been doing and point the finger at us.'

'But you said nothing,' Foxe said.

'We couldn't, sir, could we? If we spoke up, we'd need to explain what we was up to with Mrs Melanus. That would put the noose round our necks good and proper, we reckoned. If we named 'Arris, we was dead meat too. If 'e didn't come for us, Jack Beeston would. No witnesses, no trial, you see.'

'Right enough,' Foxe agreed. 'Now listen carefully. Disobey me and you'll most likely end on the gallows or being transported. Say nothing about what you were doing to anyone. Go about your business as if you'd never met Mrs Melanus and I was never here. The one or two people I'll need to tell your story to won't let it out, that's for sure. If matters proceed as I plan, within a few days you'll be able to relax and do your best to forget you were ever involved. A word of advice though. The next time you're tempted to try three in a bed, make sure to pretend it's a complete novelty. Women are rarely impressed by learning about a man's experience with others of their gender in the past.'

Foxe walked home in a fine mood after this session in the tack-room. The air was crisp and fresh, the sun rising in a clear sky for once, and the city washed clean by all the rain they'd had of late. Ned Harris was their man, fair and square! Here — most unexpected too — was the evidence they needed. He'd not escape the noose now. The only stronger evidence would be to find someone who'd watched him put his hands around Eleanor Melanus's neck and choke the life out of her. The task now was to find a way to put Jack Beeston up on the scaffold alongside his henchman. That was likely to prove a far greater challenge, though not an impossible one.

As he watched the early morning hustle and bustle of the market traders setting out their stalls, Foxe found himself humming a catchy tune he'd heard somewhere, long ago. Yes, his father used to sing it sometimes, when he was pleased with himself. What were the words?

'Good King Cole,

And he call'd for his Bowle,
And he call'd for Fiddlers three;
And there was Fiddle, Fiddle,
And twice Fiddle, Fiddle,
For 'twas my Lady's Birth-day,
Therefore we keep Holy-day
And come to be merry ...'

⚜ 20 ⚜

It was fortunate that Foxe didn't rush at once to Alderman
Halloran's house to give him the good news about Harris. He
decided to have his breakfast first and think over what he had
now learned. As he did so, and his first excitement calmed a little, he
could see what a bad mistake telling Halloran would have been. The
alderman would have insisted on bearing the good news to the mayor.
His Worship had long cherished the hope that, one day, they might
bring Harris to court with a certainty of conviction. He would have
demanded the man's immediate arrest. As a result, they would have
caught the minnow and allowed the bigger fish they wanted to escape.
Far better to wait a while until both were caught in the net.

His mind made up, Foxe took his time over his meal and, for the
first time in some days, walked to the coffeehouse to relax and read the
London papers. He did not take a walk around the marketplace afterwards, as he usually did. Instead, he went back home and spent a few
moments reading a letter which had arrived from his cousin, Nicholas.
That done, he set out to keep his promise to meet with Mistress Tabby
and Young Davey.

Young Davey turned out to be every bit as pretty a lad as Mistress
Tabby had said. Just as nervous too. He put Foxe in mind of a fawn: all

trembling limbs and huge, sad eyes, keeping as close to Tabby for comfort and protection as a fawn does to the doe who bore it. Foxe took care to keep his voice calm and speak always in a low, gentle tone. He explained what he wanted, showed Davey the keys and stressed he must leave no signs behind. The house might well be unoccupied, but he couldn't be sure. It would be best to assume there was someone inside and make as little noise as possible. Bit by bit, he sensed the boy relaxing.

'I'm afraid I can't tell you how or where to make an entry, Young Davey,' Foxe said. 'There is a way to reach one of the first-floor windows, crossing by using a plank from the roof of the banking hall next door. However, that window will almost certainly be latched and shuttered. You will have to find your own way in. Once you are inside, I can tell you exactly how to find the strongroom. I'm sure that's where the safe will be — and the press for making coins, if there is one. I suppose it's possible the press could be in the cellar, but I doubt it. Too many chances for it to be found by one of the servants. No, if it's not in the strongroom, I'll assume Mr Melanus had it located somewhere else in the city.'

'Don't you be worryin' about me gettin' inside, sir,' Davey said, his voice as soft as his eyes and bearing a strong Norfolk accent. 'You leave that to me. I reckons there ain't no place in this city as I couldn't get into if I wanted. You just give me them keys and tell me where to find this strongroom. I'll do the rest.'

It was greatly to Foxe's credit, as Mistress Tabby told him afterwards, that he accepted Young Davey's assurance immediately. He handed over the keys and described in detail the layout of the first floor of the house. That, he assured the lad, was where the strongroom was situated. When he'd finished, Young Davey simply smiled, nodded and prepared to leave.

Foxe called him back.

'You know already I don't want you to take anything from the house and why that's the case. Still, you need to live. You also need money enough to look after the old man who took you in and taught you all you know. I may not approve of how you do that, but I'm sure I'd do the same, if I had to. That's why I'm not going to ask you to work for no reward. Here's a half-guinea in payment for your services. It's yours whatever you find in that house.'

The young man hesitated, then stretched out his hand and took the money. As he did so, he looked Foxe full in the face for the first time, eye to eye and man to man. A bridge had been crossed. Trust was established. Then he turned back to the Cunning Woman and held out Foxe's half-guinea on his palm.

'You keep this for me, Mistress Tabby. 'Tis too much for me to carry around where I live. When I need some of it, I'll come to you. Keep a reckonin' of what I've 'ad and what's left. I'll be back 'ere, once I've done this little job for Mr Foxe, and you can let 'im know when to come and 'ear what I found.'

With that, Young Davey was out through the door and away in a flash.

Later that evening, at a time when he judged the servants and his apprentice would have finished their meal, Foxe summoned Molly and asked her to send Charlie up to talk with him. Foxe had more tasks for the street children. He'd already asked them to find Ned Harris and mark the house where he was lodging, then keep watch in secret to prevent his escape. Now he needed them to mark the times Harris came and went from his lodging and the commonest routes he took through the city. The part he needed the children to play in this enterprise did not end there either. When the time came to arrest Harris, Foxe wanted to ensure the constables made their arrest with the least chance of it being noted and reported back to Beeston. For that to succeed, he felt sure the street children must play a key role once again.

The longest Foxe dared wait before putting his scheme into action was two days. Any longer and he feared some whisper of trouble was likely to reach Harris or Beeston. The problem was this. To make the arrest legal, Foxe needed some of the constables to be present. That meant telling the mayor and gaining his warrant for the arrest. Even if he and Halloran obtained the mayor's promise to keep all secret until they were ready, His Worship was notoriously indiscreet. With such a prize as Ned Harris dangling before him, Foxe wouldn't put it past him to order the man's arrest at once. He might well do it on his own account, whatever they had agreed.

Two days. It wasn't enough, but it was the best he could do. If at all possible, he also wanted to hear what Young Davey had found before moving against Ned Harris. If he couldn't establish a clear link between Jack Beeston and the goldsmith, they could still prosecute Harris. However, there would be no chance of proving Beeston was behind Mrs Melanus's murder. Harris was the kind of stupid bastard who might kill for the fun of it.

FOR THE NEXT TWENTY-FOUR HOURS, FOXE FRETTED AND FUMED. Meanwhile his chosen helpers — a rabble of dirty, half-starved children and a burglar still somewhat short of his twentieth year — went about the tasks he had set them. There was nothing he could do to help them, save keep turning over in his mind all he had discovered until now.

Was he right that Mrs Melanus had not taken the keys Maria found until after her husband had left? Maria had told him she'd seen her mistress hiding things in the attic before. Had Melanus disposed of the other counterfeit coins in the way he surmised? What if Young Davey found the strong room full of the unused bullion and stock from Melanus's defunct business? That would show all his reasoning to be no more than fantasy! Foxe went about his normal business all that day as best he could. Afterwards he could recall nothing whatsoever of how he had spent his time.

Right before dinner, Charlie brought word the street children had found Harris's lodgings. They were now trailing the man himself, dodging through the tangle of alleys and yards between the market and the overgrown mass of rubble and weeds which marked the broken and fallen walls of the castle. According to those children who called this fetid, noisome neighbourhood their home, Harris was a familiar figure. He always dressed like a dandy yet was as much at home in the filthy taverns and grog shops as the cutthroats who infested the broken-down tenements and hovels which lined the streets. The man followed no regular pattern in where he went, they said. Sometimes he would disappear for hours, even days, either doing Beeston's dirty work or visiting one of his many women. At other times, he got drunk in one of the taverns, most often the Black Swan, known to everyone in those parts as the Dirty Duck.

Of late though, he was staying closer to home. They thought he wanted to avoid being seen where his presence might be noted and reported to the city authorities. Even the night-watchmen knew better than to walk into the lanes around the Dirty Duck. Constables almost never ventured there, even by day, unless they came in a group and armed with clubs and staves. If Harris was to be taken in secret and alone, it would have to be close to where he lodged. Nowhere else could his presence be predicted on any specific night.

The following morning, word came from Mistress Tabby that Young Davey had accomplished his task. He should come at once, since the lad was waiting for Foxe at her house. Abandoning his breakfast, Foxe hurried there as fast as he could.

Despite all his worries, the news was almost the best he could have hoped for. Gone was most of the nervousness which had marked Davey's dealings with him on his previous visit. Now he was a man operating in his chosen profession, an expert in his craft, happy to report success and receive the acknowledgement due to him.

Davey had entered the building with little difficulty. Inside, he found the furniture shrouded in cloths and the rooms filled with that indefinable sense of silence and dust that comes with an empty house. There might have been someone asleep on the ground floor — he didn't venture there to find out — but he doubted it. Nevertheless, mindful of his instructions, he had moved as silently as he could, ignoring all temptations along his route.

Foxe had been correct about the keys. One opened the door of the strongroom, the other a large safe, which took up a good deal of the space inside. Aside from this safe, the strongroom was lined with rough, wooden shelving, all of it empty. Whatever had once been kept there was gone. The safe, too, had been more or less emptied at some time. Not completely so, however. On its floor, Davey had found two smallish leather bags, each containing around ten to fifteen gold sovereigns. With much pride in his voice, the lad confirmed he had left all as he had found it. He might be a burglar and a thief, but he knew how to keep a promise.

After the burglar had left, flushed with pride and the richer by another five shillings pressed into his hand by a grateful Foxe, Mistress Tabby insisted her visitor take a seat in her kitchen. There he must drink the herbal tea she would prepare for him. Foxe didn't argue. More than twenty-four hours of constant worry had taken its toll. He felt in sore need of rest and refreshment — even if he did recoil at the thought of having to swallow some foul brew of who knew what herbs.

The tea turned out to be delicious, as did the fresh rolls, butter and jam that came with it. So much so that Foxe abandoned any pretence of good manners and wolfed it all down in moments. After that, at last ready to embark on explanations, he told the Cunning Woman what he guessed from what Young Davey had found — or, rather, not found.

Mr Melanus had indeed been disposing of his remaining stock of scrap and bullion, he told her. Probably the last few items he'd kept for sale as well. He'd been taking them out in small batches by night to avoid attention. Since there had been no coining-press found in the strongroom, he must have taken everything to another location. That would be where the press was sited. If he had no press — which was possible — he must have given the precious metal to a counterfeiter to turn into coins for him. Whichever of these proved to be the answer, the place he had been visiting was not far from his house. All the witnesses said he had returned home within ten to fifteen minutes.

Mrs Melanus may or may not have known what her husband was doing. On balance, he favoured the idea that she did not know, at least in detail. It hardly mattered. She did know he had money stashed away in the house, counterfeit or not. She also knew about that strongroom and safe, as well as where the keys were kept. She could have been taking small amounts for weeks before. When her husband disap-peared, she probably assumed he'd had enough of her and was planning to spend his time — and his money — with someone else. Whatever he was up to, she wasn't going to be left destitute in a strange city.

She took the keys, found the strongroom empty, save for a few remaining bags of the coins in the safe, and took some of them for herself. She didn't take them all that time. She couldn't be certain her husband wasn't coming back. If he did — and found the thirty pounds or so she'd taken was missing — she no doubt reckoned she could come up with a plausible excuse. It was a risky action, but everything Foxe had heard about her suggested it would have been completely in character. The coins she had found were, of course, the few Melanus had yet to dispose of when events caused him to leave earlier than he had intended. If she hadn't met her death, she would doubtless have gone back for the rest of the money.

'What are you going to do now?' Mistress Tabby asked Foxe, as she brought him a second plate of warm rolls.

'Go to see Halloran and tell him part of what I have discovered.'

'Why only part?'

'Asking Young Davey to help was simply to satisfy my curiosity and prove I was correct in guessing the purpose of Melanus's night-time journeys. Halloran doesn't need to know any of that — least of all how I got the information. The man's a magistrate, dammit! It's best he doesn't know Young Davey exists. The alderman struggles enough with some of the ways I choose to live my life. If he knew I was happy to break the law when it suited me, he'd probably never let me into his house again.'

Tabby laughed. 'That I doubt,' she said. 'That man is more fond of you than you or he are prepared to admit. I'll never understand why you men are so ashamed of your emotions. Now, dear Ash, I have no more rolls for you to gobble down, so you'd best be on your way. I'm glad you involved young Davey in your business as you did. It'll do him the world of good to see that not every man he encounters has only one use in mind for him. Who knows, in time I may be able to persuade him to stop risking his life as a burglar and take up an honest trade. A locksmith, perhaps, or even a steeplejack — one of those men who climb up church spires to repair the lead-work. What do you think?'

❧ 21 ❧

'This damned business is getting me down, Foxe. It's also interfering with what you should be doing — and that's unforgivable.'

Foxe had made the short journey from Mistress Tabby's house to the alderman's grand town house in Colegate. There he found Halloran in his library, gloating over some of the finer volumes in his extensive collection of rare books. It was only the alderman's devotion to duty that had caused him to wave his visitor to a chair and put down the book he had been examining.

'And what should I be doing?' Foxe asked.

'Finding me books to add to my collection, of course. It's far too long since you brought me anything at all. All you do now, when you come here, is chatter on about criminals and murders. Well, what is it this time?'

As Foxe related his questioning of the two grooms, Halloran's expression changed from irritation, through wonderment, to excitement.

'By God, Foxe, you've done it again!' he cried at the conclusion of the narration. 'That evil little bastard Harris will face justice at last; and this time he'll not escape the fate he deserves. I can scarcely credit it: two witnesses who can place Ned Harris in Mrs Melanus's bedroom immediately before she was murdered. Even a Norwich jury won't be able to find a way around that. All we have to do now is make sure Jack Beeston can't find a way to silence your witnesses before the trial. Then this business will be over at last.'

'Not quite,' Foxe cautioned. 'We still have to get Beeston up there on the scaffold alongside his creature.'

Halloran's excitement ebbed away faster than the outgoing tide from a sandbank. 'Beeston! That's a man I'd love to see hanged, but I doubt I ever will. I honestly believe he's made in the same mould as Satan himself. He's evil to the core, but somehow is never brought to pay for the wickedness he inflicts on this world. Don't let us speak of Jack Beeston, Foxe. The mere mention of his name makes me feel wretched. Go back to Harris. What do you suggest we do next?'

'We must find a way to lay hands on him and whisk him away somewhere we can question him, all without word of it reaching Beeston. I now know where he's been lodging. With the help of some constables, I think he can be arrested without too much fuss. He mustn't be lodged in the city lock-up or the castle gaol though. That would be certain to cause word of his arrest to speed on its way to Beeston in minutes. Can you think of somewhere else he can be held?'

The two men went backwards and forwards over this topic, until they had thrashed out a plan between them. Halloran would ask the mayor to allot at least two constables to make the arrest. That would ensure its legality when the case came to court. Foxe would be responsible for setting up the ambush. Once taken, Harris could be manacled and gagged, then taken and lodged in a disused part of the cellars under the old guildhall. Then he would be questioned by the two of them, with Halloran assuming his status as a justice of the peace. It wasn't quite as legal as it might be, but it would have to do. It wasn't likely anyone would risk letting Harris go free on some legal technicality.

The problem, Halloran pointed out, was not how to bring Ned Harris to justice. It was how to get him to implicate Beeston as the one who had sent him to murder Mrs Melanus. Harris would be bound to cling to the hope Beeston would find a way of securing his escape. If he turned against Beeston, there would be no chance of any rescue.

'What we have to do,' Foxe explained, 'is convince Harris that Beeston has decided to throw him to the wolves to save himself. That his sole chance to avoid the noose will be to turn King's Evidence against Beeston.'

'How, in heaven's name, do you propose to do that, Foxe? Harris has been Beeston's man for years. He'll know you're playing a trick on him.'

'With luck,' Foxe said, 'Harris's long experience of Beeston will be our best weapon. Jack Beeston has never put himself at risk if he could avoid it. All the dirty work he's ever done — and there's been plenty, as you know — has been done through others. All the beatings, the burning of business premises when demands for money have been refused, all the killings. Jack Beeston has never once dirtied his own hands. His entire criminal empire has been based on blackmail and extortion. Whenever a threat had to be carried out, or reluctant payers "encouraged" by violent means, others have been sent to do the work. That's often been Harris. He may look like a dandy, but he's a vicious bully — and the great thing about bullies is that nearly all of them are arrant cowards. Harris delights in being the one to hand out pain. I can't see him standing up for long against the prospect of suffering it himself.'

'Fair enough, but you still need to convince him Beeston will abandon him to his fate.'

'Not will, Halloran. Already has. I propose we treat Harris as if his questioning is a mere formality. First, we have witnesses who can attest he was in the woman's bedroom immediately before she was found dead. That's enough to send him to the gallows on its own. Then we suggest we're not too interested in why he killed her. Above all, we must make him believe the last thing on our minds is trying to bring evidence against Beeston. That's irrelevant. All we're concerned with is seeing Harris hang. Let's tell him this. The mayor has approached the Lord Lieutenant of the County to request His Majesty to send a royal judge to Norwich. The judge will arrive in advance of the next assize for the express purpose of trying Harris for the murder of Mrs

Melanus. How did we know where to look for evidence against him? An anonymous letter received several days ago. The writer explained Ned Harris had been extorting money from Mr Melanus, having discovered he was involved in the production of counterfeit money.

'It's obvious Harris was sent to Mrs Melanus to force her into revealing where her husband was hiding. Being the nasty piece of dung that he is, he probably went too far in "persuading" her to co-operate and managed to kill her instead. Too be honest, it scarcely matters whether he meant to kill her or not. He was responsible for her death, not by chance, but through criminal intent.'

'Is all that detail from this imaginary letter correct, Foxe?' Halloran asked. 'I thought you'd decided Beeston was the person engaged in extortion?'

'He was. What I'm hoping is that Harris will assume the only person who could have produced such a damning collection of evidence against him is Beeston. He'll think Beeston has decided to save himself by revealing the extortion and putting all the blame for it on Harris. I'm going to try convincing Harris that Beeston is intent on putting Harris in the dock for murder. If I can do that, I wager he'll be afraid enough to try to turn the tables. It's our only chance, as I see it.'

Halloran wasn't easily convinced by Foxe's arguments. He wanted desperately to put an end to Jack Beeston's criminal career, but the means proposed by Foxe carried too much uncertainty. Halloran was a man whose days of taking risks, in business or in life, were some way behind him. Foxe did win him over in the end, though it took some time. The alderman also fretted about how much to tell the mayor. His Worship's agreement was necessary to involve the constables but revealing too much would bring its own problems.

'I suggest you tell the mayor only that we have sufficient evidence to bring Ned Harris to trial for Mrs Melanus's murder,' Foxe said. 'However, we need to arrest him with as little fuss as possible. The reason for that is obvious. Beeston will try to snatch him from our grasp as soon as he knows what's happened. Don't tell him more than that.'

'You're probably right,' Halloran agreed. 'The mayor's a stickler for correct procedures. If he suspects you're going to stray so close to the limits of legality, he'll try to put a stop to the entire process. It's not that he doesn't have faith in you, Foxe. He's afraid your less conventional ways of doing things might expose him to criticism. I sometimes wonder why he accepted the position of mayor, since it causes him such worry.'

'The worst that will happen if this goes wrong is that Beeston will slip from our grasp,' Foxe said. 'I've promised the two young grooms we won't bring them into open court to give evidence, if we can avoid it. Still, if that's the only way, they'll testify. That is, they will if Beeston doesn't get to them first. That's another reason to take a few risks, Halloran. If we're too timid, Beeston will make fools of us again.'

Halloran's face grew red and he thrust his chin forward. 'Dammit, Foxe! No more delays, I say. I'd rather risk anything than hear that hateful fellow's mocking laughter and know we'd missed a chance to stop his mouth for ever. Leave the mayor to me. It's high time he showed some steel in his backbone.'

22

The seizing of Ned Harris was set in motion and everyone made ready to play their parts on the following day. The mayor sent two constables, who would be joined by the street children as guides and lookouts, plus Foxe himself to direct proceedings. The whole party was to assemble just before dark outside the rear of Foxe's house. They would then make their way, either singly or in small groups, to find suitable hiding places at prearranged spots on Harris's likeliest route back to his lodgings.

It was fortunate that Harris made no appearance that night, since the arrangements turned into a disaster.

For a start, the weather was poor. The wind blew down the streets and into the alleys in a series of chilling gusts, mixed with frequent showers. While that kept everyone else indoors, it made the event into a misery for Foxe's little band of watchers. It was too cold to stand entirely still for more than a few minutes, too wet to concentrate on anything else except trying to avoid the drips from the roofs, and too dark to see more than a few yards around you. The street children played their parts to perfection. They melted into the surrounding streets so effectively that a passer-by — had there been any — would have noticed none of them. The two constables, on the other hand, proved almost useless. They kept sighing at the cold and wet. They were too busy trying to make themselves comfortable to spend time watching out for Harris. Worst of all, they were so nervous of their surroundings that they jumped at every sound and refused to stray more than a few feet from one another in the darkness. Whether it was this nervousness or natural clumsiness, one managed to fall over a small barrel left outside a house. That — and his torrent of oaths — made such a noise people began poking their heads out of windows round about to see what was going on. After an hour or so of pure misery and frustration, Foxe gave up and sent them home in disgust.

He made a second attempt to set up the ambush the following night, using different constables. The weather had improved a little, but these constables proved just as nervous and maladroit as the last. Another failure. Despite them waiting for him for three hours, Harris failed to make an appearance.

By the third night, Foxe had come close to giving up this plan altogether. He could see no means of persuading any of the constables they could enter those particular alleyways and lanes and emerge safely. These stalwarts of the forces of law and order declared the whole neighbourhood too dangerous and unpredictable. The only way they would consent to pass within its boundaries, was in a large enough group to make any pretence at secrecy impossible.

Foxe had spent all that third day formulating an alternative plan. This time, the constables were to stay closer to the edge of the market area and safety. The actual detention of Ned Harris was to be undertaken by two stout wherrymen, supplied by Captain Brock. Foxe also borrowed Bart, Mistress Tabby's enormous servant and protector. The street children, as before, would act as lookouts and guides.

Even the weather was now in their favour. The wind had dropped. It was dry and not too cold. Soon after eleven, the moon rose at the full, bathing the streets in enough pale light to be able to see a good distance along them. There were sufficient people about early on. That made it easy for Foxe's band to enter the area without drawing any attention. Best of all, the wherrymen proved stout-hearted fellows, not afraid at the merest shadow.

By midnight, Foxe was crouched in a stinking alleyway, while unseen creatures sniffed his ankles and crawled over his feet. Something, almost certainly a large rat, attempted to scale his leg. He pushed the creature away, so that it ran off uttering an indignant cascade of squeals and chattering. He had hoped Harris would have come past by now, but that was not to be. It was going to prove a lengthy wait. At least the sky had stayed clear. The moon sailed magnificently above the rooftops, filling one side of the alley with silver light and casting the area where Foxe was hiding into dense shadow. Several of the street children had now moved further away, hoping to spot Harris's approach and put everyone else on alert.

Foxe heard the bells of St Peter Mancroft chime midnight, then one o'clock. He was chilled to the core of his body now. He was so uncomfortable he nearly risked detection by moving about and waving his arms to bring some feeling back into them. At last, when two o'clock in the morning must have been near, he heard swift footsteps. A young girl brought the news that Harris was close by.

A few moments later, Foxe heard him. Their quarry was coming at last, his footsteps faltering, his voice raised in an obscene song. Then he came into sight, keeping to the side of the lane illuminated by the full moon and still singing loudly to himself:

> 'I live in the town of Lynn,
> Next door to the Anchor Blue,
> Come day or night, I'll let you in
> . . . Tum-te-tum-te tum.
> Te-tum-te-tum-te-tum-te-tum . . .
> . . . An' you shall have my maidenhead,
> Aye, marry, and thank you too!
> 'Come let me take your strainin' yard
> An' place it 'twixt my thighs,
> Then you —'

They heard no more of the song, for the wherrymen were upon him. One clamped a huge hand over Harris's mouth, while the other pinned his arms to his sides. Then they started dragging him towards the spot where the two constables were waiting. All was done as swiftly and silently as Foxe could have hoped.

He was following after Harris and his captors, congratulating himself now on a successful outcome, when disaster nearly came to ruin it all. Once again, the bringers of bad luck proved to be the two constables.

In the brief time he had been dragged along, Ned Harris had recovered enough of his wits to be thinking up a means of escape. His chance came as the wherrymen handed their prisoner over to the constables. Quick as a flash, Harris wrenched himself free of one constable's grip. The moonlight flashed on a blade pulled from somewhere on his body. He twisted around — and the second constable let out a gasp and doubled over, releasing his grip on the man's arm too. Harris was free.

If he had run at once, Harris might well have escaped. Instead, he turned back to the first constable, meaning to use the knife on him too. That act of petty revenge proved a fatal mistake. Out of the darkness came two small figures. As Harris opened his mouth to alert the whole neighbourhood, one of them bent down, scooped up a handful of mud and filth from the street and flung it full into the man's face. That most effectively rendered him dumb and blind at the same time. The second figure paused a moment to steady herself, then planted a skilful kick hard into Harris's groin. Now it was Ned Harris's turn to double over. All he could do now was groan and clutch at the source of what must have been causing him sickening pain. Finally, the huge figure of Bart came up from behind, threw arms like tree-limbs around Harris's body and lifted his feet clean off the ground. As he did so, Bart tightened his grip around the man's chest, driving the breath from his lungs. Harris's grunts of pain turned into a frantic gasping for breath.

Harris's actual arrest was made by the constable who had first lost hold of the man. Incensed by the wounding of his colleague — and brave enough now someone else was holding the villain's arms — he stepped forward and drew his wooden truncheon. Then he called out 'I arrest you, in the name of the king!', promptly delivered a sharp blow to Harris's head, and knocked him unconscious.

The wherrymen now tied their captive as securely as only sailors could. The constable turned to help his colleague, whose knife-wound proved superficial. There was no need to gag Harris's mouth, since he showed no signs of recovering consciousness. This was just as well. In his winded state, he might have choked to death on the gag before they got him to a safe place. Finally, the constables, accompanied by a gaggle of excited street children, surrounded Bart. He had calmly slung Harris over one shoulder, ready to carry him unaided towards the place prepared in the cellars of the Guildhall. Foxe brought up the rear.

At the Guildhall, in a room so small and dark it might have been a cell, they left the wretched Harris. His fancy clothes were now caked in mud and filth from the street and he still clutched at his private parts. That one small foot, driven forward with skill as well as force, had reduced the once proud bully to a snivelling mass of self-pity. In his current state, he wouldn't have frightened a child of three.

Foxe handed out suitable rewards to the wherrymen and the children. After that, he went to his bed to take some much-needed rest. He ought to make himself ready for the interrogation he and Halloran would undertake the next day. Harris had been captured. Whether he could be made to confess and implicate his master, Jack Beeston, had yet to be seen.

𝕾 23 𝕾

It was a truculent and defiant Ned Harris who confronted Alderman Halloran and Mr Foxe soon after noon the next day. He'd been given food and water, but he still bore the dirt from his detention in the early hours of that same morning. Whether he had slept was questionable. That he had devoted a good deal of time to planning what he would say was quite plain. He was not the cleverest of men. Still, many years surviving in the back alleys, grog shops and gambling dens of Norwich had honed his survival skills to a sharp edge. It was not going to be easy to catch him out.

'I demand that you release me from this vile place,' he said, the moment Foxe and the alderman entered the room. 'I'm surprised at you having any part in this illegal attack, Alderman Halloran. You bein' a magistrate an' all. As for you, Mr Bookseller, you're always poking your long, foxy nose into matters what don't concern you. One day, someone'll grab you by the end of it and slit your bloody throat, which is no more'n you deserve.'

'Save your breath, Harris,' Foxe replied. 'I've been threatened by many better men than you and I'm still here. I had come to do you a favour — though why I cannot imagine — but if that's going to be your attitude, I'll be on my way and leave you to your fate. Which is the hangman's drop, by the way, in case you still nurse any misguided hopes of seeing out many more months on this earth.'

'Listen to you talk big, Mr Bookseller. You ain't got nothin' as'd interest a proper court o' law in my case, 'ave you? That's why you 'ad me grabbed by ruffians and brought 'ere. This ain't the proper gaol an' I ain't been brought before a magistrate, as is my legal due. This is unlawful detention, that's what it is. I'll see as you pays for it too. You just wait until Mr Beeston 'ears what you done to me. Ah, that shook you, didn't it? You thought as 'ow you'd seen the last o' him. Well 'e's back an' very much alive, I tell you. 'e was no friend o' yours before. This attack on one o' his most valued associates is goin' to convince 'im its long past time 'e settled your 'ash for good an' all. You see if it don't.'

'Beeston? Nasty piece of work, but nothing to do with this matter. If you're relying on Jack Beeston to help you out, you're even more stupid that I thought. This time, Harris, even the Archangel Gabriel himself couldn't save you from dangling from that rope. You wanted to be brought before a magistrate. You acknowledged yourself, a moment ago, that the alderman here is a magistrate, so you've got your wish. I've already given him more than enough evidence to bring you before a judge on charges of ... let me see ... resisting arrest, wounding an officer of the law, extortion, rape and murder. That's to say nothing of the extra charge of treason you'll face in due course.'

'Treason? What fuckin' treason?'

'Counterfeiting. Our men found a bag of counterfeit gold sovereigns when they searched your lodgings.'

'But ... 'Ow did you find —'

'How did we find the coins? We knew where to look, thanks to our anonymous letter writer.'

'That ain't treason.'

'Didn't you realise counterfeiting counts as treason in the eyes of the law? Well, it does, believe me. They don't simply hang traitors either, you know. They hang, draw and quarter them. That means cutting them down, half dead but still conscious, slitting them open, pulling out their innards and burning them before their eyes. Oh, and cutting off their private parts into the bargain. Then, after they're dead, they cut their bodies into quarters and hang the pieces over the city gates for the crows to eat.'

'You can't frighten me with fairy tales like that, Foxe. I seen a woman 'ung for counterfeiting and they didn't do any o' that stuff to 'er.'

'No, not to a woman. It's different for a man. I don't say they will do it, Harris, but that's the penalty on the statute book, and in view of all your other crimes ...'

No convicted traitor had suffered that barbaric, medieval penalty for many long years, but Foxe hoped Harris wouldn't be aware of that.

'What other crimes? You talks big, Mr Bookseller, but I don't 'ear no evidence against me. You're very quiet too, alderman. Ain't you got anythin' to say to me? Or do you know all this is just a load o' bollocks?'

'Not at all, Harris,' Halloran said coldly. 'I've simply been marvel-ling at your brazen impudence. We have proper witnesses who can attest to you being present at the place where an unfortunate woman — and a respectable one at that, the wife of a leading citizen of this place — was raped then strangled. Present at the very time between the witnesses leaving and her dead body being discovered by her maid-servant. A matter of so little time, as it seems to me, that you have to be the one who attacked and killed her. No jury in the kingdom can fail to convict you after they've heard that. You're a doomed man, Harris. I tried to persuade Mr Foxe to leave you to your fate, but he insisted on coming to give you a final chance. Even after that letter and what it contained ...'

'That was why we knew precisely where to find your cache of coun-terfeits, as I explained already,' Foxe added. 'Our public-spirited corre-spondent gave us all the details.'

In reality, finding the small bag of coins was no more than luck. To be fair though, there weren't many suitable hiding places in the wretched room Harris lived in. He'd chosen one of the most obvious ones as well.

'Think about it,' Foxe said. 'Ask yourself how we know so much of what you've been doing. How we knew about your attempt to extort money from Mr Melanus as the price for you staying silent about his counterfeiting activities. How I knew where to go to question the men who you found with Mrs Melanus when you burst in on her.'

Foxe could sense Harris was wavering. His fear of death was starting to overcome his faith that Beeston would, as so often before, find a way get him out of facing justice.

'So 'oo is this writer of far-fetched letters then. Give me 'is name!'

'Sadly, he failed to sign the letter he sent us. No matter. Even a dullard like you should be able to work out who it must be. Who else could know so much about what you've doing of late?'

'Liar!'

'As you wish. Of course, sacrificing you means saving himself. He's never been known to do his own dirty work, has he? That's what fools like you are for. "I had nothing to do with it," he'll say. "I wasn't even in Norwich that night. I can prove it." All true enough, naturally.'

'Beeston would never —'

'Turn you in? Of course he would, if it was his neck or yours. Plenty more useful halfwits like you about. What's one less to a man like Jack Beeston?'

Thanks to Foxe, Harris by this time thought his master had thrown him to the wolves to save his own neck. He had made quite sure he, Ned Harris, would be taken and bear the blame for everything, while his betrayer escaped scot free. As this realisation sank in, Foxe could see fear take complete hold of the man. That was when all Harris's attempts at bravado failed and his resistance collapsed completely.

'Please, Mr Foxe.' It was "Mr Foxe" now, not "Mr Bookseller" or plain "Foxe". 'You said as 'ow you was plannin' to do me a favour, didn't you?'

'I was, but that was before you became so unpleasant. I don't know whether to bother anymore.'

'I'm sorry for sayin' what I did. Truly I am. I thought that bugger Beeston was goin' to be my friend, didn't I? Now I sees what a treacherous swine 'e is. Gawd! An' I trusted 'im. 'E was the one what did all them things you said — tried to squeeze money out o' the goldsmith, after 'e caught on as to what Melanus was up to. 'E sent me to rough Melanus up a bit — encourage 'im to pay like. Only I never 'ad to do it. The lily-livered cove practic'ly got on 'is knees and swore 'e was going to send the gelt in a day or so. That's what 'e did an' all, only Beeston told me 'tweren't good money, just more o' what 'e were passin' off. Then I 'ears as Melanus 'as run off, so I tells Beeston right away. Bloody 'ell! Were Beeston fuckin' mad or what? Right off 'e tells me to get 'old o' Melanus's wife and make 'er tell me where Melanus's gone.'

'He didn't tell you to kill her though, did he?'

'Yes, 'e bloody well did! Told me I could 'ave a bit o' fun with 'er first, if I wanted, 'cos she were well known to be no more 'n a London whore what the goldsmith 'ad taken a fancy to. Then I was to finish 'er, 'e said. Teach 'er 'usband a lesson for tryin' to cheat Jack Beeston.'

Maybe Harris hadn't quite realised until this point what he'd been saying; that he'd now confessed to the murder of the goldsmith's wife. All the colour left his face and he grabbed wildly at Foxe's hand.

'Gawd 'elp me, Mr Foxe! What've I done now? You said you'd do me a favour, didn't you? I don't want to swing! Me mother always said I'd go to 'ell, if I didn't mend me ways. Beeston told me to do it! I swear 'e did! I'll even turn King's evidence, if it'll save me from the drop. 'Elp me, Mr Foxe. Please!'

The sight of the arrogant Ned Harris begging for his life would have caused most respectable citizens of Norwich a good deal of satisfaction. All Foxe felt was sadness, tinged with more than a little pity. The fact that he was the one who had brought Harris to this state — deliberately too — was more a reason for him to feel ashamed than triumphant. When he spoke next, his tone was almost gentle.

'I promise to do what I can for you, Harris, though it may not be much. Your fate won't lie in my hands.'

'No, it will not.' The sound of Alderman Halloran's voice made both the others in the room jump. It was so long since he'd said a word, they had forgotten his presence altogether. 'The judge will decide on that, not Mr Foxe here, nor me.'

'I will speak up for you,' Foxe said. 'That you can rely on. Tell the court you co-operated with us. Even if your wish to turn King's evidence isn't allowed, I'll try to get you sentenced to transportation to the American colonies, rather than hanged.'

'That's all for later anyway,' Halloran said. Now they'd achieved what they'd set out to do, he was eager to get away and put proceedings back on a more conventional legal footing. 'We'll send a clerk to take down your confession, Harris, so you can sign it or fix your mark, if you can't write. After that, the law will take its course.'

Harris nodded, then another thought came into his mind; one just as terrifying as the scenes of execution he'd been imagining for the past few minutes.

'You won't let Jack Beeston get me, will you? You'll keep me safe an' all, till I gets to tell me story to the judge? If that filthy bastard Beeston knows I've turned 'im in, 'e'll sure as 'ell send one of 'is men to shut me mouth afore I can peach on 'im. I knows 'im, gentlemen. 'E'd not 'esitate to send someone to murder 'is own mother, if 'e thought it might suit 'is purpose, let alone to save 'is miserable neck.'

❦

'IT'S CERTAINLY A WORRY,' HALLORAN SAID TO FOXE AS THEY WERE walking away together from the Guildhall. 'Beeston has spies everywhere. At least, he used to have, when he lived in this city. Do you think he still does, even after his time in hiding and the fact that he's now causing problems in Great Yarmouth, rather than here?'

'We'd better assume so,' Foxe replied. 'At least, without Harris, it'll take a bit longer for word to reach him and for his orders to get back here. If you'll take my advice, you'll ask the mayor to have Harris kept in the Castle gaol. Put him in solitary confinement until he comes to trial — or we have Beeston safely locked up there as well. That's got to be our next step.'

'With his confession, we've more than enough evidence to get Harris convicted of murder,' Halloran said. 'The counterfeiting charge is different. Do you still believe he was involved in that business?'

'Aside from being told to encourage Melanus to pay what Beeston was demanding, I doubt it,' Foxe said. 'That little bag of coins is more likely to be his payment from Beeston. If not that, Mrs Melanus could have given it to him to try to buy him off. We don't know that the sovereigns Maria found were the only ones her mistress had taken. No, it's all too vague to form the basis for a successful prosecution. He might be charged with handling false money, but that's almost insignificant compared with the murder charge. All those things I told him about treason were said to scare him. They did too!'

'You're a cunning fellow, Foxe. Well named, I'd say. Let's get back to Beeston though. Suppose Harris sticks to his plan to save his own neck by turning King's evidence. Will that be enough to get a conviction in Jack Beeston's case? Can we even find twelve jurors in this city ready to defy Beeston's threats and send him to the gallows?'

'On the last point, we can always have him tried in London on the basis of there being no possibility of a fair trial here. Your earlier point is a good one though. It seems to me Harris's confession must provide at least enough evidence to have Beeston arrested. That is, if we move fast enough to stop him slipping away, like he did last time. Can you get the mayor to send an urgent letter, by special rider, to Great Yarmouth? He should ask the mayor of that place to order Beeston's arrest right away, then send him here for us to interrogate.'

'I'll go to see His Worship at once.'

'One more point.' Foxe's brain was working furiously. They'd come so far, he couldn't bear to be cheated out of finishing Beeston off for good. 'Could someone persuade the commander of the local garrison, here or in Great Yarmouth, to assign a group of troopers to guard Beeston along the way? We don't want any of his band of ruffians to spring him loose before he gets here.'

'I know the commander here socially, Foxe. I'll send him a note. He's a good chap and I'm sure he'll do it if I ask him. Either that or ask the officer in charge in Great Yarmouth to see it done. Right, I'm off to find the mayor, then I want to go back home and have a drink to wash the taste of Ned Harris out of my mouth. What about you?'

'Home too, probably to fret and worry until I hear Beeston has been taken and is on his way here under guard. No. I'll call on the Cunning Woman first. I need to thank her for letting me borrow Bart last night. If it hadn't been for him and the street children, Harris might well have escaped. Then he'd have run to Beeston and both of them would have vanished.'

❧ 24 ❧

Whether it was the herbal tea she made him drink, the soothing effect of her presence, or the encouragement she gave him, Foxe left Mistress Tabby's house an hour or so later in a very different frame of mind. He was still anxious over whether Jack Beeston would be arrested, before he had time to escape, yet the despondency he had felt over his part in bringing Ned Harris to confess had gone. It had been replaced with the quiet satisfaction that comes from completing an unpleasant job and knowing it had been done well. By the time he reached the door to his shop, Foxe was almost cheerful. So much so, that he decided to go inside and tell Mrs Crombie about the latest events. He would begin with his part in the capture of Ned Harris and end with the man's confession and his offer to turn King's evidence against Beeston.

Fortified still further by his partner's expressions of amazement and her praise for his achievement, Foxe ate a hearty dinner. He also rewarded himself by consuming a little too much brandy afterwards. Finally, he retired to his bed more than ready to make up for the sleep he had lost the night before.

Of course, as a result of his indulgence, Foxe rose late and with a severe headache. He behaved in a surly manner towards his servants.

He was unable to eat more than a single roll for his breakfast. When he left to walk to his usual spot in the coffeehouse, there was considerable relief among those he left behind. Even in the coffeehouse, his expression of furious concentration and distracted air made sure everyone gave him a wide berth.

It took Foxe twice his usual number of cups of coffee, followed by a decidedly brisk walk around the great marketplace, to restore his normal temper. He arrived back at his house ready to turn his attention to something he had ignored for many days. It was high time he read through the various book catalogues which had arrived from his suppliers in the London trade. Perhaps he would discover something in their lists of rare volumes to offer Alderman Halloran the next time he went to visit.

While Foxe was engaged in this pleasant activity his maidservant, Molly, came to tell him the alderman's manservant had brought an urgent message from his master. Mr Foxe was to go to the house in Colegate right away. An unexpected event had occurred, and it was bound to have a profound effect on the whole business of the missing goldsmith and his murdered wife.

The event turned out to be a lengthy letter, which the mayor had received only that morning. Recognising its importance, His Worship sent it on to Halloran, with the unnecessary instruction that it should be shown to Mr Foxe as soon as possible.

'You'll scarce believe who sent it,' Halloran said. 'None other than Mr Melanus himself. Our missing goldsmith and probable producer of those exquisitely crafted counterfeit sovereigns. Look at the signature at the end. "Samuel Melanus", as clear as day! I even had Mr Richards rush over here from the Norwich City Bank to confirm the letter is definitely in Melanus's own hand. What's more, Melanus says he's written to supply the evidence we need to seize Jack Beeston on a charge of making and distributing counterfeit coins! Can you believe it? Here, read it for yourself.'

To His Worship, The Lord Mayor of Norwich
 Sent from Liverpool

Your Worship,

By the time this letter reaches you, I will have left the shores of England for a new, and I hope better, life far away. I had planned to write it earlier. However, business in the capital delayed me somewhat, and a series of unfavourable winds kept all the ships here tied up and unable to go to sea. Only now, after nearly a week, is the master of the vessel on which I propose to take passage prepared to leave the harbour. And that is only after I had pressed him hard and offered him a large bribe to do so. I have no notion of what may have been happening in Norwich since my departure. Still, you can well imagine my anxiety to be away and safe before there is any chance of pursuit reaching me here.

You must understand this is not a confession. I do not give a jot for English law, for I shall soon be beyond its reach. You should see it rather as a sop to my conscience. Whatever I have done, you must realise I am, at heart, a law-abiding man. My most recent dealings with the Norwich City Bank should offer ample evidence of that. I needed it to furnish me with the necessary bills of exchange and notes for my forthcoming journey. Nevertheless, I made sure proper payment was made and deposited in the bank's vaults. My fellow directors and shareholders may sleep easy. I have left the bank in a most prosperous state. I have also sent another letter to my attorney in the city. He has been directed to distribute my own shareholding in equal shares to the other partners. This will, I trust, compensate them for all that I have done.

Why have I written to you? I wish to ensure justice is done. If you act quickly, an undiscovered maker of counterfeit coinage can be apprehended. His master in those crimes is a vicious criminal and extortioner well-known to all in Norwich: one called Jack Beeston. By providing the evidence against them, I will implicate myself in a serious crime, but that is of no matter, as I have already explained. I will also need to lay bare a great folly of my own doing; one that is responsible for my present position. I offer no excuse for my past stupidity. I did it of my own free will and am now paying the price.

First things first. Jack Beeston is in Great Yarmouth, where I have no doubt he is causing as much trouble to the authorities as he did in Norwich. You will find him lodging in rooms next door to The Green Dragon. I understand he began his business in that town by seeking to gain leadership of the gang of smugglers who use the port. I do not think he succeeded. Maybe that was why he later turned his attention to the profitable crime of coining. Since then, he has gradually brought almost all the counterfeiters in both Yarmouth and Norwich under his control. Since I did not know what he was doing when I started on my plan for escape, I fell into his hands. Extortion has always been part of his nature. It is hardly surprising he saw me as a fat and stupid sheep, ready to be shorn and shorn again. If you do as I say, he will soon discover his error in that respect.

I have married three times. My first marriage was happy, but short-lived. My wife died of the smallpox within the year. The second marriage lasted longer but gave neither of us much pleasure. My wife failed to give me children, as I wished. I failed to keep up even the pretence of finding her company desirable. She had grown into something of a bitter shrew and I made the error of telling her so on many occasions. One of us had to go. Fortunately, it was her, thanks to a fall from an expensive horse she had nagged me into buying for her.

My third marriage has eclipsed both the previous ones in the depth of my initial infatuation; then in the havoc it has brought to every aspect of my existence. Within three months, I found it regrettable. Within six, it was proving intolerable. Lacking the courage and the depravity to resort to murder, I resolved instead to free myself by going overseas and assuming a new identity. That was why I pretended not to know of my wife's repeated adulteries. While I gave in to her ridiculous extravagance, all the time I laid my plans to escape.

I am a wealthy man, Your Worship. However, not even Croesus himself could have satisfied my wife's constant demands for baubles and fashionable clothes. I had planned to sell my original business in gold and silver work anyway. I am no longer a young man. It is time for me to take my ease and enjoy the fruits of my past labours. Now, of course, I had neither the time to find a buyer, nor the wish to make my departure known. The best I could do was to close the business down in an orderly manner before I left.

It was while I was working out a way of doing this that I hit on the means to produce sufficient funds to be able to live my new life in considerable comfort. My legitimate income was, of course, being eaten up by the greed of my wife. I could not sell my business or my property. I had no time to do so, and I wished to leave in secret. Then I hit on the first of my stratagems. I could use the property as security for a series of modest loans, such as any businessman might enter into. Perhaps to pay for some expansion to his commercial activities or to enter a new market. I will not be able to repay the money. However, seizing and selling my house will be enough to ensure the lenders are not out of pocket. Happily, the debts produced will also deny my wife any hope of living on there after I am gone. Certain other ways of obtaining funds also appeared to me at that time. I need not explain. What I have done will become clear in due course.

My other solution to gaining the extra money I needed was simple. I am a skilled engraver, so I used that ability to produce a single set of dies capable of stamping out gold sovereigns. I did not know the proportions needed to produce the correct alloys to adulterate the gold. Nor did I possess the means of stamping each blank to produce a coin. I therefore sought out a person who did. That was how I came to the notice of Beeston. You will find the man who turned my gold and silver into coinage in the third house on the left side of the alley that lies behind The Golden Cross Tavern. If you are quick, you will also find his stamping machine and dies. He makes many different values of false coinage, though I was interested only in sovereigns. I let him have all the silver and gold I could. After taking a proportion as payment, he gave me false sovereigns in return, stamped from my own die.

There you have it. For many months, I used the counterfeit money for my normal expenses, and to pay for my wife's extravagances. That allowed me to amass genuine coins to the same value. The total amount, together with the loans I mentioned, I set aside to take with me when I left.

Beeston, of course, tried to exact payment for keeping silent about my arrangements. The fool even threatened to harm my wife, if I did not meet his demands. I almost laughed in his face. If he had killed her, all he would have done was remove a person I had come to hate with every fibre of my soul. He could chop her into pieces if he liked and good luck to him.

I hope you will now act as my agent, Your Worship, in taking revenge on Jack Beeston, thereby freeing the world of a most wicked criminal. If you search his lodgings, you will find a significant cache of counterfeit coins. He had, as I said, been engaged in that trade for many months before I came along, having failed in his attempt to become the leader of the existing criminal fraternity in Great Yarmouth. Norwich is his preferred location and I imagine he is trying to find a way to return there.

His principal agent in Norwich calls himself Ned Harris. He is an arrogant dandy and scapegrace to all appearances. Within, he is a man every bit as evil as *his master. Him I have met face to face. He brought his master's demands and would, I imagine, have carried out his threats, if the money was not paid on time and in full. That is work I am certain he would enjoy. I noticed a deep seam of coarseness and violence behind the boastful manner.*

I could have slipped away quietly, for I doubt anyone could have discovered my plans and prevented me in time. I did not do so, because it must have handed a kind of victory to Beeston and his pack of thieves and murderers. I am too old, too weak and too much of a coward to attempt vengeance on my own account. I have therefore done my best to arrange matters so that the full force of the law will descend on these rogues as a direct result of my escape. I will not know the outcome, but I will at least know that I have tried.

Along with the message about my shares in the bank, I have given my attorney instructions for the disposal of my other remaining assets. Since I will never return, you may see this as my last Will and Testament, for I am as dead to England now as if I lay in my grave.

I have no children, which is perhaps the worst cross I must bear in what remains to me of life. My relations are few and distant. They deserve nothing from me. The same applies to my wife. As she chose to betray me, so I now choose to betray her and leave her penniless. She brought nothing to the marriage and, by God, she will bear nothing away. After my debts have been paid, all my property is to be sold. The proceeds will be given to that fine charitable organisation known as the United Friars of Norwich.

Farewell to Norwich and to England! I do not ask for your understanding for what I have done. I care not whether you admire my cunning or curse my effrontery. I have made very sure you will never see me arraigned for my crime and that is enough.

I am, sir, your former fellow-citizen and most reluctant law-breaker,
Samuel Melanus

'Harris said Jack Beeston was furious against Melanus. That was why he sent Harris to carry out the threat to harm his wife,' Foxe said, when he had finished reading. 'Melanus must have paid at least part of the price Beeston demanded for his silence but did so in counterfeit coins. By sending this letter, Melanus hopes to have the rogue seized at once, while he still has the false coins in his possession. He must have known Beeston would have spotted the forgeries right away; especially since he knew what Melanus was doing.'

'Won't Beeston have disposed of them?'

'Not him! You know what good forgeries they are. He'll have hung onto them. I wager he's planning to pass them off in small amounts. That way, he'll add their value to the extra money he is doubtless hoping to extort from Melanus as the price of his "betrayal". That was why he made good on his threat to harm Mrs Melanus. He was showing what must happen if there was any deviation from his demands in the future. As if Melanus cared! His plan all along has been to avenge all the wrongs done to him, including — no, especially — those perpetrated by his wife.'

'The man's a devil — and a damned arrogant one too!' Halloran said. 'To think I invited him to dine in this house on more than one occasion.'

'You have to admire his ingenuity and planning though,' Foxe replied. He couldn't help grinning at the alderman's indignation at the thought he had entertained a man who had cheated His Majesty's Treasury. One who was even now bringing about the certain death of those who had transformed him from local worthy to criminal fugitive. 'Melanus arranged things so that, by the time this letter arrived, he'd be aboard ship, heading for a new life. He also ensured all those bills and notes he has with him will be honoured. They were properly and legally issued in return for genuine coins of the realm, he says here. From what Mr Sedgefield has discovered, I'm sure that's correct. Whatever else he's done the bank has no grounds to refuse to honour that paper — not if they want to retain the trust of their other customers.'

'Yet none have been presented for payment.'

'Not yet. I'm sure they'll arrive back at the bank sometime though. Most likely from some bank in our American colonies. That's where Melanus is heading, if you ask me. That's why he waited to write until he reached Liverpool; the post from where much of our trade with America departs. He's already set up his new identity as Mr Joseph Smith, silversmith of Boston. While he was in London he used the Royal Mint to add to his bona fides. He's either going to Boston or to some place such as Philadelphia or New York. There he can be Mr Joseph Smith from the start.'

In this, however, Foxe was proved wrong. When the first paid bill returned a few days later, it had been made over to a Mr Emanuel Janowicz and cashed in a bank in Rotterdam.

❧ 25 ❧

During that day and the next, the Norwich and Great Yarmouth mayors busied themselves in arranging arrests. Jack Beeston was to be seized in Great Yarmouth. The counterfeiter in Norwich, whose name proved to be Abel Greenleaf, was also to be taken into custody.

Foxe decided to accompany the constables in Norwich. He would have liked to be present at the arrest of Jack Beeston. However, he dared not delay matters by asking the Mayor of Great Yarmouth to wait until he could arrive there.

The mayor sent two constables and his Swordbearer to arrest the counterfeiter at the house to which Melanus's letter had directed them. It proved to be one of an unremarkable row of buildings set along one side of a narrow, wretched alley, roughly midway between the marketplace and Tombland. All these houses were made of wood, their upper stories overhanging the pathway below. Most of their roofs were of thatch. The whole area looked as if a single neglected fireplace or cooking range would be enough to clear the ground ready for new and better buildings to be erected.

There were still quite a few such corners of the city, where buildings dated from the time of Good Queen Bess, or even earlier. Over the years, all had become more and more neglected so that now they sagged against one another, like drunken men. Few had, as yet, been replaced with modern buildings of brick and tile. Such alterations were to be found only in places where the most prosperous artisans and shopkeepers lived. Even in these better quarters, the seeming replacement of wood by brick and tile might be only skin-deep. The rebuilt houses might well present a fine frontage to the street, complete with large sash windows and pillars either side of the doorway. But go to the side or the rear, and you would see the old timber framing and steep-pitched roofs making up the bulk of their fabric. In the streets inhabited by labourers and the rest, change had yet to come. The landlords of the poor found no reason to improve these wretched hovels, though they charged rents far higher than was warranted.

The two constables proved to be the very ones who had so nearly fumbled the arrest of Ned Harris. Foxe therefore decided he should, once again, take his own measures to ensure the success of the operation. As the group moved down the side of the marketplace, it attracted a good deal of attention. Soon, a gaggle of loafers, scroungers and general ne'er-do-wells followed behind them. Amongst these, Foxe spotted several of the street children. They had also seen Mr Foxe. It took little more than a nod and the wave of his hand to bring them clustered around him. He selected one of the older girls to act as their leader. Now he gave his instructions to her, using a low voice that would not carry to other ears in the general hubbub about them.

Exactly as Foxe expected, the three city officials marched directly to the door of the house where they had been told that the counterfeiter lived. They banged on the door with their cudgels, hard enough to produce substantial dents in the woodwork, and demanded entry in the name of the King. Foxe, bearing no such authority, but far wiser in the ways of the criminals of Norwich, waited quietly some steps away. After a moment or so, one of the street children plucked at his sleeve and led him down a narrow passage to come out at the rear of the property in question.

He had scarcely arrived, when a door flew open and a thin man of some forty or fifty years of age, still dressed in nightshirt and nightcap, tumbled out. The fellow was aiming to take refuge in the tangle of yards and overgrown gardens to the rear. That was where householders had once grown vegetables for the table or kept a pig for ham and bacon. His plan was thwarted by one of the street children, who darted forward and tripped him up. By the time he had struggled back to his feet, Mr Foxe was standing before him, with a loaded pistol levelled at his chest. He gave a quick glance to the ring of street children surrounding him; another at Foxe's calm expression and the steadiness of his hand holding the gun. These convinced Abel Greenleaf that surrender was his only option.

Next, one of the constables came out through the door Greenleaf had left open in his haste. Obtaining no answer to their furious knocking, the constables had broken down the front door. Naturally they had found the house empty and their bird flown. It was only thanks to Mr Foxe that their enterprise had proved successful. They looked at him with sheepish expressions, then put the shackles on Greenleaf, prior to leading him away. Doubtless, in boasting to their friends, they would somehow overlook the part Foxe had played in the arrest.

Once Abel Greenleaf was manacled, the constables and Sword-bearer made ready to lead him back to the lock-up. Foxe stopped them. They had, he pointed out, fulfilled only one part of their orders. They had yet to discover the equipment needed to produce counterfeit coins. To do that was as essential to securing a conviction as the arrest of the man himself.

While Foxe and the Swordbearer guarded Greenleaf, the two constables searched the house from the cellars to the attics. Even so, they found no trace of the means to stamp out blanks into coins; nor the furnace and crucibles needed to melt and mix the metals to make the blanks. When they returned to announce their failure, the counterfeiter was triumphant.

'This be false arrest,' he crowed. 'A man's lying peaceable in 'is own bed, when some ruffians come beating on 'is door demanding entry. Is it any wonder if 'e nips out o' the back door, intending only to save 'imself from foul assault or worse? You ain't found nothin' and you won't, because there never was any counterfeiting tools in that 'ouse. You got no evidence against me, 'ave you? So why don't you all bugger off and leave a man in peace. Aye, and pay for the cost of repairin' my front door too.'

For a few moments, even Foxe was forced to admit the truth in the man's words. Had Melanus given them false information? Had Melanus's disappearance alerted the counterfeiter to his danger? Maybe the delay in finding him had provided time to clear away all the incriminating evidence. Should he insist Greenleaf was taken into custody anyway for further questioning, or now release him. His dilemma was solved only when the girl he had put in charge of the street children came up to him and put her hand on his arm to attract his attention.

'Don't you worry, Mr Foxe, we found it. The 'ouse next door's a bit of a ruin. Nobody living there. Not for some time, I reckons. That's where you'll find the stuff you're lookin' for. He's turned the old kitchen into a place where 'e can melt 'is metal and make the blanks. What must 'ave been the room where the family lived has got a big machine in it now for stamping the blanks into coins.'

'That ain't my house,' Greenleaf yelled, hearing what the girl had said to Foxe. 'I ain't never even been in there. You can't prove whatever's in it 'as got anything to do with me.' Foxe ignored him and went next door instead to take a look for himself. Greenleaf was still protesting his ignorance of what the other house contained when he returned.

'Stop your noise!' Foxe said to him. 'I found the door you had made so you could go through from your own house without stepping into the street and risking being seen. I also found that beautiful set of dies for stamping out gold sovereigns which Mr Melanus, the goldsmith, gave to you. Couldn't bear to dispose of them, could you? I expect you even went on using them. If you want to blame anything for your undoing, blame your own greed and stupidity.'

'It weren't me!' the man wailed. 'It were Jack Beeston. He wouldn't let me destroy them dies. Said they was too good. I could make 'undreds more sovereigns — thousands, even — all so good 'ardly anyone would find them out. Beeston's behind all this. 'e put me up to it. I were an honest craftsman until I fell in with that rogue. If I'm for the drop, mister, I'll sure as 'ell take him with me! I'll turn King's evidence, that's what I'll do. I'll tell you all you wants to know about Jack Beeston and what he's been up to.'

Later, after Foxe and Halloran had finished questioning him, they knew the story of Abel Greenleaf's entire, sorry life. He'd learned his skills while apprenticed to a master silversmith and engraver in London. He would have stayed there too, if he'd not been discovered making free with the silversmith's young daughter. As a result, he found himself driven from the household, his apprenticeship uncompleted. He left London then, hoping to find work elsewhere. To do so, he made the false claim that he had finished his apprenticeship and was entitled to style himself a journeyman silversmith. Unfortunately, his remarkable ability to entice women into his bed ensured he had to move on, time and time again. To look at him — thin, slightly stooping, the kind of man who always seems to be in need of good meals and someone to tell him how to dress himself properly — Foxe couldn't imagine what all these wives, daughters and maidservants found so attractive. Eventually, Greenleaf explained, he settled in Norwich. Once again, he tried to stay away from the women long enough to earn some honest money.

He failed, of course, and soon found himself pursued by yet another irate husband. That was when Jack Beeston offered him a deal. He would give him refuge from his pursuer and set him up in a suitable property as his own master. In return, Greenleaf must agree to use his skills to produce counterfeit coins of various values for Beeston to pass off. Beeston even provided him with a series of young whores to act as maidservants and save him from getting into trouble again with his neighbours. That had been almost a year ago. Since then, Greenleaf had only worked for Beeston; until the goldsmith had turned up one day and offered him a deal he hadn't been able to turn down.

All Melanus had asked of him was to produce around fifty gold sovereigns each week. The goldsmith would supply the stamping-dies needed for the front and back of the coins, together with a more than suitable supply of bullion. The silver he brought was far more than what would be needed to mix with gold for the sovereigns. Greenleaf was free to use a third of it on his own account as payment for his work. Any left over, he was to return to Melanus in the form of counterfeit coins of small denominations. The only other stipulations were that his work for Melanus was to be of the highest quality and no one else was to know what he was doing.

How Beeston had found out, Greenleaf never knew. He had expected Beeston to be angry. To send his bully-boys to extract revenge — or at least throw the counterfeiter back onto the street. Beeston did neither. He simply instructed Greenleaf to continue with the arrangement with the goldsmith as if nothing had happened. Even when word went around that the goldsmith had vanished into thin air, Beeston had sent word that the counterfeiting should continue without interruption. That included production of sovereigns from the goldsmith's dies. Beeston would supply the metals needed. Everything produced was to be handed over to Ned Harris, who would act as Beeston's agent and collect Greenleaf's output on a regular basis.

❦

In contrast to the counterfeiter, Jack Beeston in Great Yarmouth put up no struggle or protest when he was taken. Calmly maintaining the pose of an innocent citizen, he protested he was the victim of mistaken identity. That came to an end when his house was searched and several bags of counterfeit sovereigns and other coins were found in his possession.

Events now descended to the level of farce. Greenleaf, all of whose counterfeiting equipment had been seized, duly turned informer against Jack Beeston. In response, Beeston claimed he was the victim of a plot where Melanus, Harris and Greenleaf were trying to save themselves by shifting the blame onto him. The counterfeit sovereigns found in his house were false evidence, planted there by Melanus. He knew nothing about them being so-called 'Spanish brass'. Indeed not. They were nothing more than a loan made to him by Melanus on a personal basis. If they were bad, that was Melanus's crime and not his.

No one believed his explanation.

Beeston's fate was finally sealed by his past attempts to supplant the local gang leaders. He'd tried to push them aside and become the most powerful figure amongst the criminals and smugglers operating in the port of Great Yarmouth. Now, seeing him trapped by the authorities — and no longer in a position to see his threats enforced — the local criminal fraternity closed ranks against him. The true leaders of the gangs of smugglers in the area made it known that anyone trying to save Jack Beeston from the gallows would have to answer to them.

There would be no need to send Beeston to London for trial. Freed from the threat of reprisals, jurors in Norwich could be relied upon to bring in a conviction. Beeston was certain to face death on the gallows, given the mass of evidence against him. The authorities therefore refused Ned Harris's request to turn King's evidence. Greenleaf's offer was accepted. He would be sentenced to transportation instead of death. Thanks to Mr Joseph Smith's visit to the Royal Mint with his bag of counterfeits, the government had been longing to discover the source of those counterfeit sovereigns. Now they were determined to make an example of all those involved. They had the chance and they took it eagerly. Mercy was not on anyone's agenda.

When the time came for his trial, Foxe made good on his promise to speak up for Harris. He stressed the way in which Harris had co-operated in bringing an end to what had proved to be a truly pernicious counterfeiting ring. Although the trial judge duly forwarded a note of Foxe's evidence to the ministry in London, His Majesty refused to grant a reprieve. Norwich was to be treated to the spectacle of two of its most notorious criminals suffering the ultimate fate alongside one another.

❦ 26 ❧

During the time Beeston, Harris and Greenleaf were in custody in the castle gaol in Norwich, further elements in the story of Mr Melanus, his foolish and unhappy wife, and his plan to escape to begin a new life elsewhere, slowly came to light.

First, the Norwich City Bank received a paid and receipted bill of exchange in the sum of one thousand pounds issued to Mr Joseph Smith, but made over to Mr Emanuel Janowicz. Subsequent enquiries showed Mr Janowicz was a diamond merchant. He was based in Rotterdam but travelled regularly to London to buy and sell gems. Three days later, another similar bill, this time for the sum of two thousand pounds, was received. It had been countersigned in favour of one Geert de Hooven; another diamond merchant plying his trade between London and Rotterdam. The next day, the remaining banknotes and bills arrived. All had been paid into an account in Rothschilds Bank in London. An account opened there by Mr Joseph Smith, a visitor from Boston in the colony of Massachusetts. Rothschilds declined to say whether any withdrawals had been made from the account. In a polite but firm letter, they pointed out there was no evidence a crime had been committed. Nor had it been proved that Mr Smith was anything other than an honest subject of the king.

'So there the matter must rest,' Brock said, when Foxe told him about it. 'Unless you can prove Mr Samuel Melanus and Mr Joseph Smith are one and the same person, Rothschilds are not going to accept that there are any irregularities. That goes for both the deposits and the account itself.'

Foxe nodded in glum agreement. 'You're right,' he said. 'We all believe that Joseph Smith is Melanus's alias, but we have nothing to prove it. It looks to me, Brock, that the fellow is going to get away.'

'Why should that matter to you?' Brock said. 'For the present, you are a popular and respected person in this city, at least amongst the merchants and traders. That means with those who fill all the places on the Common Council and the Mayor's Court, along with all the offices pertaining to the government of this city. I doubt it will last. I know your tendency to ignore conventional standards of behaviour. Why not enjoy it while it does? Forget about Mr Melanus and the rest. Your part in this business is over.'

'I hate to leave loose ends, Brock. The news about the diamonds and the large deposit with Rothschilds Bank make it quite clear, to me at least, that Melanus is heading overseas. He has probably got a small fortune in gems sewn somewhere inside his garments. He also holds a small fortune in Letters of Credit from Rothschilds. They'll be directed to one of their overseas offices — in Boston, or perhaps New York or Philadelphia. Seeing him escape irritates me a good deal. What feels even worse are the puzzles he's left behind. For example, why did the fellow go to so much trouble to find ways to take what I would guess to be less than half his total fortune away with him? Why not take all of it? Why leave so much behind? It niggles away at my mind, Brock. I won't feel content until I know the answer.'

'You may have to settle for what you do know.'

'I realise that, but I won't give up until I'm convinced — utterly and completely — I have no alternative.'

'It's your life. If you want to waste some of it knocking your head up against a brick wall, nobody can stop you. Look, Foxe. Be sensible for once. If you can't put the problem out of your mind, try some suit-able distraction. Go to that bagnio you like so much. I'm sure the girls there can find suitable ways to make you forget about murder and counterfeiting — at least for a time. Go to the theatre. You've always had the knack of picking out some pretty young actress who's willing to become your bedfellow. As a last resort, you could even try paying attention to the business of selling books.'

Halloran's advice was similar. 'Look, Foxe,' he said. 'Think about something else. Thanks to you, we've got the rogue who produced the counterfeit coins. We've also got Beeston and his creature Harris, the actual murderer of Mrs Melanus, locked away. They've been tried, found guilty and sent to the gallows. It's all over.'

'I suppose so,' Foxe said, his face revealing that he supposed nothing of the kind. 'By the way, I finally got around to looking through the latest correspondence from my suppliers in London. I think I may be able to lay my hands on two or three books which would make fine additions to your library.'

'Splendid! That's exactly what you need: to get back to normal life and forget about Melanus, Beeston, Harris and all the rest. Now, when can you be ready to tell me in detail what you've found? Do you know whether they're still available?'

Foxe tried to follow Brock's advice. He visited the bagnio; the one which had once been run by Gracie Catt. After a little time talking with several of the girls who now worked there, he finally invited one — a pert little redhead with a cheeky face and a distinct gleam in her eye — to be his bedfellow. In one sense it worked. He had a thoroughly enjoyable time with the girl, who proved as adventurous and passionate as he could have hoped. In another sense, his visit changed nothing. He'd known for some time the real attraction of the place for him was Gracie Catt. Not only was she perfect as his lover, she also had the knack of calming his mind and helping him bring his life into perspective. If all he'd wanted was a bout of serious, all-consuming passion, her actress sister, Kitty, could be relied upon to leave him happy and exhausted. She wasn't interested in him the way that her sister was. At the same time, she wouldn't bother him with her own problems or expect more than the best time he could give her. The girls at the bagnio were all like Kitty: delightfully skilled and accommodating playthings, but not interested in listening to anything more serious than pretty compliments or the kind of sexually titillating talk likely to spur both parties on to a repeat performance.

His trouble, Foxe told himself, was that he hated unresolved mysteries of any kind. He was also lonely. Brock was the best of friends, but, like Halloran, he was a bluff, no-nonsense kind of companion. You shared stories and jokes with Brock, but stayed away from anything too emotional or personal. Mrs Crombie was a fine sounding-board for his ideas and the most reliable of business partners. However, their relationship flourished because both of them kept it on an appropriately professional basis. Neither, for example, ever ventured to call the other by their Christian name. It was always "Mrs Crombie" and "Mr Foxe", even when nobody else was present. There was another drawback to sharing his problems with her too. Although Mrs Crombie was indulgent towards him and accepted his unconventional way of life, she had always made it clear it was not one that met with her approval.

Two more weeks passed. Foxe went to the theatre, where he endured several mediocre offerings and one excellent one. He flirted with several of the younger actresses but went no further than that with any of them. His servants, noting this uncharacteristic spell of celibacy, grew nervous. They began whispering amongst themselves that the master was unwell. In the end, Charlie was despatched to consult Mistress Tabby. Perhaps she could suggest some way of raising Mr Foxe's spirits — or at least diagnose what it was that was ailing him.

Her response, as relayed by Charlie, did not seem encouraging. 'Wait,' she told them. 'The matter on which he has been so deeply engaged is not yet over. When he's ready, he'll come to speak with me of his own accord. Such matters of the heart and mind cannot be hurried. I sense that your master's life will soon enter on a new course. Indeed, the first signs of this change are already stirring in the depths of his mind. Go about your duties as usual. Above all, stay cheerful. Don't worry about this lack of intimate female company. With your master, that has never been more than a temporary state.'

❧ 27 ❧

Alderman Halloran, the mayor, and the other leaders in the city now declared themselves convinced the affair of Mr Samuel Melanus and the Norwich City Bank was completely resolved. Mr Reuben Sedgefield, leading Quaker and partner in the Cawston & Sedgefield Bank, was not so sure. The directors of the Norwich City Bank had sought his assistance to make sure Mr Melanus's disappearance did not presage problems or irregularities in the business of the bank. They wished to be informed of anything likely to cause them embarrassment or — far worse — significant financial loss. That task Mr Sedgefield intended to carry out to the letter. It didn't matter to him how deeply he needed to delve into the bank's affairs, nor however long it took him. The reports he had submitted so far were no more than preliminary and provisional — as least as far as he was concerned. If they chose to assume that because he had found nothing quickly there was nothing to find, he had certainly reached no such conclusion.

Now, thanks to Mr Sedgefield's diligence and determination to leave no part of the business of the Norwich City Bank unexamined, another strange part of the affair connected with Mr Melanus came to light. At least, that was what he later claimed. In truth, the catalyst which set these fresh events into motion was no more than the passage of time.

Two months after the murder of Mrs Melanus and her husband's disappearance, the first instalment of interest on a certain loan fell due for payment. No payment came. The clerk responsible for monitoring such matters at once reported this default to Mr Paul Richards, the chief cashier. Another week passed with no payment received and no explanation from the person who had taken out the loan. That was a Mr Nathaniel White, described in the loan documents as a ship-owner of King's Lynn, engaged in the whaling trade located there.

Several urgent letters were sent to Mr White, but he did not reply. A bailiff, employed by the bank, was instructed to go at once to King's Lynn. There he should locate Mr White and point out his default. If he obtained no payment, he should request the harbourmaster to issue a ban on any ship belonging to Nathaniel White leaving the harbour. According to the loan agreement, security had been offered in the nature of a lien on two of his whaling ships, the "Walrus" and the "White Bear". Now, if the interest due was not paid at once, the whole debt would fall due. The ships would be seized and sold to discharge what Mr White owed to the bank — which was the considerable sum of nine thousand pounds.

The bailiff returned empty-handed. He had not found Mr Nathaniel White at the address he had given, nor anywhere else in the town of King's Lynn. His enquiries after the supposed ship-owner had met with blank stares and much shaking of heads. To be blunt, he reported, no Nathaniel White, ship-owner, was resident in King's Lynn; nor, according to those in a position to know, had such a man ever lived there.

Worse was to follow. The harbourmaster told him no vessels named the "Walrus" and the "White Bear" were registered at the port. Neither had been taking part in the annual whaling fishery nor in any other trade. If they existed — which he very much doubted — they had not been moored at King's Lynn in the eleven years in which he had held the position of harbourmaster.

This news from King's Lynn threw the directors of the Norwich City Bank into confusion. The effect could best be compared to probing an ants' nest with a large stick. When Mr Sedgefield added that, so far as he could tell, all the dealings with this Mr Nathaniel White had been conducted by Mr Melanus in person, confusion became panic. Every mind turned at once to the only man they thought could save the bank's reputation and their money — Mr Ashmole Foxe.

That was why, later the same day, Foxe was to be found seated with Mr Sedgefield in a private room at the bank. Before he did anything else, he needed all the details the careful Quaker could provide.

According to Halloran, the prevailing view amongst the directors of the Norwich City Bank was that Mr Reuben Sedgefield was honest to a fault and an excellent banker. He was also 'a dry old stick, the kind of fellow who counted the teaspoons every day to make sure none had slipped away without leave during the night.'

Foxe's impression was different. Sedgefield was certainly careful and thorough — his examination of the Norwich City Bank's affairs proved that. He also had the typical dress and manner of a Quaker. Yet behind this calm and serious demeanour, Foxe sensed a lively mind and even a whimsical sort of humour.

'I gather thou hast been trying to make sense of this affair, Mr Foxe,' Sedgefield said to him. 'It doth occur to me that might prove to be a hopeless task. The ways of men are rarely rational, in my experience. People make great decisions on nothing more than a whim. Then they change their minds because the food they ate the previous night is sitting a little too heavily on their stomach. There is also a most dangerous age in a man's life. A time when he comes to believe the world has passed him by. Had he but chosen differently, he tells himself, he might have done great things or enjoyed pleasures now denied to him. He therefore has no option but to snatch at what he reckons will be his last chances to savour the delights of this world he has missed. Believe me, if that happens, the fellow is likely to commit acts of such unbelievable foolishness even he is amazed at them afterwards.'

'Is that what you think Mr Melanus did?' Foxe said.

'Ah ... There I have the advantage of thee, sir. All that has been asked of me is to discover what actually happened, at least as regards the affairs of the Norwich City Bank. To seek to discover the reasons for them is outside my remit. Speculation is an activity quite foreign to bankers. We are men who abhor risk as the righteous abhor sin. What Mr Melanus did, in this case, may be discovered by any who, as I have done, sifts through the copious records all bankers maintain. That is as far as I am asked to go.'

Foxe smiled. 'I suppose that is where my work and yours overlaps, Mr Sedgefield. I too am interested in facts, but more for what they may tell me of what I do not yet understand, than for their own sake. Very well. Let us begin with the facts you have uncovered. There must be something suspicious about this loan for you to have drawn particular attention to it. Banks make loans all the time. It is their business to do so. Yet this loan somehow drew your attention. Why was that?'

'There were three reasons, Mr Foxe. The first arose simply because I was especially interested in business conducted by Mr Melanus himself. I believe thou knowest he had, of late, taken less and less of an active role in the bank's day-to-day business. His name appeared only rarely in the records. Yet here was a customer and a loan which he had dealt with in person. No other director or servant of the bank was involved in any way, so far as I could discover. When I questioned Mr Richards, the chief cashier, on the matter, he could neither recall this Mr Nathaniel White, nor any of his dealings with the bank.'

'That is indeed odd.'

'More than odd, Mr Foxe. Nine thousand pounds is a substantial amount of money to be lending to anyone. I would expect such a loan to be given only to a person well-known to the banker who made it. A person of sound reputation in the city, whose antecedents and business dealings in the past would be a matter of general knowledge. Yet this Mr White, apparently a resident of King's Lynn, had no links to Norwich before this. His business was also one with which the Norwich City Bank had no prior experience. I know little of whaling myself, Mr Foxe, save that its success depends on taking tremendous risks. No profit will accrue without the most favourable conjunction of weather and the movements of vast living creatures. When all goes well, I believe enormous wealth is there to be gained. The whaling fleet of Lynn is a small one, yet a good year's hunting can double the income of the town. In a bad year, many lives and considerable fortunes will be lost. I would not expect a banker, asked to invest as much as nine thousand pounds in a venture of that type, to do so as casually as Mr Melanus seems to have done.'

'Indeed not. Perhaps this Mr White was known to him from another context?'

'Ah, there we return to speculation, Mr Foxe, and I cannot accompany thee any further.'

'I understand, sir. So, what was your third reason for taking especial note of this loan?'

'The matter of security. According to the records, liens were granted over two ships owned by Mr White. You understand the nature of a lien, Mr Foxe?'

'The right to hold ultimate ownership of some valuable property belonging to another person, until he discharges a debt owed to the person making him a loan,' Foxe said. He must have read that somewhere.

'Thou art correct, sir. I could not have put it better myself. Wouldst thou not expect some details to be given of the nature and worth of this property? How else is the person making the loan to know that, if the debt be not discharged, taking possession and selling the item will be enough to cover the loss? Imagine my surprise, when I found the only details given in the records regarding these two ships was to be their names.'

'Nothing else?'

'Nothing. I could not discover their size or displacement, their location, the business on which they were engaged, nor any independent proof of their worth. Even of their existence. I would, at the very least, have expected proof of ownership on the part of Mr White, together with a statement from an independent person of their assessed value. A ship is a risky piece of collateral, Mr Foxe. It may be lost or badly damaged at any time, thus reducing or removing its worth as a security. I myself would be most reluctant to secure a loan on such a basis, unless I was certain the value of the ships far exceeded the loan amount by a large margin. I would also demand that my interest be protected by proof of suitable insurance against loss or damage. None of this appears in the records made by Mr Melanus.'

'It all smells to me of corruption, Mr Sedgefield,' Foxe said. 'I think Mr Melanus was well aware that no such ships existed.'

'Back to speculation, Mr Foxe. On a purely personal basis, I share thy feeling. In relation to the task set me by the directors of the bank, I must offer no opinion.'

'One last thing, Mr Sedgefield. Was there anything unusual about the nature of the loan itself?'

'No. The loan was for a period of five years at an interest rate of six percent per annum. A little high, perhaps, but not if thou dost consider the amount of risk involved. The principal was to be repaid at the end of the loan period, with interest paid every six months.'

'And it was not paid?'

'The first instalment is now outstanding.'

'Can you tell what happened to the money lent?'

'Only that it was all deposited with the West Norfolk and Lincolnshire Bank in King's Lynn, to the credit of Mr White. I understand those sent to try to obtain the interest, or recover the loan itself, found it gone. It had been paid, in its entirety, into Rothschilds Bank in London, having been made over to a Mr Joseph Smith.'

'Ah ...' Foxe said. 'I have met his name before. Many thanks to you, Mr Sedgefield. You have made the facts admirably clear. It is now up to me to pursue them and see where they take me.'

'To success in your endeavours, I trust, Mr Foxe. God will punish sin, sir. No sinner can escape from his justice. I pray that thou wilt find thy man, but thou shouldst remember that God's time is not ours. His punishment may be applied in the next world, rather than this. If Mr Melanus is at fault in this matter, he will not escape the consequences, however cunningly he hides himself. Good day to thee, Mr Foxe ... and good hunting!'

Mr Joseph Smith and Rothschilds Bank! Whatever the cautious Mr Sedgefield said, Foxe needed no more proof. This was yet another piece in Melanus's complex plan to escape carrying as much of his personal fortune as he could. The sum of this so-called loan must be added to the value of the notes and bills the Norwich City Bank had issued to Mr Joseph Smith. Add in the loan Melanus had taken out against his house and other properties and you reached the grand sum of twenty-two thousand, five hundred pounds. That was a fortune in anyone's terms.

The purist might argue Foxe still had no clear proof that the two Mr Joseph Smiths were one and the same, or that either represented an alias for Mr Melanus. Foxe was no purist, nor did he believe in coincidence as an adequate explanation in this — or any other — case. Mr Nathaniel White was a false identity. If "he" had signed over the money to this "Mr Joseph Smith", it could only mean Melanus himself had done so. That must be why the transaction had to take place away from Norwich, where Samuel Melanus would not have been recognised. The problem now was to track down where Mr Smith would appear next — and do it quickly, before that proved to be beyond the reach of the King's justice.

Just a moment! The colonies in America were part of His Majesty's dominions and subject to his laws. They had all been assuming Melanus was heading there, purely on the basis that Mr Smith had described himself as a silversmith of Boston, Massachusetts. That and the letter Melanus had headed "From Liverpool". Yet America would not leave Melanus free from the possibility of arrest. True, it was a large continent, much of it still unexplored. Was Mr Melanus planning to throw himself on the mercy of the natives who lived beyond the lands held by the colonies, armed only with letters of credit from Rothschilds Bank and a fortune in diamonds? Surely not! On the other hand, if he stayed within the bounds of the colonies themselves, he might be tracked down, even if he changed his name again. Foxe chided himself for a fool. Arresting Mr Melanus in America might be possible in theory, but it was most unlikely to be practicable. To stand any real chance of apprehending this fugitive, they would need to do it before he left England — if he had not done so already.

For a start, they had to discover the total value of the letters of credit Rothschilds Bank had issued to "Mr Joseph Smith", Melanus's alias. They also needed to be certain to which of Rothschild's many offices and agents around the world the letters had been directed. That could be achieved, he assumed, by official means. The Norwich City Bank had been defrauded by this fake loan, so Rothschild's could no longer claim there was no crime. Even so, it would take weeks — many, many weeks — for their request to grind through the official channels. Foxe needed something quicker, even if it involved a certain degree of deception and a less than legal approach.

The next day saw Foxe in a meeting with Mr George Handy, the senior partner of his own bank. He had to find a way to persuade Handy to comply with a somewhat unusual request. He therefore couched what he had to say in as modest a way as he could, carefully emphasising the informal nature of the whole conversation. He only hoped it would work. He was relying on his status as one of the bank's most valuable customers; one with a very large sum in credit to his account. If his luck held, that might persuade Mr Handy to bend the rules a little to do as he asked.

Foxe explained that a gentleman from the American colonies had recently been in Norwich on some business and had come to his book-shop. Being a collector of fine and rare volumes, this American, a Mr Joseph Smith, sought out Foxe himself. He hoped to be able to make some additions to his collection. There was one item in particular — Foxe would not trouble Mr Handy with the precise details — he was most anxious to track down. Sadly, Foxe had not been able to oblige him. Such a book came on the market only in the most unusual instances. When it did, it was snapped up at once by any collector discriminating enough — and wealthy enough — to understand its worth.

By the most amazing chance, Foxe explained, he had heard this very item was about to be offered for sale in London. Since he knew the person who was arranging the auction, he had obtained a promise to delay the sale for a short time. In that period, Foxe explained, he intended to acquaint Mr Smith with the opportunity and thus secure the large commission such a sale would provide.

Mr Handy could well understand his eagerness to contact the American, Foxe went on. Unfortunately, the piece of paper on which the man had written the details of his address had been mislaid. All Foxe knew was that Mr Smith hailed from either Boston, New York or possibly Nantucket. He had relied on the missing note and could not now recall even the town precisely.

All might not be lost, if Mr Handy could assist him. Mr Joseph Smith said he was returning to London for some days more, before taking ship for home. He had also mentioned he had some significant business to conclude with Rothschilds Bank. Foxe knew Mr Handy's bank was the agent in Norwich for that prestigious financial institution. He therefore wondered if Mr Handy might consent to make enquiries on Foxe's behalf — entirely unofficially, of course. All Foxe wished to know was the name of the town in America in which Mr Smith resided and whether he had yet departed to return there. If Foxe knew the town, a letter addressed to such a prominent citizen as Mr Joseph Smith would be bound to find him.

George Handy hardly hesitated. He would be delighted, he said. He knew one of the senior officials of Rothschilds Bank on a personal basis and would be happy to speak with him on Mr Foxe's behalf. The information wanted was not of an especially confidential nature and he anticipated no problem in the bank supplying it. He would also stress the urgency of the request. If all went well, he should have what Mr Foxe asked for in no more than the time it would take for the post office to deliver the letters in both directions.

Foxe departed in a state of considerable satisfaction. What he would do with the information, if he secured it, was another matter. By this stage in his investigation, satisfying his own curiosity was becoming more important than seeing the law upheld.

28

'**R**othschilds Bank offered more information than I asked for,' Foxe told Mistress Tabby, when they met a little over a week later. 'Thanks to them, I believe I can now reveal the whole of this most complicated drama. Save only for the very last moments of the last act, which must, I fear, elude me for ever.'

'You cannot always know everything, Ash. There are limits even to your powers of investigation. My advice would be to stay content with what you do know. I am sure most men would not have uncovered half as much as you have. Now, tell me all. You know I am as curious as any of my cats.'

While she spoke, she was stroking the back of a sleek, black and white cat, still barely past kittenhood. The creature lay curled in her lap, its soft purring the only sound in the room besides their voices. That sound, both gentle and insistent, seemed somehow appropriate to their conversation. Both signalled the end of a hectic period of action and the return of Foxe's life to a more restful state.

They were in Tabby's small parlour, seated one either side of the hearth. September had passed with cold winds and sullen rains. October brought a last glimpse of rich sunshine, before the rains returned. Now, with the start of November, winter had set in. Bitter easterly winds once again blew across the German Ocean, trapping ships in port and signalling the end of the year. That day, there was the scent of frost in the air and Tabby had lit a cheerful fire in the grate to warm their feet.

Foxe's closeness to the Cunning Woman had been renewed only recently. Too much pain and confusion had followed his father's unexpected death at too young an age. Then, he had somehow associated his widowed father's young, much-loved mistress, Tabitha Studwell, with all the wretchedness he felt. At that time, she was only just establishing herself as a Cunning Woman and herbalist. She was as uncertain as him in dealing with the grief of loss and death. At first, he accepted her lessons in the art of love-making. When she also attempted to offer him advice on dealing with his father's death he rejected both the advice and the one who gave it. They quarrelled, and he more or less cut himself off from her for more than a decade.

She had come back into his life barely four months earlier. She had gone out of her way to help him in his investigation of the deaths at The White Swan Playhouse. That was when Foxe at last realised what a fool he had been. His method of coping with the loss of his deeply-loved father had been to pretend he needed no one. Never again would he allow himself to become close to someone else. The pain was too much if you lost them, as he had lost his father. From now on, he would face life on his own.

Of course, this strategy — if you could call it that — hadn't worked. He had found himself alone at the very times he most needed wise counsel or a shoulder to cry on. For a time, Gracie Catt had provided both. Now she and her sister had left Norwich, probably for good. He was on his own again — and he was coming to hate it.

Foxe would have denied it, of course, but it was already evident he was starting to see in Mistress Tabby something of the mother he had never known. An hour or so in the soothing atmosphere with which she surrounded herself acted on him like the strongest balm. He didn't share the view of many in Norwich that the Cunning Woman possessed the Second Sight. Foxe didn't believe in the supernatural in any form. What others saw as uncanny knowledge of future events, he saw in natural terms. It was the combination of the woman's considerable intelligence and a deep insight into human behaviour. All those years of listening to others describing their problems, aspirations and most intimate fears had left their mark.

He told himself his visit to her today was simply a wish to acknowledge the help she had given him. That was true, but it was far from being the whole truth. There was also a strong element of the feelings of pride any young man would have in telling his mother of his latest success in the world. That Tabby was also the best of listeners was the final incentive.

'Mr Melanus had reached that stage of life,' Foxe began, 'in which some men come to think they have missed too many opportunities. Success — business success — had lost its savour. He had neither a wife nor children to comfort his old age. His previous marriage had brought him little but irritation. Even his wealth felt more of a burden than a benefit. Now he dreamed of escaping from the humdrum, care-worn nature of his present circumstances. That way, he hoped to find excitement and joy again, before the last darkness rolled in.'

'You ought to write books, not sell them,' Mistress Tabby said. 'You and the Rev Mr Laurence Sterne have much in common. His tale of Mr Tristram Shandy might yet contain a chapter with a similar opening.'

Foxe frowned, but pressed on.

'He decided to break free and catch up on what he had missed. In the attempt, he married a saucy, sensual young actress from the London stage. That proved a disaster and left him worse off than he had been before. Rather than bringing home a pretty bride, who would bear him the children he craved, he had saddled himself with a profligate, demanding and utterly selfish woman. A woman who was also openly and repeatedly unfaithful to him. The true parentage of any children she bore would never be certain.'

'Surely he must have known earlier what kind of woman she was?'

'If he did, desire blinded him. Think about the situation, Tabby. An elderly man, tired of a life of dull respectability, encounters a young woman half of London was lusting after. What's more, she appears to prefer his clumsy compliments and tentative caresses to the young bucks who flock to see her on stage. She's an actress, Tabby dear. How many times would she have played the role of the young wife, who must keep an aged husband sweet, while indulging herself elsewhere?'

'She wasn't a very good actress, from the rumours which went around after her death.'

'Good enough in this case. She aided in her role by possessing a figure ideal for attracting eyes away from her performance towards her physical assets. Assets she was more than willing to display to the greatest effect.'

'I suppose so. Go on.'

'Once again, Mr Melanus needed to escape. This time, he planned with greater care. Not only would he contrive a means of starting afresh, with a new name and in a new location, he would take revenge on his adulterous wife at the same time. You already know the details. How he undertook the secret production of counterfeit money to be able to take a good part of his fortune with him. Getting hold of the rest was bound to be more difficult. You can't sell your house, or your shares in a bank, without the news becoming public. He began by arranging a legitimate loan in his own name, with no intention of paying it back. That suited his second purpose. He pledged his house and other Norwich property as security for the loan. When that loan was left unpaid, his creditors would seize it and deny its use and value to his wife. Some vengeful husbands try to encompass the death of an unfaithful wife. Melanus settled on ruin and destitution. Since she behaved like a whore, she should have to become one to survive.

'The solution to his other difficulty — realising the value of his shareholding in the bank — was to break the law in a second way. This time he abused his position as the Norwich City Bank's senior partner. He embezzled funds through arranging a false loan, handling the whole deal himself. By setting payment of the first tranche of interest six months away, he also bought himself time to disappear with the money.

'This second loan was issued to a fresh alias, a Mr Nathaniel White — our man was not imaginative in choosing names. White was said to be a shipowner engaged in the whaling trade established in King's Lynn. Much of the rest of what I am going to tell you is conjecture on my part. Even so, I do not think I will be found to have strayed too far from the truth — should the truth ever be known.'

'The guesses of an educated mind are often as close to the truth as we can ever get,' Mistress Tabby murmured.

'Indeed so,' Foxe said. 'especially in this case, as you will see. By locating his new alias in King's Lynn, Mr Melanus made it possible to transfer the loan money away from his own bank. He then went to the bank in Lynn, where he had set up an account earlier, posing as Mr White. There he obtained bills of exchange for the whole amount of the loan. Once that was accomplished safely, he headed for London and to Rothchilds Bank. On the way, posing once again as Nathaniel White, he signed over the bills to his previous alias, Mr Joseph Smith. Finally, he paid them into the account at Rothschilds. That was where he had already deposited the funds from his counterfeiting operation and his own loan against his house.'

'So complicated!' Tabby sighed.

'I imagine that was part of the pleasure he took in carrying out his plan. He must have felt as if he was taking the leading role in a melo-drama he had written himself.'

'Where was Jack Beeston in all this?'

'I am coming to that. All these pieces of monetary sleight-of-hand should have proceeded smoothly. None should have been discovered until long after Melanus was far away from England. The unforeseen complication which marred the whole scheme was Jack Beeston. He'd found out about Melanus's involvement in coining. Being Beeston, his response was entirely predictable. He determined to force his way into what was obviously a successful criminal enterprise. He would also extort money from Mr Melanus at the same time.

'Melanus had already planned to punish his wife by leaving her destitute. He now added a few changes to his plan to send Beeston and the actual maker of the counterfeit coins, Abel Greenleaf, to the gallows.'

'Why punish Greenleaf? He seems to have done all Mr Melanus asked of him.'

'I imagine he blamed Greenleaf for letting slip something which drew Beeston's attention. Whatever the reason, Melanus's stratagem to

BLACK AS SHE'S PAINTED

bring both to justice was simple. He sent a letter in his true name to the mayor of Norwich. In it, he explained the whole scheme in detail and pointed to the parts Beeston and Greenleaf had played. He sent the letter just when he was on the point of leaving England. By the time it arrived, he calculated, it would be too late to use any of its information to apprehend its sender. Just to make sure, he indicated this in the letter that had been sent from Liverpool. That would be the obvious port to choose, if you were making for our American colonies. As a banker, Melanus always wanted to make security more secure. In this case, he did it by strengthening our assumption that was his destination. He'd already made his alias, Joseph Smith, a silversmith from Boston, in the Massachusetts colony.

'When Beeston threatened to harm his wife, if he didn't follow orders, Melanus didn't care. What he couldn't have known was that Beeston's threats amounted to more than bruises and broken bones. That kind of harm Melanus would have welcomed, as he told us himself in his letter. However, when Beeston found Melanus had cheated him by first delaying payment of the money demanded, then sending it in the form of forged coins, he ordered his minion, Harris, into action. Harris should see if he could squeeze information on Melanus's whereabouts out of Mrs Melanus, then rape and murder her.'

'Ned Harris would probably have done that anyway,' Tabby said. 'That kind of mindless ruffian enjoys hurting others too much to hold back.'

'I agree. By the way, the man stoutly denies raping Mrs Melanus. According to him, she was willing — even eager — to let him do as he wished. Sheer nonsense! You cannot free yourself from the charge of rape by pointing out how you terrified your victim into compliance. It's still rape, as I'm sure the court will agree.'

'Of course it is. Forced compliance can never be counted as willingness. Ned Harris always was a heartless brute. Now he'll reap the reward of his cruelty and arrogance.'

'Even after working out all that,' Foxe continued, 'something still bothered me. I didn't know where Mr Melanus actually intended to go on leaving England — always assuming he truly planned to leave these shores. I therefore prevailed on one of my contacts to enquire from Rothschilds Bank. He asked them whether Melanus had said anything which might offer some indication.'

'Had he?'

'It seems he had, though the answer leaves me no clearer in my mind than before. When depositing the first amounts there, our Mr Joseph Smith hadn't described himself to Rothschilds as a silversmith of Boston. He said he was the owner of a fleet of whaling vessels based in Nantucket. Still in the American colonies, as you'll appreciate, and oddly similar to Mr Nathaniel White's representation of himself. Both involved in the whaling trade. That trade, as you may know, produces vast profits in certain years. He might have made the change to account for travelling overseas with so much wealth in his possession. I don't know. It could be he was enjoying acting various parts, so decided to add one more. What I do know is this. When Mr Smith requested letters of credit covering the full amount of his deposits, he specified that they should be directed to the bank's office in Venice. Now why should he do that?'

'Another case of covering his tracks? He might have gone there, then moved on to yet another destination.'

'It's quite likely he hasn't gone anywhere,' Foxe said. 'Those letters of credit were ready by a date now more than three weeks past. They are still awaiting collection. And that makes no sense!'

'Perhaps I can offer to guess at a solution,' Tabby said quietly. 'About a year ago, well before any of this business came to light, Mr Melanus came to consult me. I never disclose anything about those who seek my help, Ash. That's why I haven't mentioned it before. It seemed irrelevant to what you were doing.'

'Tabby!'

'You will not persuade me I was wrong. If I am telling you this now, it is because I suspect Mr Melanus may be beyond caring whether I keep his secrets or not. He told me he was suffering severe headaches. Several times he had found his left arm becoming numb and useless. He had consulted two physicians, who had both bled him and taken the usual, large fees. Their ministrations brought about no change. He spoke with an apothecary, who made him a potion to help lessen the pain. Then another to improve what he diagnosed as a temporary wasting of the muscles in his arm. Mr Melanus brought both with him. From their smell and colour, as well as the effects he described to me, I judged the principal ingredient of the one was laudanum. The other contained a strong dose of cocaine.'

'Did you treat him?' Foxe asked.

'I told him he was beyond my treatment, Ash. What he should do was avoid all tension and excitement. He should also eat sparingly and avoid over-indulgence of any kind. To my eyes, there was something odd about his face, almost as if the one side of it was distorted. I have seen such distortion before. It warns of an approaching apoplexy. The problems with his arm spoke to me of a deep-seated malady of the heart. Taken together, I reached a worrying conclusion. Mr Melanus had driven himself into a state which neither heart nor brain can cope for long without serious consequences. Hence my advice, which I backed up with a harmless herbal draught useful in calming the nerves and promoting relaxation. He took what I gave him, offered me money, which I refused, and went on his way. I never saw him again.'

'You think he may be ill? That's why he hasn't been to collect his letters of credit?'

'I fear he may be dead. From all you have said, he did not heed my advice to stay quiet and avoid becoming worried or excited. In such circumstances, I don't believe he could have lived even twelve months longer, probably much less. I'm sure you've heard the old saying about those who sup with the devil needing a long spoon, Ash. Mr Melanus placed himself in the company of dangerous and violent men — devils, if you will. He would have needed a great deal of luck, as well as cunning, to escape unharmed. I fear he has not done so.'

'If you sup with the Devil, you need a long spoon ...' Foxe mused. 'That could apply to everyone involved in this wretched tale. Mrs Melanus thought she could enjoy the benefits of being a wife and the pleasures of illicit affairs at the same time. She paid for her actions with her life. Beeston and Harris have been the Devil's boon companions for years. Now he has betrayed them. Even Melanus himself, for all his planning ...'

For a while, the two sat in silence, considering the probable fate of

Mr Melanus. How it had come about as a result of telling himself his hitherto prosperous, quiet existence indicated missed opportunities, rather than prudence and sound endeavour. If you believed in evil as an intelligent, supernatural presence — which Foxe did not — the fates of Melanus, his wife, Beeston, Harris, and even Greenleaf, would offer proof that those who followed its promptings would find it always betrayed them in the end.

It was Mistress Tabby who broke the silence.

'You promised to visit Lady Cockerham, Ash,' she said. 'Have you done so?'

'Not yet, Tabby dear. I have had other matters on my mind. I know I promised I would do so, but —'

'There can be no "buts", Ash. A promise is a promise. Always remember that. No more excuses or delays! I will expect to hear you have been to see her within a week from today at the most. If that is not so, I'll send Bart to sit outside your shop and grimace to frighten your customers away until you do.'

'You would too! Very well, Tabby. I surrender. I will send Alfred to Lady Cockerham's house this very day to enquire when it would be convenient for her to receive me.'

'You won't regret it, that I can promise you. Now, we have talked for long enough and I have much to do. The same should be true of you, but you lead such an indolent and pampered existence I rather doubt it. Be off, Ash! Do not come again until you can look me in the eye and say you have spent at least thirty minutes in Lady Cockerham's company.'

❧ 29 ❧

Foxe was as good as his word. Alfred was sent to bear his card to her ladyship within minutes of his master returning home that day.

Despite Foxe's reluctance and irrational fears, his visit to the home of Lady Cockerham two days later proved a considerable success. To be correct, this was her town house. She had another, somewhat larger property too, situated some twelve miles outside Norwich in the direction of Fakenham. If she went there rarely, that was due to its remoteness and the limited opportunities for anything other than hunting on the estate or fishing in the two lakes. Her late father, the third Baron Gawston, had spent almost all his time there. He, being a man deeply devoted to country pastimes, rarely, if ever, ventured anywhere else. The memory of being forced to spend long periods at Gawston Hall as a child had left Lady Arabella Cockerham with a severe aversion to the place.

Thankfully, her husband had shared her dislike of rural surroundings. Indeed, he had done so to such an extent that the whole of their mercifully brief married life had been spent in London. Now, as a widow and her father's sole heir, Lady Cockerham owned the Gawston estate. She also held the lease on a neat house in Kensington. However, it was this house she owned in Norwich, which had proved to be her favourite place to live.

On his arrival, Foxe was greeted not by the usual stiff, disapproving and corpse-like butler. Instead, the door was answered by a cheerful and comely lady of perhaps forty years of age. She was also dressed as befitted the housekeeper to a mistress said to be the most elegant and fashionable lady in the city of Norwich. Smiling broadly upon their visitor, she conducted him through a hallway rather more splendid than his own and into a library of still grander proportions; its walls lined with four or five thousand volumes, all most handsomely bound. There she left him to await her ladyship's arrival.

Foxe was never able to resist the pleasure of inspecting other people's choice of books. He was nodding in approval of what he had found in the first stack, when the door opened and Maria Worden slipped inside to greet him. Working for Lady Cockerham clearly agreed with her. That day she seemed even prettier than when he had seen her last. Her grin of pleasure as she curtseyed neatly before him warmed his heart.

She could not stay long, she whispered, for her ladyship would be with him very soon. Still, she was determined to take the opportunity for a few moments with him on her own. At once she threw her arms around his neck and treated him to a passionate kiss. It was a kiss of such nature that the urge to lead her to the large desk at one end of the room and use its top as a makeshift bed came close to over-whelming him. Foxe had, thankfully, been raised to value decorum over lust. The notion that Lady Cockerham might arrive to find her visitor and her maid engaged in amorous sport on top of the library desk proved enough to restrain him. Even so, he made sure to return the kiss in ample measure.

All too soon, Maria slipped deftly from his arms and hurried away — and only just in time too, for heard her greeting her mistress in the hallway outside the room.

Foxe had remembered Lady Cockerham as being elegant above all else. In this, his memory proved correct. What he had not recalled so well was the quiet beauty in her face, nor that certain look in her eye, which mingled keen intelligence with the suggestion that laughter was never far below the surface. She greeted him graciously and invited him to sit and take some refreshment — exactly as etiquette demanded. Then she discarded all convention by enquiring whether he approved of such of her library as he had been able to inspect (he did); and whether he had found Maria as delectable as she had proved to be in his bedroom.

Foxe was rarely taken aback in quite such a profound way. He was usually the one to shock others with some forthright or risqué remark. This time, he could do nothing but stare at his hostess with his mouth hanging open. His surprise drew from her ladyship a delicious giggle, followed by a peal of delighted laughter.

'Forgive me, Mr Foxe,' she said, when she had recovered herself sufficiently to speak. 'That was very wicked of me, but I could not resist it. Your reputation naturally precedes you. I assumed that you would not be offended by my reference to one of your more recent conquests. Dear Maria is quite enamoured of you, sir. She has told me, at length and with graphic attention to detail, of the single occasion when you and she were able to share the pleasures of the bed chamber.'

Somehow, Foxe forced himself to speak. 'You find her satisfactory as your maid?' he said weakly.

'Indeed, I do. I am most grateful to you for sending her to me. She has been with me for only a few weeks, but we have already formed a closeness between us. I have high hopes of polishing her manners somewhat and persuading her not to drop her aitches all the time. If I succeed, I will have turned her into almost the perfect lady's maid — as well as one of the prettiest. But now, let me stop baiting you and prove I can behave with exemplary propriety, when I choose to. Let us walk around this room a little, sir, so that you may inspect the rest of my library and give me your opinion on its contents.'

Foxe had intended to stay for only the thirty minutes he had promised Mistress Tabby. In fact, it was more than an hour and a half before he left Lady Cockerham's house. He left then only because her ladyship indicated she expected her dressmaker to arrive at any moment. Throughout all that time, Lady Cockerham proved to be the most intelligent, witty and cultured lady whom Foxe had encountered in many years. It was thus no hardship at all to pledge himself to call on her again and invite her to return his call at such time as might prove convenient to them both.

Foxe walked back to his house, still amazed by the warmth of his reception and the pleasure he had found in their conversation. He could only wonder why he had avoided Lady Cockerham for so long. It was clear her ladyship was well aware of his feelings towards her maid, Maria, and felt no disapproval of them. That, in itself, was remarkable enough. Coupled with her wit and learning, her cheerful freedom from the bounds of strict convention — at least in private — had left him both entranced and bewildered. He had found her a most delightful person to spend time with. There was no doubt about that. That he could feel that way without immediately finding that pleasure in her company spilt over into intense physical desire was new. Never before had he found himself wishing to spend time with a most attractive young woman in ways other than bedding her.

Foxe struggled with what it might mean to form a close relationship with a young woman based more on shared interests than shared passion. Lady Cockerham's thoughts, had he known it, had begun to move precisely in the opposite direction. As their friendship grew, they became fully at ease with each other. They exchanged remarks and gossip in ways which would have been unthinkable in more conventional persons. All the while, her ladyship became more and more determined to join her maid in enjoying Foxe's company in the closest and most intimate way as well.

But that is to jump ahead too far.

❧ 30 ❧

Long before the relationship between Foxe, Maria and Lady Cockerham had reached its full flowering, the final pieces in the puzzle concerning the plans and whereabouts of Mr Melanus were put into place.

It was well into November, when Foxe, responding to a request from Alderman Halloran to discuss the final elements in the affair of Mr Melanus and the Norwich City Bank, arrived at the alderman's mansion in Colegate. Halloran had been joined by Mr Henry Humboldt, Mr Lancelot Gregg and Mr Nathaniel Farmer, the bank's remaining directors. These three greeted Foxe gravely, as was befitting such luminaries amongst the city's mercantile elite, and repeated their thanks for his efforts and their congratulations at such a successful outcome. From this, Foxe judged, quite correctly, that substantial amounts of money were involved — and that most of it had accrued to the credit of the Norwich City Bank and its shareholders.

Since the three visitors told their story in a confusing and jumbled manner, each interrupting the others and correcting their explanations, it would be far too tedious to follow what they said verbatim. It is therefore set down here in summary; and in the logical order they so signally failed to observe.

At the conclusion of Foxe's investigations, the directors of the Norwich City Bank had set out to convince the senior officials of Rothschilds Bank in London that a good part of the money deposited there in an account in the name of Mr Joseph Smith of Boston, Massachusetts, had been obtained from the Norwich bank by various types of criminal deception. They therefore requested that it should be returned to them as swiftly as might be convenient.

The first response was not encouraging. The mighty institution that was Rothschilds was not accustomed to receiving demands from what they deemed to be a minor, provincial bank of no importance. The bank's response, signed by the chief clerk of its London branch, was suitably ponderous and magisterial in style. Stripped of its verbiage, however, it offered no more than a blunt refusal. Rothschilds Bank was, the chief clerk wrote, in no way minded to do as the Norwich bank requested. Before he could even place their request before the bank's partners, he would require full and convincing documentary evidence to substantiate such a surprising claim; nor was he hopeful of securing the partners' agreement even then. He had reviewed the account in question personally and found it was opened and operated in a proper manner. There, in his opinion, the matter ended.

The merchant princes of Norwich were unused to being treated in this way. How dare this group of foreign bankers turn their request down! Their displeasure was profound and was swiftly followed by practical action. The mayor contacted the lord lieutenant of the county in person. As His Majesty's representative, he was asked to bring the matter to the king's attention as speedily as possible. The county's two members of parliament were also briefed on the affair. As expected, they expressed their support and undertook to raise the case in Parliament. Finally, a lengthy letter was sent to the Master of the Royal Mint, with a copy to the Governor of the Bank of England. It gave details of the entire affair and how it had come to light. The proper rule of law, the directors of the Norwich bank wrote, demanded that this money should be seized and their share of it returned. If not, a person guilty of the treasonable crime of producing counterfeit coins might well be able to escape justice, along with all his profits, by using the services of a foreign bank.

Within two weeks, Rothschilds had sent another, very different response. This new letter, the directors of the Norwich bank told Foxe, was much better in tone and content. To Foxe's relief, it also vindicated his reconstruction of Melanus's motives and actions.

'We taught those foreign bankers to mind their Ps and Qs in dealing with us,' Mr Farmer told Foxe, his voice full of satisfaction. 'Just because they have some grand office in London doesn't mean they can treat us like rustics. I imagine they quickly discovered His Majesty's government expected a more co-operative attitude. If, that is, they wished to continue enjoying its custom on the same scale as in the past.'

The Norwich City Bank's directors plainly believed their proper importance had finally been recognised. Foxe was far more of a realist. Unlike them, he was not weighed down by a mountain of self-esteem. It seemed to him any explanation for Rothschilds' change of heart was going to be far more prosaic and based mostly on finding a means of saving face.

As the story unfolded, his view was proved to be the correct one.

In their second letter, the chief clerk of Rothschilds attributed their change of heart entirely to certain recent events. The bank, he explained, had been visited by representatives of the magistrate of the Bow Street Office. They brought news that a man's body had been found in a superior lodging house not far distant from Rothschild's place of business. At the inquest on the dead man, the medical examiner gave evidence he had died as a result of a massive cerebral embolism and haemorrhage. A verdict of death by natural causes was therefore returned.

However, the case had not ended there. As was routine, constables had searched the man's room seeking to establish whether there were any signs of foul play. While doing so, they found a letter of introduction to Rothschilds Bank, signed by a Mr Samuel Melanus of the Norwich City Bank. The inquest had been told this letter appeared to establish the dead man's identity as Mr Joseph Smith, a silversmith

WILLIAM SAVAGE

from one of our American colonies. The magistrate now wished to confirm this identity, if possible. He could then write to the appropriate authorities in Massachusetts and ask them to inform the next of kin.

In approaching Rothschilds, the representatives of the magistrate explained that they sought but one piece of information. Could they be told, they enquired, whether any person of the name of Mr Joseph Smith, hailing from America, was known to Rothschild's Bank?

Foxe guessed that, following this unexpected turn of events, attitudes within Rothschilds Bank had changed in an instant. Adding this new information to that contained in the earlier correspondence from the Norwich City Bank must have produced a series of most unwelcome conclusions. The bank's good name might now be at stake. The bank's partners, probably already under pressure from official quarters, would have issued peremptory orders. All remaining links with Mr Joseph Smith were to be severed at once. The slightest suggestion that Rothschilds were prepared to hold funds arising from the proceeds of such a serious crime as counterfeiting was to be avoided at all costs. The tainted account must therefore be closed without delay, and the balance handed over to the authorities. A letter explaining the banks' actions was also despatched in haste to Norwich.

This letter was, naturally, much more to the liking of Messers Humboldt, Gregg and Farmer. It began by accepting the proposition that the man Rothschilds knew as Mr Joseph Smith was indeed Mr Samuel Melanus. It also accepted that he had almost certainly been involved in criminal enterprises. The earlier suggestion that the money deposited in Mr Smith's name represented the proceeds of crime now rang true. Rothschilds Bank had no wish to be involved in assisting the transfer of such money overseas; nor did it knowingly accept deposits from criminals. They had therefore handed over the remaining amount in the account held in the name of Mr Joseph Smith to the magistrate at Bow Street, who would doubtless see to the speedy return of the amount due to the Norwich City Bank.

'Most satisfactory,' Mr Humboldt said, when the end of the directors' narration had been reached at last.

'Very much so, from your bank's point of view,' Foxe said. 'The bills and notes first made payable to the fictitious Joseph Smith were, by Melanus's own admission, paid for fully and in legal tender. You will soon also have the money from the false loan back again. In place of the substantial losses you feared, you find yourselves in the happy position of losing nothing.'

The directors beamed at Foxe. Unfortunately, his next remark caused their smiles to waver, then fade.

'It could, of course, be argued,' Foxe went on, 'that, once the bills and notes were presented for payment to Rothschilds, your own obligations in the matter ceased. On the other hand, the money passed to Rothschilds in payment for those bills has now been returned. A pretty dilemma, surely? If the amount returned to you contains most of the value of those bills and notes as well as the loan amount, that will represent a substantial profit for your bank.'

'There is that,' Mr Gregg said. 'I suppose.'

'There are also the diamonds Melanus bought,' Foxe went on. 'Where are they? Who owns them now, since they were purchased with money obtained through crime?'

'Surely they will be seized by the Exchequer,' Mr Farmer said.

'Rothschilds returned the entire contents of the bank account to the London magistrate,' Mr Humboldt explained. 'He has indicated that the amounts drawn on our bank will be sent to us in due course. Nothing has been said about diamonds. Even if they are found, we have no claim on them. Do you agree, gentlemen?' They did. 'As to the value of the paper money Melanus bought from us, if the authorities do not ask for its return from the amount paid over by Rothschilds, ...'

'Which they seem unlikely to do, having overlooked the matter thus far,' Foxe said, filling the silence that followed Humboldt's last remarks.

'Perhaps it would be seemly to make some suitable payment to a charity with part, at least, of the money.' Mr Gregg sounded embarrassed. 'That is, assuming the authorities do not demand it from us.'

'After a suitable lapse of time,' Mr Farmer added. 'Not too large a part either. We've been put to a good deal of trouble by this affair. There's also the fee we agreed to pay to Mr Sedgefield.'

At this point, Foxe and Halloran intervened. Such a discussion, they said, was best discussed at a formal board meeting of the Norwich City Bank. The other three took the hint. Yet when they took their leave, they were still arguing about the ethics of accepting such a windfall profit. The 'suitable charity' might well have a long time to wait before any money passed into its coffers — if it ever did.

Left on their own, Foxe and the alderman made their way into the alderman's library. There they drank a celebratory glass or two of champagne and talked about Halloran's favourite topic: adding more books to his collection. Foxe had recently located several volumes of interest. The two of them therefore spent a happy half-hour discussing his discoveries. That was followed by a similar period spent considering how far Foxe might be able to persuade the London dealers concerned to lower the ridiculous prices they were asking at the outset.

IT TOOK A FURTHER WEEK FOR THE FINAL NEWS CONCERNING Melanus and his affairs to make its way from London to Norwich. The mayor heard it officially from the Bow Street magistrate. Halloran heard it from the mayor and hastened to pass it on to Mr Foxe.

As a result of the letter sent from Norwich, representatives of the Royal Mint had been despatched to the rooms once occupied by Mr Joseph Smith. Their task was to make a more detailed search than the one undertaken by the constables, with an emphasis on seeking out evidence of counterfeiting. As a result, they made three fresh discoveries. The first was a fine pocket-watch in a gold case. On the rear of the case was an engraving of the coat-of-arms of the Earls of Belstone. Enquiries had been at once made at the earl's London address. By sheer good fortune, his lordship was in residence, attending to parliamentary business, and had expressed great delight at the finding of the watch. It seems he had sent it to a goldsmith in Norwich, one Mr Samuel Melanus, for the engraving to be added. After that, Mr Melanus went missing and the watch with him. Until now, the earl feared his watch had been either stolen or lost.

The second find was a leather purse, containing twenty-four gold sovereigns. On close inspection, all were found to be fakes, though of a far higher quality than usual. The third of their discoveries consisted of two packets of diamonds, sewn into the lining of one of Mr Smith's coats. The sovereigns and diamonds had, of course, been seized at once and handed over into the possession of the relevant authorities.

'So Melanus is indeed dead, as Mistress Tabby suspected,' Halloran said. 'He doesn't seem to have enjoyed much good fortune at any stage in his life, does he?'

'You shouldn't feel too sorry for him, Halloran,' Foxe replied. 'It's true he lost two wives to illness and accident, but he caused all his most recent problems by his own actions. He didn't have to marry such an unsuitable woman; nor was he compelled to deal with the difficulties this caused by turning to crime.'

'You have to admit his plan was ingenious.'

'Certainly, even if it proved in the end to be flawed. Too much relied on what is euphemistically termed "honour amongst thieves". Such a thing doesn't exist, in my experience. Perhaps we should be grateful that he became more interested in punishing those he counted as his enemies than securing his own escape.'

'Why so?'

'Had he not,' Foxe explained, 'he would have been far away before we could discover his plans.'

'I suppose he would. I still tend to think of Samuel Melanus as the respectable businessman we once thought he was. I have to keep reminding myself he became a clever criminal.'

'He should have been prepared to take his time. That's what ruined him. That and dabbling in a world of which he had no experience. I don't doubt the world of merchants like yourself contains a good many rogues. However, few of them will be as ruthless or cunning as Jack Beeston. Poor Melanus was out of his depth from the start, had he but realised it.'

Halloran sat quiet. Foxe assumed he was musing on all they had discovered over the past weeks.

'I wonder why he had those letters of credit issued for payment by the bank's office in Venice,' the alderman said after a few moments. 'Why not head for our American colonies, as we guessed was his plan all the time?'

'I still believe that must have been his intention. Nevertheless, delaying his arrival until the search for him had died down would have been no bad idea. Why Venice? I believe it's a beautiful city, Halloran. It's also ideally placed as a starting point for what is usually called The Grand Tour.'

'What? Like some young offshoot of the nobility, sent to better whatever passes for his mind by inspecting the antiquities and art of Italy? The kind who come home weighed down with paintings and baubles to decorate their grand mansions?'

'Exactly so. Remember this. Melanus was seeking to fulfil the fantasies of an ageing man. He was convinced he had been denied much of what should have been the best parts of his life. He'd just tried acting like a young buck and dallying with an actress. We know where that got him. Maybe this time he thought he'd indulge himself in more decorous entertainment. He could furnish the home he planned in America at the same time. Of course, he might have listened to stories of young English milords enjoying the mercenary attentions of all those sloe-eyed, Italian beauties. Either way, I expect spending time in Italy seemed a good way to use some of his wealth, while avoiding his enemies — and English justice — at the same time. A far cry from running a business in Norwich, wouldn't you say?'

'You're probably right, Foxe. Anyhow, it's finally over and with all the loose ends tied up.'

'The Cunning Woman told me Melanus didn't have long to live,' Foxe said. 'She was right, as usual.'

'Has she the Second Sight?' Halloran asked.

'More likely it's experience and intelligence, backed up by common sense,' Foxe replied. 'Those are more valuable possessions than an imaginary ability to foretell the future.'

They both fell silent. Then Foxe, forgetting he was not on his own, began musing aloud.

'I wonder if that other prophesy of hers will come true?' he murmured. 'As I recall, it was "companions", in the plural. Yes, that's what she said.'

'What prophesy was that?' the alderman asked.

'Never you mind,' Foxe told him — then refused to say another word on the subject.

ABOUT THE AUTHOR

William Savage is an author of British historical mysteries. All his books are set between 1760 and around 1800, a period of great turmoil in Britain, with constant wars, the revolutions in America and France and finally the titanic, 22-year struggle with Napoleon.

William graduated from Cambridge and spent his working life in various management and executive roles in Britain and the USA. He is now retired and lives in north Norfolk, England.

www.williamsavageauthor.com
www.penandpension.com

ALSO BY WILLIAM SAVAGE

THE ASHMOLE FOXE GEORGIAN MYSTERIES

The Fabric of Murder

Follow Mr Foxe through Norwich's teeming 18th-century streets as he seeks to prevent a disaster to the city's major industry and tracks down a killer with more than profit on his mind.

Dark Threads of Vengeance

Mr Ashmole Foxe, Georgian bookseller and confidential investigator, has a new case: to find the murderer of a prominent Norwich merchant and banker before his businesses collapse and the city is crippled by financial panic.

This Parody of Death

Eighteenth-century Norwich bookseller and dandy, Ashmole Foxe, is asked by the local bellringers to look into the death of their Tower Captain, found in the ringing chamber with his throat cut.

Bad Blood Will Out

Ashmole Foxe investigates two cases, both involving poisoned relationships from the past. A wealthy man dies amongst his own guests and a series of murders occupy centre stage at one of Norwich's main theatres.

ALSO BY WILLIAM SAVAGE

THE DR ADAM BASCOM MYSTERIES

An Unlamented Death

When the body he trips over in a country churchyard proves to be a senior clergyman, Dr Adam Bascom expects a serious inquiry to follow. Instead, it looks as if the death is to be left unsolved.

The Code for Killing

Dr Adam Bascom, called to help a man who's been brutally assaulted, is drawn into solving a series of murders in a world of deceit, violence and treachery.

A Shortcut to Murder

18th-century Norfolk physician Dr Adam Bascom longs to get back to his medical work. Fate, however, is determined to keep him off-balance as he is asked by his magistrate brother Giles to investigate the death of Sir Jackman Wennard, rake, racehorse breeder and baronet.

A Tincture of Secrets and Lies

A Quack doctor leads Dr Adam Bascom into a mystery which includes a series of local murders and a plot to destabilise the country, and ends with Adam directing a thrilling climax on land and sea.

Made in the USA
Coppell, TX
04 January 2021